HALCYON CHRONICLES:

HARBINGER'S
END
HERALD

Books by Elliott Michaelson

HALCYON CHRONICLES:
HARBINGER'S END
HERALD

HALCYON CHRONICLES:
HARBINGER'S END
THE TIME OF MEETING

HALCYON CHRONICLES:
HARBINGER'S END
ENDGAME

www.halcyonchronicles.com

Dedications

To my family and friends
who read and reread this book in all its incarnations:
your feedback and support were invaluable.
This publication would not have been possible
without you.

To the campers and staff at
Camp Shalom from 1993-1996:
for giving me an excuse to write and to dream.

Preface

It's been a long and circuitous route to publication. *Harbinger's End* began as a thirty-page short story called "Orb of Prophecy" that I wrote for my campers in my second year as an overnight counselor at Camp Shalom north of Toronto. It was the spring of 1993, and as I had already developed a reputation as one of the official camp storytellers the previous summer, I decided to get really creative with my campers' bedtime routine. But what to write for a cabin full of preteen boys?

I'm an avid collector of movie soundtracks, so one night for inspiration I popped in a CD from a fantasy movie (lousy movie, terrific music). As the music ebbed and flowed in time to the scenes from the movie, I began to wonder what it would sound like if I wrote a fantasy adventure story that moved to the music. What a great way to put the kids to bed! "Orb of Prophecy" was born.

The story was meant to be read over four nights (this is a great way to bribe campers into good behavior — if you work at an overnight camp, I'd highly recommend trying it), and in the summer of 1993 it was an instant hit. Before long, I was coming around to every cabin in the unit. The following summer, I visited nearly every cabin in camp.

From 1993 to 1996, I wrote one new "musical adventure story" every year, each set to a different movie soundtrack, and each for a different age group. Perhaps one day I'll turn those other stories into full-length books, too.

I started exploring "Orb of Prophecy" without music in the school year of 1993-1994 to see where the narrative would take me. But for that part of the story, you'll have to stay tuned for book two...

Harbinger's End now bears very little resemblance to the original short story I wrote eighteen years ago, but the spirit of "Orb of Prophecy" remains at its core. I hope you enjoy reading it as much as I enjoyed writing it.

— *EM, March 2011*

Notable Citizens of Halcyon

PRAETORIAN OFFICERS

Duncan Milius —
>   Praetorian captain, Valandov garrison; junior officer under Marshal Corinn Wallace; foster-son to Premier Leodore Milius

Dorian Bowen —
>   Grand-General of the Praetorship

Corinn Wallace —
>   Praetorian marshal; commander of the Praetorian garrisons in Valandov Province, Federated States

Elliss Blaine —
>   Praetorian captain, Valandov garrison; junior officer under Marshal Corinn Wallace

Rupert Baldwin —
>   Praetorian marshal; commander of the garrison in Fargon, Torinn Province, Federated States

Elenna Bronnaugh —
>   Praetorian general; member of Grand-General Bowen's advisory council

Evelynne Tarran —
>   Praetorian lieutenant; commander of an infantry platoon in Duncan Milius' unit

RELIGIOUS OFFICIALS

Arlyne Corbonne —
  Kahanne of Assize

MEMBERS OF THE CIRCLE

Cain —
  Circle Chieftain

Quinn —
  Inner Member

Reeve —
  Inner Member

CITIZENS OF THE REPUBLIC OF GHAULT

Cedric IV Deis —
  Padishah of the Republic of Ghault

Cecil du Langue —
  Duke of the duchy of Langue

Robert du Dijinn —
  Duke of the duchy of Dijinn

Edwin du Lamans —
  Marquis of the duchy of Lamans; aide-de-camp to the dukes
  Cecil du Langue and Robert du Dijinn

Dane Orreil —
  Marquise of the Padishah's court; intelligence chief to Padishah
  Cedric IV Deis

CITIZENS OF THE HANSIC ALLIANCE

Yarena Hanser —
  Chancellor, Hansic Alliance

Lawrence Hanser —
  Husband of Yarena Hanser

William Lessander —
  Governor of the Great Sea District

CITIZENS OF KHADASH

Glendon Fortinbras —
  Premier of the Dominion of Khadash

Dannia Fortinbras —
  Daughter of Glendon Fortinbras

CITIZENS OF THE FEDERATED STATES

Jarren Entingen —
  Chief-of-staff to General Cyril Hawkwin

Cyril Hawkwin —
  Overall commander of the Federate militia

Leodore Milius —
  Premier of the Federated States; foster-father to Duncan Milius

Bethany Manallo —
  Colonel in the Federate militia

Major Events in the History of Halcyon

An introduction for initiates by Svetla,
Sixth-Level Circle Member

GOLDEN AGE

1

Appearance of the Spirits

(Note: before this time, no known records exist outside of the Library of the Elders, to which we have no access)

AGE OF RUIN: 132-200

132

Demeter Ahenak is born

159

Ahenak's First Codex is written

161

Demeter Ahenak rises to power

162

Scientific community flees the ancient city of Halcyon

165

Ahenak's Second Codex is written

166-172

Assault on technology

173

Settlement of Khadash is founded

Teivan groups begin to coalesce

First northern settlements are founded along the rivers leading into Lake Caeligen

174

Ahenak ascends to offices of Kahanne and Padishah of Halcyon

175-179

Ahenak writes his Third Codex

186

Ahenak is assassinated

188

Cedric I Roussa becomes first Padishah of Ghault; Zacharias Eldorad becomes first Kahanne

188-200

Separatists flee from Ghault to the West

Age of Disquiet: 200-463

200-300

City-states of Gottingen and Gath are founded; expansion along the River Amzan

Coastal towns established in the west, along with inland trading posts

283-290

First underground complex in the Fingers of Khorshim is completed

401

Elders are created

403

The Dominion of Khadash is founded

425

Western towns form the Hansic League

451

Padishah Mauriss III Deis builds up his army

454

Ghault establishes the outpost of Kennedor

460

Kahanne Roland Demeter demands the secret of the Elders

461

Dominion of Khadash and the northern city-states build up their defenses; Maurice III Deis interprets this as a sign of war

The Great War: 463-470

463

Ghault overruns Khadash's border towns

Ghaultian forces seize the region around Lake Caeligen

464

Ghaultian forces besiege Gottingen from the Oboddon River and from the Great Sea

465

Ghaultian forces march for Irbirah; Hansic League declares war

467

Siege of Gottingen is broken; Ghaultian forces retreat to Kennedor

468

Padishah Mauriss III is assassinated; Kahanne Demeter becomes Regent

Ghaultian forces pull back to prewar positions along the border with Khadash

Armistice between Khadash and Ghault; terms of reparations are negotiated

470

Truce is declared in Kennedor

Establishment of the Commonwealth Council

475

  Establishment of the Praetorship

488

  Establishment of the Circle

545

  Founding of the Federated States

547-556

  Kennedor war between Ghault and the Federate

556

  Kennedor joins the Federated States

564

  Five western governates replace the Hansic League with an economic Alliance

567

  Kahanne Fenric Gauchon promotes institutional change in Assize

570

  Office of Kahanne breaks with the Padishah

584-587

  Days of Attrition between the Hansic Alliance and the Federate

Following the Days of Attrition, the Commonwealth Council agreed to expand the role of the Praetorship as a peacekeeping force by permitting the establishment of garrisons in most major cities and towns. It is due to the presence of these garrisons that the destructive conflicts, which characterized Halcyon's past, have largely been avoided. Thus, there have been no external events of any lasting significance to the Circle since the year 587 After the Appearance.

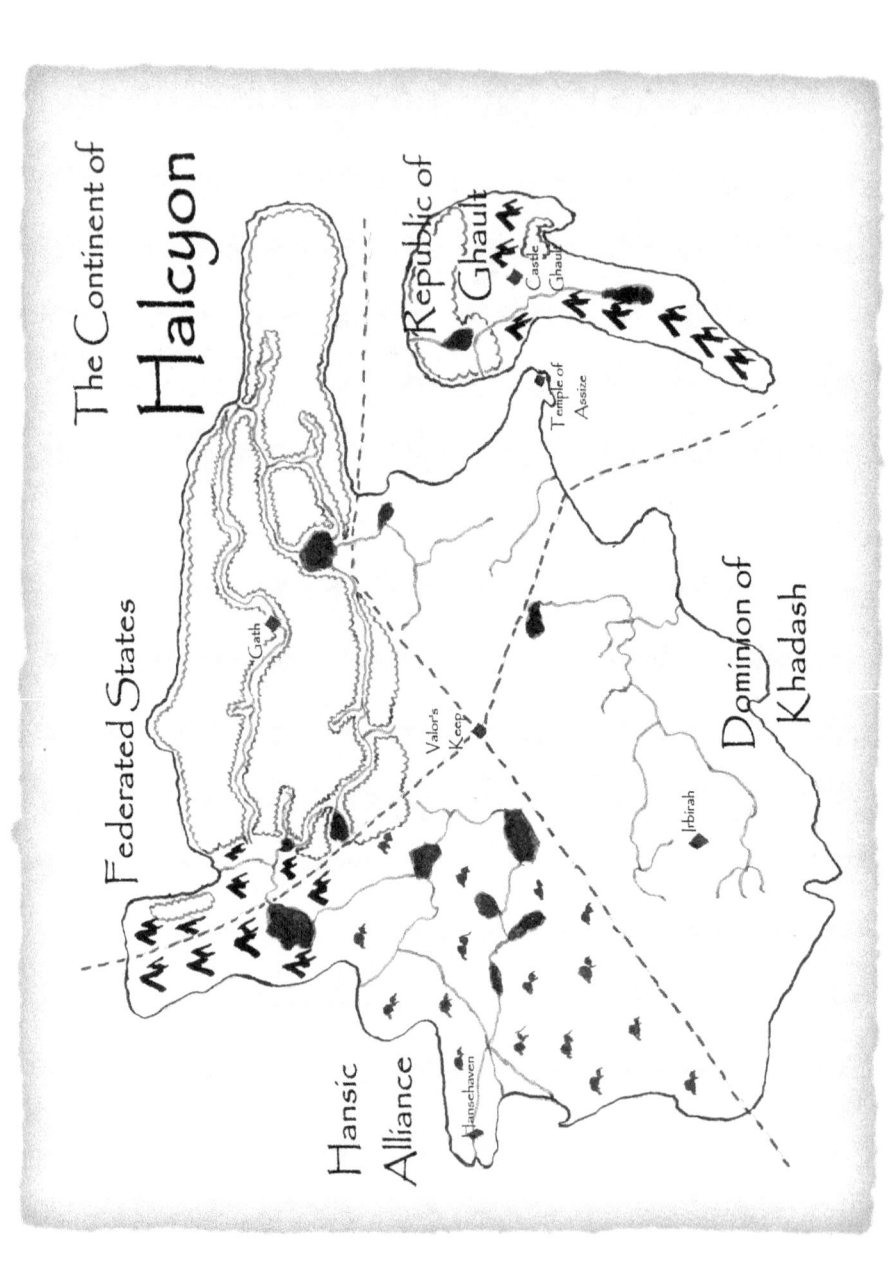

The Continent of
Halcyon

Republic of Ghault

Castle
Ghault

Temple of
Assize

Federated States

Gath

Dominion of
Khadash

Valor's
Keep

Irbirah

Hansic
Alliance

Hanschaven

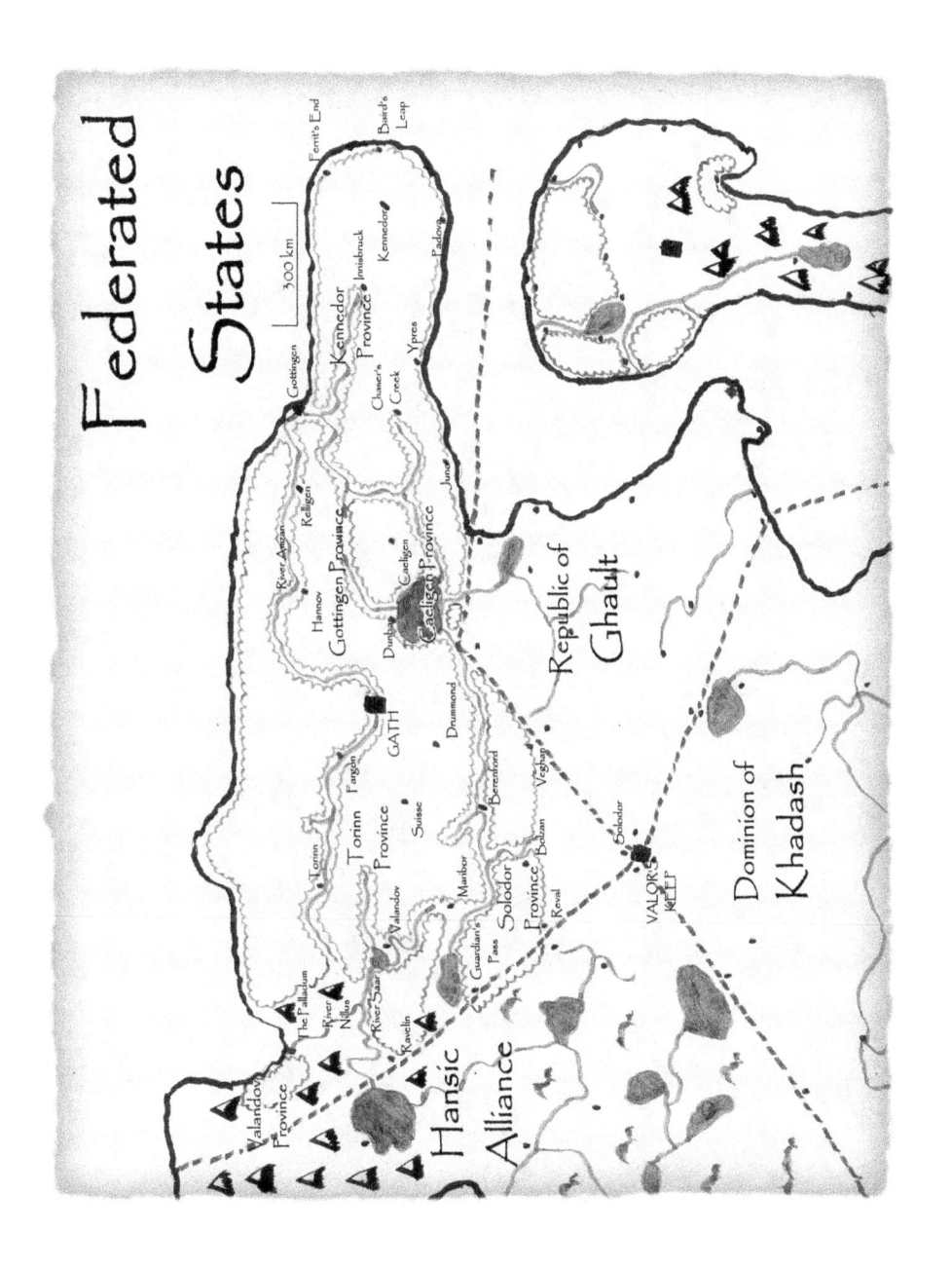

Federated States

300 km

Ferrit's End
Baird's Leap

Gottingen
Kennedor Province
Innisbruck
Kennedor
Padova

Religen
Chaser's Creek
Ypres

River Anisan
Hannov
Gottingen Province
Caeligen
Jund
Dunbar
Caeligen Province

GATH
Fargon
Drummond

Torinn
Torinn Province
Suissec
Maribor
Breszford
Veghan

Valandor
Solodor

The Palladium
River Nitus
River Saar
Ravelin

Guardian's Pass
Solodor Province
Reval
Balzan

VALOR'S KEEP

Valandov Province

Hansic Alliance

Republic of Ghault

Dominion of Khadash

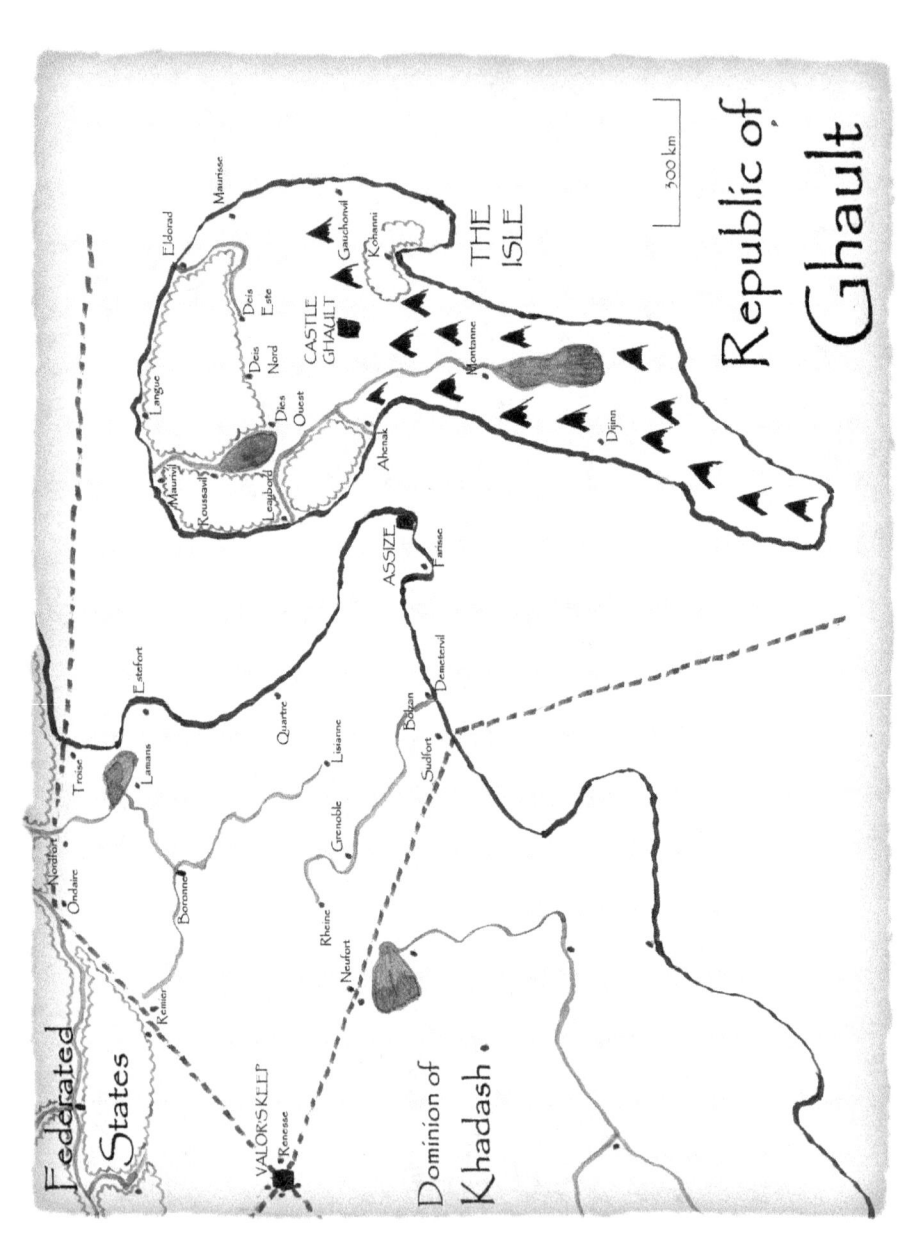

Republic of

Ghault

THE
ISLE

CASTLE
GHAULT

Maurisse
Eldorad
Dics
Este
Dics
Nord
Langue
Dics
Ouest
Maurivi
Kousauvil
Leighard
Gauchouvil
Kohanni
Montanne
Ahcnak
Djiun

ASSIZE
Fantasc
Estefort
Troisc
Latsains
Quartre
Lisearne
Bodgan
Denecterval
Sudfort
Grenoble
Rhaine
Neufort
Ajoufort
Ondaire
Baronne
Remer
Kenner

Federated

States

VALOR'S KEEP
Renesse

Dominion of
Khadash.

500 km

Hansic
Alliance

300 km

Montagne

Liebland

Reghenport
Alpas

Riga
Alpas
District

Federated
States

Kaiden

Danzik

Helsing

Gerenspen

Frau

Ilien

Lufthane

Kiel

Rugen   HANSEHAVEN

Lubec

Raskilburg

Great Lakes
District

VALOR'S
KEEP

Great Sea
District

Borgal

Kanterburg

Revenna

Central
Highlands
District

Malmo

Mayam's
End

Stettin

Yorling

Yarma's
End

Stettinburg

Southern
District

Dominion of
Khadash

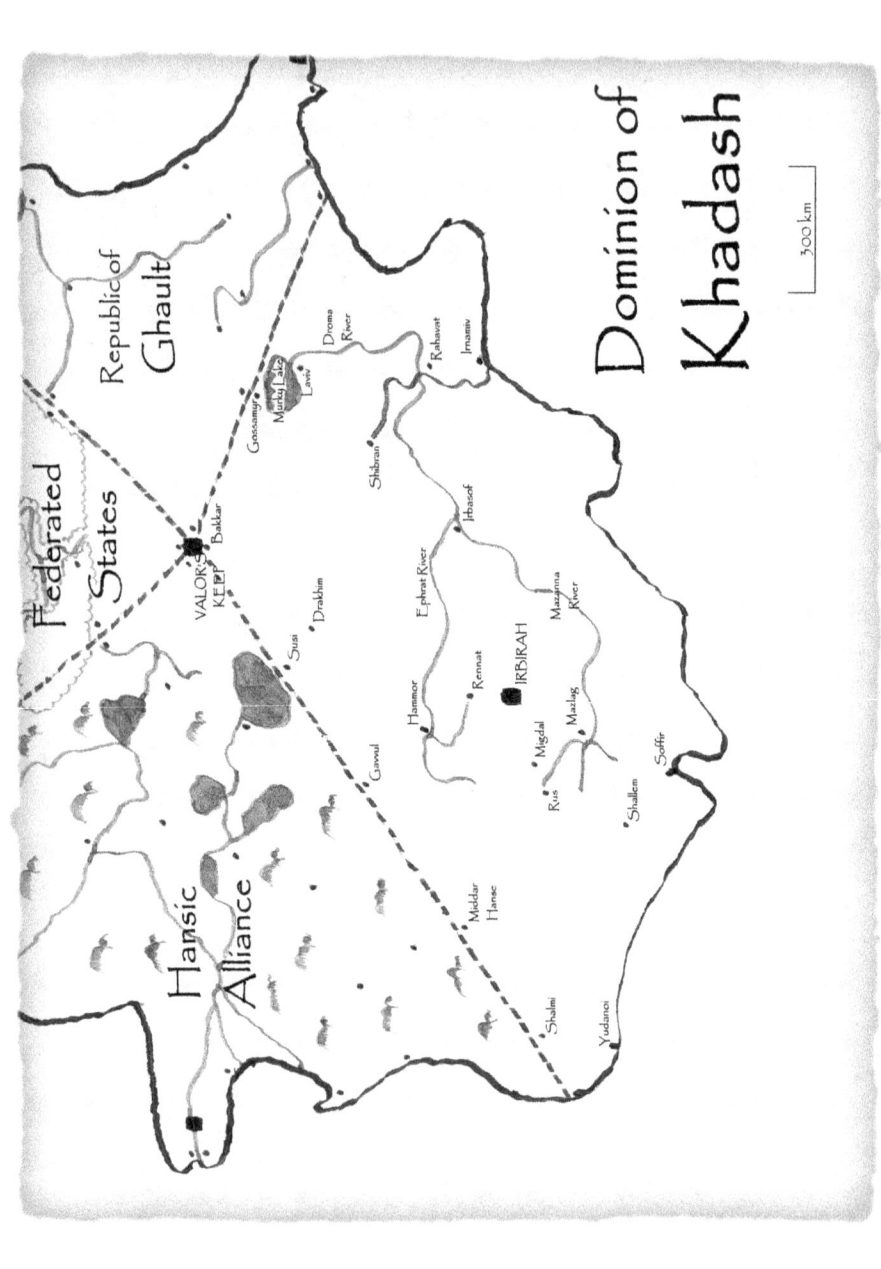

Dominion of Khadash

300 km

Republic of Ghault

Federated States

Hansic Alliance

Drona River
Murky Lake
Lavix
Gossamyr
Rahavon
Imasov
Shibran
Irbasof
Bakkar
VALOR'S KEEP
Susi
Drakhm
Ephrat River
IRBIRAH
Mazanna River
Rennat
Hammer
Gawul
Mygdal
Mazlag
Rus
Soffir
Shallem
Meldar
Hanac
Shalmi
Yudanoi

PROLOGUE

The Ancient City of Halcyon

I have to reach the Kahanne!

The Mayor of Halcyon pushed frantically through the stunned crowd that packed the central square. The appearance was so sudden – so unexpected – that no one knew what to do or how to proceed.

Where's the Kahanne? Why isn't he responding?

Nothing in the Mayor's political or personal experience prepared him for this. A crush of people pushed him back as everyone pressed into the square to see if what they had heard was true. The Mayor tried to ignore the questions that seemed to come from a hundred directions at once.

I need to reach the Kahanne!

The Mayor finally arrived at his office and grabbed for one of his aides. After a moment of frantic instructions, the aide nearly stumbled over himself as he headed for one of the transports.

The Mayor returned to the central square to join thousands of his fellow citizens. The mood was a curious mix of fear and anticipation.

The Kahanne will know what to do.

*

Nathan Kohani sat cross-legged in a corner of his study. Before him was a bronze statue of a fox-bear accompanied by a smoking incense pan. Behind that was a large, oblong window that afforded him a magnificent view of the surrounding woodland. His home was built on top of a mild grade on the shore of Lake Paix, a region rich with life. Normally, Kohani would have stood before the window and soaked up the environs: large deciduous trees crowding the lake shore, small rodents darting about for a quick drink, birds and insects of every kind, and dozens of species of flora and fauna that even after two hundred years had yet to be catalogued. Nathan Kohani would have noticed all this had he been alert.

Several soft raps on the door drew no response. The Kahanne was too deep in meditation.

Kohani inhaled deeply, filling his lungs with the hallucinogenic smoke that enabled him to reach Communion. Every muscle was relaxed, though his mind was aflutter. Images of his surroundings flashed in front of him — fern trees with their wide flat leaves, a squirrel scrambling after its mate, the cool mud under his paws... Then he realized that he *was* the fox-bear, dashing through the forest that occupied the northern third of this island.

Communion!

The experience started to wane. His mind began pulling back. He no longer saw through the fox-bear's eyes — his perspective had shifted, as if his head rested between the animal's pointed ears. It slowed to a trot, and Kohani now floated above it. By the time the fox-bear stopped to munch on a berry bush, Kohani's consciousness had reached the tops of the trees. He continued his journey skyward, away from the island and into the clouds.

As he pulled further away, other sounds became audible, as if he was hearing them through water. The soft pat of footfalls on wood... A beep from a communicator... A muffled conversation...

Blackness.

Kohani opened his eyes and blinked quickly to get them to focus. The last wisps of incense smoke were diffusing into the air, and the intoxicating sweetness that filled his nostrils was slowly being replaced by the woodsy aromas of his home. He rose gracefully to his feet and stretched. He felt refreshed. He stood there for a moment to reflect on his experience. Kohani was very old by any standard, though he was unusually robust. He credited this partly to his daily regimen of exercise, healthy eating and antioxidants — the standard fare for anyone over eighty years of age — but nothing maintained his youthfulness more than his daily Communions. It was his search for unity with Nature that brought him here some fifty years ago. His Communions were responsible for his heightened sense of spirituality, and his aptitude at achieving them enabled him to attain the highest office of religious advisor.

When he finished his moment of reflection, he turned to face the door. "Entrer." The voice was light, almost musical.

At Kohani's bidding, the door opened and the Mayor's aide nervously stepped inside, visibly relieved that the Kahanne was finally awake. "Pardon, Monsieur," he ventured.

Kohani studied him. He was a young man in his twenties who had the look of a spiritual acolyte. A frock was draped over his body, and his pants stopped halfway up his shins. As with most of the people here, he was barefoot. Kohani's attire was hardly more formal. He wore a light shirt that partly covered his baggy pants, neither of which did much to hide his tall, wiry frame. The Kahanne grinned warmly at his visitor. He was probably working in the Mayor's office to pay off his university tuition.

The aide continued. "Le Maire a appelé a vous."

Kohani sighed. The Mayor always seemed to treat him like he was on call. "Bien."

As they walked through his home, Kohani glanced at his message board. There were twelve calls from the Mayor in the past three hours! Something serious must have happened while he was communing. No wonder they sent someone to fetch him!

The aide led Kohani out of his home. There was a comfortable breeze blowing so he decided to leave the front door open — locks were unheard of around here and crime was nonexistent. They clambered into a waiting transport, and once they were seated, Kohani's escort fired up its engines. It lifted off the ground and headed out to the mainland. Kohani glanced back at his home — a simple wood cabin nestled in a forest by a lake, and a stark contrast to the technological marvel he was sitting in. After twenty minutes, they had passed over the channel and the city was in sight. It was a majestic collection of spires and low buildings with a large, open square in the middle. Everything about it betrayed a strong sense of simplicity. Thousands of homes, schools, research facilities and businesses without a shred of excess. The people kept and used only what they needed to live comfortably. Anything beyond that was a distraction from the one thing they all strove for: unity with Nature.

Raising his hand to shield his eyes from the sun's glare, Kohani studied the city as it grew closer. It was usually a bustling place, with transports such as this flying all about. Now, though, there seemed to be no activity whatsoever, as if the city had been abandoned. A shiver crept through Kohani's body as he thought about this. Where was everybody and why did the Mayor issue such an urgent summons for him? Evening prayers weren't for another three hours.

"Qu'est-ce qui a?" he asked the aide.

No answer was forthcoming as they began the landing cycle. After a few minutes, the transport touched down on a landing pad and the aide turned to Kohani. "Le Maire va vous montrer."

They exited the transport and Kohani was greeted by the Mayor, who bowed his head. He was shorter than Kohani and heavyset. His dark skin glistened with perspiration. Like the others, he was dressed plainly in loose-fitting clothes and he wore no insignia.

"Kahanne, thank God," he sighed. "You won't believe what's happened."

"I am not supposed to be needed until evening prayers, Hanan," admonished Kohani. His rolling accent, along with his light voice, gave his speech an almost lyrical intonation. "You know that I Commune in the afternoon."

"Believe me, we wouldn't have summoned you if we had another choice. We need you."

"For what?"

Hanan ushered him past one of the spires that marked the city's limit. It looked like a small, smooth mountain peak. "Something extraordinary has happened. I can't describe it, you simply have to see for yourself. They've been here for hours. I tried calling you all afternoon. They appeared out of nowhere. We've had experts of every sort examine them — scientists, doctors, physicists... All we've been able to determine is that they're real!"

"What is real? What is causing all this excitement?"

The central square was just beyond the next spire and the hushed voices of thousands of people could be heard. The Mayor stopped for a moment and grabbed Kohani by the shoulders, gently pushing him into the spire's shadow. He sounded edgy. "We don't know. That's why you're here. We think they've been here all along, but that they've made themselves known to us now for a reason. We need someone to talk to them, and no one is more qualified than you."

As they rounded the bend and began to wade through the crowd, a flash caught Kohani's eye. Still being dragged by the Mayor, he glanced back and saw a faintly gleaming aura. Squinting, he made out the shape of what looked like a man dressed in ancient armor. The armor was part of a military uniform, though Kohani couldn't make out any identifying marks through the light. The man appeared to be watching them. Then their eyes met and their gazes locked. Enthralled by the shimmering specter, Kohani began to feel drawn to the phantom warrior even though the Mayor was tugging him in the opposite direction. He blinked and rubbed his eyes, thinking it was somehow the residue of his Communion, though he had no idea what it had to do with a fox-bear. When he looked back, the aura was gone.

Kohani suddenly became aware of the mass of people around him. No one else appeared to have seen the image. As they made their way through the press of people, deference was shown to him, with the word "Kahanne" muttered throughout. Kohani didn't notice. With his eyes downcast, he shook his head, trying to make sense of what he had just seen. The Mayor stopped short. Kohani looked up and saw that they were standing in front of a small brown hill. He didn't remember this being here before. He turned around and saw thousands of people facing it. He was stunned. Every last citizen must be here!

They quieted down to see what would happen. Kohani glanced at the Mayor, who was staring at the hill. "Well," demanded the Kahanne, "where are these mysterious arrivals you were talking about?"

The Mayor pointed straight up.

Kohani turned back around. It took him a few seconds to realize that the hill was actually a huge booted foot. His gaze followed the foot up along the giant leg, which was attached to a body that would have looked human had it not been for its colossal size. Swashes of royal blue and soft purple adorned a black, tight outfit that allowed the proportions of a well-muscled man to show through. It towered above the crowd, standing almost as tall as the spires surrounding the square. Behind it stood eleven others, all dressed the same way. Only their genders and skin tones set them apart from one another. They wore no jewelry or decorations of any kind but they exuded a regal authority.

Kohani was awestruck. "Mon Dieu," he whispered.

He slowly stepped back to join the crowd of people that was giving the giants an increasingly wider berth. The Kahanne put a hand across the nape of his neck as he strained to regard the face of the one in front.

It had a clear, hard expression, and its dark eyes scanned the crowd, marking their presence. Apparently reaching a decision, it turned to the two who stood immediately behind it. There was a brief, silent exchange between the three of them. The first one then turned back to the people. It opened its mouth, and a deep, rumbling basso filled the minds of everyone present. The booming sound resonated across the square. Although everyone heard the same voice, the people would later disagree as to the precise wording of the pronouncement, since they all heard it in their own native languages:

"This, we give you to know: that your world shall pass through seven ages in its time. Three shall be times of Order and three shall be times of Chaos, in which your world will be laid waste.

"Let it now be known that upon the third coming of Chaos, the bones shall be tossed in a contest of wills to see which shall emerge dominant in the struggle between Order and Chaos and that the victor shall determine the fate of all that is to proceed.

"Everything past, present, and future shall meet at that appointed time to act as witness. Two will enter; one will survive. And the One shall rule them all."

The giant paused for a moment, and as the echo of its voice faded away, it resumed, indicating each of its companions as it spoke.

"Rasqu'il and L'Xar will contend. Samlah, Elren, Teyull, Rukh, Avari, Shakar, Qedem, Yarmah, and Arya will bear witness. I, the Unknown, will judge. I have spoken. Let the Game commence."

With that, the twelve giant visitors vanished, leaving behind a crowd of confused and frightened civilians.

Herald

Eve of the Age of Redemption

Beyond space and time was a location that did and did not exist. This was the place of meeting, where the matches were played and the fates of whole worlds decided. Now, though, it was empty.

Presently, the fogginess of the place retreated to reveal a tiled floor. There were benches at the edge of the mist so the others could sit and watch — and judge — to ensure that the match was being played according to the rules.

This contest had been a stalemate for a millennium, a draw that was about to come to a decisive end. The situation had changed. The time for the final round was drawing close. Once the players returned, the Game would be renewed.

Six Months Before the Time of Meeting

THE PRAETORIAN

The morning air was still and frosty. A caravan of enormous galleasses slowly skimmed the surface of the River Saar, traveling west toward the Alpas Mountains. The sails were completely furled and there was no visible activity above deck.

The gray water reflected the light of an overcast sky, with only a bright patch to indicate the sun's location. The river was as lifeless as the air. Only the rhythmic motion of the galleass' oars disrupted its tranquility.

The Saar had spent the last few millennia carving its way eastward from its source in Lake Kristalvas, which was high up in the Alpas range. It snaked through the Alpas foothills and into the rugged terrain of Valandov's interior. Like the rest of the Federated States, Valandov was covered by a thick, mostly coniferous carpet of trees that seemed to glide by the galleasses. The rolling forested hills climbed as high as three hundred and fifty meters, making the country nearly impassable to anyone not using the Federate's roads or extensive river system. The beauty and serenity of this vast country were deceptive — beyond the paths eked out by humans and the rivers lay great danger.

All along the shoreline, the wildlife was awakening. Movement could be seen at the water's edge. A faunn appeared from behind a bush and dipped its snout in the water. Suddenly it jerked its head up and listened intently. It watched the first galleass travel upriver, but it was far from shore. Satisfied that it posed no threat, the faunn returned to its drink. It pretended not to notice eight other galleasses pass by.

Soon the forest came alive and animals of every kind ventured out to the shore. Winter was finally retreating, which meant that hibernation season was over. Most of the animals ignored the crafts that moved smoothly along the River Saar.

The galleasses were designed simply with three decks and a cargo hold. Since the Federated States couldn't afford a large navy like the Hansic Alliance or the Dominion of Khadash, it had to resort to the cheapest system of transportation for its rivers. Galleasses were an efficient and inexpensive way to move raw materials and manufactured goods. They also made effective troop carriers. One galleass was big enough to carry two entire platoons — nearly one hundred soldiers, plus supplies and provisions — in addition to the normal crew of seventy-five.

The first people to get up were on the second galleass. One of them was a herald who put a horn to her lips. Her commander laid a restraining hand on her arm. He spoke quietly, and with a measured cadence that betrayed his Teivan heritage.

"Not this morning, Sergeant. I want to enjoy the peace. Wake them personally."

The sergeant nodded and headed below decks. While she went about her business, her commander alerted the other galleasses by signaling to the captains of the watch. Once that was done, he returned to the bow of his craft. He nodded curtly to the helmsman, who was wrapped tightly in a thick cloak, and inhaled deeply. How he loved these mornings! The crisp air refreshed him. He stood there and gazed at the shoreline, which was a short swim away. The foliage wasn't as thick in this part of the Federate as it was in the rest of the country because of its altitude and its proximity to the Alpas Mountains. He noticed a faunn taking a drink. It looked up at the galleasses for a moment before returning its attention to the water.

Duncan Milius displayed the hardened expression that was typical of military commanders. If his visage betrayed a sense of youth, it was because he had achieved his rank faster than anyone ever before. He was of medium height, burly, and had sandy hair that lay flatly on his head. The man wasn't ugly, though he wasn't handsome, either. A jagged scar ran the length of his left cheek.

He stretched his cramped muscles and the distinct sound of creaking leather was heard. The Federated States were the only parts of the Commonwealth in which metal armor was prohibited. Steel protection was very expensive, and although the Praetorship could afford to equip its troops this way, they recognized that steel provided poor range of motion in the densely forested country, and good mobility was necessary to combat the constant threat from grimal clans.

The sun broke through the cloud cover and for a moment, its glint reflected off the rank insignia on the soldier's shoulders: the likeness of two wolvan's teeth overlapping three chevrons, indicating a commander of a company that was only now beginning to wake up. Above these symbols was the depiction of an attacking vulturn with a bow in its claws and a sword and pike crossed behind it — the crest of Valor's Keep.

"Captain Milius!" The sergeant approached him. She had put away the horn. "The other companies have reported in, sir. The battalion is awake." This woman was youthful, short and stocky. She was called Terrel. Not much to look at, mused Duncan, but then his thoughts in this regard dwelt on someone else. He closed his eyes, and his love's image flashed before him. Long, dark hair framing a milky, oval face… almond-shaped eyes the color of oak… thin, inviting lips… He had memorized every square millimeter of her face, and he could still remember her body's scent even though weeks had passed since their last meeting. With an inward sigh, he opened his eyes. His reverie had lasted only a second and he found himself matching the sergeant's gaze again.

Terrel didn't carry what most people in the service referred to as the "Praetorian Air" but she had passed her training and served her time as a cadet. Duncan studied her for a moment and recalled everything he knew about her. He had seen her type before: loyal, efficient, but not particularly creative. She was certainly no career officer. It was most probable that she would finish a long and honorable tour of duty as a squad leader before returning to Valor's Keep as a cadet trainer. It wasn't illustrious, but she filled a need.

Duncan nodded curtly. "Thank you, Sergeant. If I'm not mistaken, meal duty goes to Sergeant Parsons' squad today."

"I believe so, sir. I'll remind them right away."

Duncan's stomach grumbled loudly. "You'd better hurry," he added.

Terrel smiled and headed off.

*

After breakfast, Duncan received a summons from Marshal Corinn Wallace, who was traveling with the first platoon. Two privates detached a small lifeboat and rowed him over. He was escorted to the marshal's cabin and ushered inside, where the battalion commander and the other three captains waited. They were seated around a map of the Ravelin region that lay three hundred and fifty kilometers south of the Palladum, the closest major Federate garrison.

Duncan saluted. "Sir."

The marshal didn't get up. "At ease, Captain. Have a seat. The next time you decide to wake up early, try to let the herald do her job. The entire unit was four minutes off schedule this morning."

"I apologize. It was a peaceful morning and I didn't want to disturb the tranquility. It won't happen again, sir."

Marshal Wallace eyed Duncan with annoyance, an expression that Duncan could see was shared by the other senior officers. Wallace had never been very good at hiding his feelings. He wasn't a very attractive person and Duncan found his abrasive demeanor hard to get along with, though he had a reputation for being a vicious fighter.

"Captain Milius, I appreciate your concern for the tranquility of our environment, but this is a military venture, not a Teivan pleasure trip. If you're looking to enjoy yourself then resign your commission and return to your father's parliament."

Duncan averted his gaze, humiliated. "Sorry, sir." The barb about his Teivan background was unnecessary.

Wallace gestured to the map. "I want ideas on how to relieve the siege of Fort Ravelin."

"What's their supply situation?" asked Captain Blaine. Duncan studied her. Fair skinned with auburn hair, he had heard that her promotion was due more to a display of valor in battle than to any real expression of intellectual skill.

"When we left Valandov they still had three months of rations," answered Wallace, "and they'd been siphoning water from a glacial stream which flows beside the fortress. They were well-stocked with ammunition for their ballistae and catapults, and they had plenty of arrows and bolts, though it's impossible to speculate on the situation now."

"We've been out of contact with them for weeks," mentioned Captain Lecy. "There could be munitions shortages of every kind." Duncan wasn't sure about this captain — he hadn't met or heard of her before this mission. She had blond hair and skin like Blaine's, though Lecy was considerably more attractive. 'She wears her armor well': it was a saying he had heard during his cadet years that referred to the more desirable female proctors and cadets. The wisecrack infuriated them.

"Shortages may not be the only problem," stated Blaine. "We don't even know if there's a fortress left to relieve."

Captain Alren concurred. He was an exceedingly tall man with simple features and, from what Duncan could discern, an intellect to match. The chair he sat in was too small for him and he shifted uncomfortably.

"I think we have to assume the worst," suggested Alren.

Wallace nodded. "Agreed, we have to proceed on the assumption that the fortress has been overrun by Hansic forces or is still under duress. In any event, we should expect no support from them at all." The marshal glanced at each of his executive officers for approval. "Captain Milius, we haven't heard from you. Have you something to add to our discussion, or should I fetch your senior lieutenant instead?"

There was no visible response to the insult from anyone, but Duncan felt Wallace's sting. His foster-father was always warning him about receiving such treatment, and he was right. Duncan's short career already featured more promotions and commendations than most Praetorians saw in a lifetime, but most of the officer corps still believed that he had something to prove. *Except the Grand-General,* he mused. *He sees everything and judges honorably.*

Duncan was by far the youngest person at the table right now and he knew the others resented it. He could see that they were awaiting his response. He decided not to take Wallace's bait and dealt instead on the matter at hand. "The last message from the fortress mentioned that they were besieged by an unidentified force, so we're assuming that the Hanse is involved. But there haven't been open hostilities between the Hansic Alliance and the Federated States in years. Why pick a fight now?"

Wallace straightened himself up. "We're not politicians. As far as we're concerned, the motives of the two sides are irrelevant. Our job is to enforce the Commonwealth Treaty which both of these countries signed in good faith and have since renewed."

"All the more reason to suspect a group other than the Hanse."

"Who else has the resources or the manpower to assault a fortress like Ravelin?"

Duncan inhaled deeply. The others weren't likely to accept his answer. "Grimals."

Alren treated this remark disdainfully. "Excuse me?"

"I've dealt with grimms all my life. I spent my childhood living alongside them before I was… taken in by my foster-father. I even fought in skirmishes against them when I was in the Federate militia. Cutting off communication and supplies, starving the fort into submission: this is their pattern."

"And I suppose you're writing the book on grimm tactics," jibed Alren.

Duncan pressed on. "The problem is that there *aren't* any such books. If there were, they would say that this situation bears all the signs of a grimm attack. Expecting to meet Hansic troops makes no sense."

"Why not?" challenged Lecy.

Wallace cut off any further debate. "Captain Milius is correct on one count. We can expect that the only route through the forest has been cut off. So, presumably, has the pass Ravelin guards into the Hansic Alliance."

Duncan examined the map. It displayed the region around the fortress in a twenty-five kilometer radius. "These marks represent the Ravelin garrison's patrol routes?"

"Yes, red corresponds to Federate troop movements and blue is for the Hansic patrols that we know about."

Duncan studied it intently while the others discussed possible strategies. Their voices faded into the background as he focused his attention on the map.

"We should cut east and come around the fortress from its south flank with our backs to the mountain," suggested Blaine.

"Send two companies out to break the blockade on the road to Ravelin while the others continue through the forest in flanking positions," said Alren.

"We're assuming that they're blocking the road, but they may not be," countered Lecy. "They could be entrenched in the forest anywhere along the route."

"Our biggest problem is that we can't know for certain where they're positioned," voiced Wallace. "Our most recent information is two weeks old — before any engagements took place between the two forces, assuming there were any. It seems most probable that they're spread out around Ravelin in small groups to better avoid detection."

The three captains nodded.

Duncan was still trapped in his reverie. Images from his militia days flooded his mind… and then he was back at his outpost near Gath. His regiment was stationed in a fort twenty kilometers north of the capital city. The fort had been placed there in advance of a new settlement that was to be built around it. A scout party was ambushed by a small group of grimals, and Duncan's regiment was being dispatched to clear the immediate vicinity of enemy activity. He heard echoed shouts from officers as they barked orders to form offensive lines to drive the grimms out of human territory. He heard cries of pain as his comrades fell and recalled the adrenaline surge as his regiment tried to cut a swath through the defense. He remembered the shouts of success as the grimms kept falling back — it was almost as if they were trying to draw the humans away from something…

He returned to the present. "I know where they are," blurted Duncan. The memory had been so vivid, he felt like he had actually traveled back fifteen years. He felt a bit dizzy, so he steadied himself against the table.

"What are you talking about?" sighed Alren.

"The grimals."

Wallace's eyes narrowed.

Duncan ran his fingers through his hair. "They're just keeping enough of a presence to make us think they've surrounded Ravelin, but really they haven't. There's a pattern here. Look!" Duncan pointed out the markers indicating the patrol routes. "Both the Hansic and Federate troops avoided this border area northwest of Ravelin. It's unexplored territory, and for a reason: that's where the bulk of their forces are concentrated."

"The phantom grimm army," muttered Wallace.

Duncan ignored the quip and continued. As the conversation became more heated, his accent became more pronounced. The others shifted uneasily, uncomfortable with the reminder that one of their battalion's senior officers was a Teivan. "We can send an expeditionary force along the road — at least a platoon, something large enough to make them think we're serious — and divert their attention from our main strikes in the forest northwest of Ravelin."

"And just what do you expect to find there?"

"I don't know… a camp… a settlement…"

Wallace laughed. "I think you're giving these creatures too much credit! They're primitive, incapable of employing the strategies you're ascribing to them. We're fighting a more intelligent enemy, a *human* enemy, and our best bet is to flush them out. Captain Milius and Captain Blaine, your companies will take the road south to Ravelin." He leaned over the map as he spoke. "The other units will begin a day in advance so they can assume flanking positions in the forest, here and here. Captain Alren's company will take up a posture to our west and Captain Lecy on our east. You two will flush the Hansic troops north along the path towards the main force, where we'll issue our ultimatum: return to the other side of the border or be wiped out. Brief your lieutenants and sergeants accordingly and prepare your troops. We'll be disembarking before nightfall."

*   *

Within thirty minutes, the supplies were organized and the troops were ready. The Praetorians spent the rest of the morning in their platoons being briefed by their lieutenants. After lunch, Marshal Wallace made his rounds from one galleass to the next inspecting the soldiery. Following that, the Praetorians spent the remainder of the day chatting quietly, relaxing and concentrating on the next few days. They weren't afraid of dying in battle — to Praetorians, falling in combat was an honor. A Praetorian's greatest concern was for the lives of others. No one wanted to be remembered with the dishonor of failing his or her own squad.

Duncan sat alone as he often did before entering combat, though his thoughts were not on the coming battle. He had been unable to convince Wallace of his tactical oversight when the marshal boarded the galleass on his inspection tour. A nagging sensation told him that they were headed for disaster. The problem was that he could find no fault with Wallace's strategy. The marshal was making the most logical conclusions based on the available data. Duncan simply *knew* that his commander was wrong, but there was no way to convince him without evidence.

He looked up and saw the eastern end of the Alpas Mountains looming before them. Two giant, jagged peaks: one right next to them on the north and one to the distant south, which was their destination. Ravelin lay at the foot of that one. Duncan sighed and stood up. The dock would soon be in sight. It was time to rally his troops.

*

Sergeant Terrel was chatting with two corporals when she heard a loud voice in her head.

Terrel.

She broke off the conversation and excused herself. She looked all around for the source of the voice, but she only saw soldiers sharpening their weapons and checking their gear.

I've hidden myself, Terrel. Speak telepathically, and for the Spirits' sake, behave normally! You look like you're about to break down!

Terrel composed herself. *Sorry, I wasn't expecting any contact. Chieftain, is that you?*

It is. I've been watching your captain very carefully. He put on quite a show today in the strategy session.

You were there?

The Chieftain sounded proud of himself. *I certainly was.*

How did you get in? Surely, they didn't invite you...

Oh, come on, he snapped, *do you honestly think I asked permission? I was hidden, just like I am now. But don't think I wasn't tempted to reveal myself. It would've caused quite a stir. Now that would have been something to see.*

The sergeant shook her head. *They probably would've tried to kill you on the spot. Sometimes I wonder why they tolerate our presence at Valor's Keep.*

They don't have a choice, really. They know that the Circle gets what it wants — better then to agree to our terms and keep us in plain sight where they can monitor our movements.

The Chieftain said this sarcastically, and Terrel laughed inwardly at the irony. *What do you want me to do?*

Watch Jehorom Galaddi carefully, but at a distance. Don't draw too much attention to yourself. Let us know if he does anything unexpected.

Like what?

I'm not sure, you'll know when you see it. Right now, it's just a hunch, but I've had a feeling about this one for a long time. He may be the culmination of our work. I must return to the Enclave, so you'll be on your own for now. Report everything directly to Phylar, no matter how insignificant.

I'll do my best.

With that, the contact ended. Terrel stood there for a moment shaking off the echo of the Chieftain's voice when Duncan called the troops to attention. The dock had been sighted. Alren's and Lecy's companies were disembarking and settling in for the night. Tomorrow, they would assume their flanking positions and begin the three-and-a-half-day trek to Ravelin. Twenty-four hours after that, the rest of the army would follow along the road. The battle would be joined soon enough.

$$*\qquad*\qquad*$$

Four tense days passed before the remaining half of Marshal Wallace's battalion set out. Captain Duncan Milius led his company in a steady march southward, the eastern end of the Alpas Mountains looming before them. There had been no contact with Alren's and Lecy's companies. No progress updates, no scouting reports. Duncan shrugged — according to the plan, there should be no sign of their flanking units until the enemy was practically upon the main force.

Wallace had ordered Duncan and Captain Blaine to deploy their troops into standard defensive formations. Each company marched in a square, with three infantry squads forming double lines on each side with pikes and swords. In the middle of the squares were the companies' command teams (Wallace marched with Blaine), their attendants and the supply carts, as well as four squads of archers.

The road was just wide enough for the formations to pass, though Duncan had argued that smaller groups would allow for greater mobility and spontaneity — should they be attacked en route, platoons could be redeployed more quickly and efficiently than whole companies could. Wallace had opted instead for a more traditional defense.

They were progressing very slowly. Duncan's company marched ahead of Blaine's, and he instructed his front lines to be on the lookout for the scouts he had sent ahead as warning against any advance. So far, the scouts had been reporting regularly that there were no hints of the flanking companies, enemy forces, or signs of battle. Duncan considered the possibilities: the flanking companies had not yet met the enemy; they had been forced to hole up inside Ravelin; or their troops had been completely wiped out — a possibility that no Praetorian ever considered.

As they marched, many soldiers shifted their gear uncomfortably. Every person carried a backpack that contained a bedroll, rations, a sewing kit, extra leather patches for their armor, and basic medical supplies like bandages and tourniquets. Their bedrolls were water-resistant and had built-in head coverings. This was the standard issue for every Praetorian. Although it was generally understood that a tour of duty in the Federated States meant a greater risk to one's life, troops assigned to other parts of Halcyon were envious of the fact that in the forests of the Federate they didn't have to march with an ungainly backpack *and* heavy steel armor.

Leather protection may have made for easier travel, but this thought was far from the minds of the troops who marched to Fort Ravelin. With every new step, the tension increased. With every negative report, the soldiers' anxiety deepened. Their training kept their emotions in check, but no amount of preparation could suppress the human need for action. They could deal with being a small force facing superior numbers — it was a fact of life in the Praetorship and a source of pride that they enjoyed such success in spite of it. To the contrary, the apprehension on the road to Ravelin stemmed from the unknown. Had their companions engaged the enemy? Had they faced death honorably? Duncan had often remarked that the worst part of battle was waiting for the fight to begin. He decided to ease the tension by starting a marching tune. Soon, every soldier in both companies was humming along. Duncan knew he would hear about it later from Wallace. The marshal considered singing a distraction.

It was midmorning now and the weather was clear, just as it had been for the last two days. The coniferous forest spilled over onto the side of the road. Pines stretched up from the ground in light clumps — many of them were as tall as a two-story building. The ground was frozen but not hard. There had already been one spring thaw, though most farmers were saying that there was still time for one last gasp from winter before it was finally chased away for the year. The air was chill but refreshing.

And a good thing, too, mused Duncan. *It'll keep the troops alert.*

The captain looked about uncomfortably. This place was too still. He signaled a halt and the troops obeyed his command immediately. A second later Blaine's company stopped as well. The echoes of the marching and singing faded away. Now there was no noise at all — the area around the road was completely silent. Duncan beckoned to two privates and ordered them to boost him up. They cupped their hands at their waists and hoisted him above their shoulders. At the same time, the troops readied their weapons: the infantry set their pikes, balanced their shields and steadied their swords, and the archers loaded their bows and prepared to fire. Blaine's company did the same. Everyone awaited Duncan's next move.

He stood above his privates' shoulders and surveyed the scene. His searching gaze swept slowly and methodically over their surroundings. There was no movement in the forest, no natural sounds of animals or insects. It was as if the wildlife had been evacuated. Duncan suddenly felt out of place in the forest in which he was raised. Something was wrong — he could sense it right in front of him. He knew the answer was there, but his mind danced around it.

Blaine silently placed her company on high alert while Wallace watched Duncan intently. Didn't he know that he was exposing himself needlessly by raising himself over the heads of his troops? He glanced at Blaine, who shrugged. They would have to wait and see what Milius was up to, and hope that a Hansic archer hadn't managed to slip past their scouts.

Duncan returned to the ground and ordered the second infantry line from his rear flank to reinforce the front. Blaine and Wallace merged the second company with Duncan's into one long rectangular formation. The three senior officers met in the middle.

"What did you see?" whispered Wallace.

"I don't know," answered Duncan. "I just had a feeling, that's all."

"What kind of feeling?"

Duncan shook his head. "It's hard to describe. It's an intuition that hits me whenever I enter battle. I felt like we were being studied."

"Studied? What the hell is that supposed to mean? You're a professional soldier! If I want to know what someone *feels*, I'll consult a psychic. Give me hard data, not intuition!"

"Sorry, sir, it's just that I've come to learn to trust my instincts, and I'm telling you that something's out there watching us."

Wallace surveyed the pine trees that stretched above them along the sides of the road. "No-one's reported any movement. There's nothing here."

"That's the problem, sir."

Wallace and Blaine looked questioningly at him. Duncan was getting desperate. He knew this was his last chance to sway Wallace. "Look, I know you don't trust me because I'm Teivan —" Wallace glared at him "— but you have to believe me. I know things about this forest that you don't. I can detect subtle signs… the movement of animals and insects, disturbance of leaves, certain kinds of trails designed to look real but they're not—"

The marshal grabbed Duncan by his collar and pulled him close. He whispered harshly, "Listen carefully, Captain, because I'm not going to repeat myself. I am responsible for seven hundred and sixty-eight lives. I don't care about overturned leaves or footprints on the ground!"

"Then listen to someone who does. We're being watched."

Wallace released Duncan. "Watched…"

A moment passed while the marshal considered his options.

"Sir," ventured Duncan, "I recommend that we close into a tighter formation to protect our flanks and our rear. Each side should be four squads deep with double lines of pikes and swords backed by cover fire from the archers."

"We're fine, Captain," assured Wallace.

"Our perimeter's too thin! They can break through too easily!"

"At ease, Captain! I'm warning you, I've heard enough!" He turned around to face the south perimeter.

All the soldiers had their backs to the officers, but if they heard the conversation, they flatly ignored it.

Duncan half-shouted at his commanding officer. "Sir, we're boxed in!"

Wallace wheeled on his junior. "You're relieved of duty! Captain Blaine, strip him of his weapons!"

At that moment, a corporal came running up to them. "Marshal, our scouts are reporting back from Ravelin!"

Presently, one of the scouts approached the marshal and saluted. Wallace returned it and demanded a report.

"We assumed our position in the forest, as per orders," she began. "It took us three days to reach Ravelin, but we encountered nothing, not even a single person. When we reached the fort, the main gate was barred shut. There were no answers to our hails. We decided to scale the wall and see what was going on inside." She paused. "Sir, Ravelin is deserted."

"What...?"

"Not a soul remains. We unlocked the gate and I toured the place myself. There are signs of a struggle everywhere — judging by the amount of blood we saw, it was a hell of a fight — but there are no bodies."

"Are you saying that the Hansic militia abducted everyone?" asked Blaine incredulously.

"I'm saying that they're not there. I don't know what happened to them. The gate was locked from the inside, but no one seems to have remained behind to secure it."

"A militia garrison of fifteen hundred soldiers doesn't simply vanish!"

"There's something deeper happening here," stated Wallace. "I was sure that two whole battalions could hold out. We're not dealing with Ghaultian militia here, either — these Federates can fight."

Wallace and Blaine stood there for a moment contemplating the new situation. The troops around them waited patiently, poised for action. Duncan was standing slightly behind the marshal, his gaze fixed on a tree.

"Wait a minute," continued Wallace, "what about our own two companies? Was there any sign of them?"

The scout exhaled slowly and averted her superior's intense gaze. "We found no trace of them."

"They're dead," stated Duncan. He hadn't moved his gaze from the tree.

Wallace turned to glare at him. "Captain Blaine, didn't I order you to relieve him of duty?"

"Sorry, sir, I got sidetracked with—"

"Hold it." Wallace moved to stand beside Duncan and follow his line of sight. "What are you staring at?"

"That tree, sir, directly ahead of us, to the left of the tall one."

"What about it?"

"There's a grimal crouched on that branch, sir, about two and-a-half meters from the ground. It's staring right at me. I've locked eyes with it."

"I don't see it."

"I do. Remember that feeling I had? It's even stronger now…" Duncan's voice grew distant. "I can see what they're planning. My God… they've outmaneuvered us. We have to get out of here, sir. Fast."

Wallace wasn't sure what to make of his captain. He had heard stories of Duncan's uncanny ability to anticipate an enemy's moves, but as far as the marshal was concerned, this man was a spoiled, insubordinate, rich man's kid who was obviously sick in the head. To suggest that the Praetorship should retreat? This was an affront to everything Wallace held dear!

Duncan spoke as if he read his superior's thoughts. His eyes were still trained on the tree. "We're only an expeditionary force, sir, half the size of the garrison we were ordered to relieve, and we've already lost half of our number. We don't have the supplies or the people to man that fortress properly. We need to come back here with an army and teams of experienced trackers. Grimals did this, sir, not Hansic militia."

"Ravelin's less than half-a-day away at a fast march," suggested Blaine. "We can hole up there and send a carrier bird to the Palladum advising them of our status."

"The fortress may be deserted, but it's well-stocked," added the scout. "All the garrison's supplies were left behind."

Wallace nodded but was disappointed. The last thing he wanted to do was relieve one of his senior officers from duty. "We'll go to Ravelin. I'll assume direct command of Captain Milius' unit. His weapons will be surrendered and his hands bound. I'll decide what to do with him when we reach the fort. Redeploy the troops. We'll march in separate companies with the defensive box pattern."

No sooner had the order been relayed to the lieutenants than Duncan cried out.

"Marshal Wallace!"

"What is it now? Do I have to gag you?"

Duncan motioned wildly at the front lines. "Get them away from there!"

At that moment, a low rumble sounded from the ground. The earth shook and everyone lost his balance. It was over in a few seconds and order was immediately restored.

Wallace grabbed Duncan. "What the hell was that?!"

"Marshal!"

The shout came from a sergeant at the front. Wallace and the captains jogged up and pushed their way through. Their eyes widened in shock, except for Duncan, who backed away. He had seen this sort of thing before.

The entire front line had vanished — in its place was a yawning ditch in the ground. The elongated pit was a half-dozen meters deep and at the bottom lay nearly a hundred Praetorians. Some of them were dazed from the fall and others were clearly wounded. Many of them were impaled on wooden spikes that protruded from the pit's floor.

Wallace's jaw tightened and his hands clenched. "Reinforce our position," he whispered.

Blaine answered, "Sir?"

"You heard me. Do as Captain Milius said: a formation to protect our flanks and our rear. Four squads to a side with double lines of pikes and swords backed by archers."

"What about our wounded in the pit?"

"Now, Captain!"

As the marshal's orders were relayed, Duncan pointed at the trees. "Grimals!"

The Praetorians were just breaking formation when the attack came. The forest came alive with hundreds of brown blurs as grimals detached themselves from the trees they were using as cover. The sergeants on the front lines quickly gained control of their troops, but the left and right flanks, which still had only two defensive lines, were breached almost immediately. The attackers were smaller than most humans and were covered entirely in brown fur, but what they lacked in size they more than made up for in catlike speed and agility. The Praetorians immediately broke out of their large formations and into squads, and the grimals danced between them, avoiding pikes and swords. The archers were having only moderate success — it was difficult to aim and fire without hitting one of their own. Soon the well-ordered defense had completely devolved into a large melee, with only a few squads of infantry forming a tight defensive shield around a dozen archers. The pikemen had dropped their gangling weapons in favor of the swords at their sides. Total bedlam ensued — except for Sergeant Terrel's group, the archers had been completely taken out in the first minute of battle.

The grimals darted back into the trees and the attack ended as abruptly as it began, allowing the confused Praetorians to regroup. Officers barked orders all over the place, but eventually the defensive pattern that Duncan originally suggested was established. They were now packed tightly together, with at least three meters of open ground between the flanks and the forest wall — enough space to provide some reaction time for the infantry. Most of the archers had been killed and many pikemen lay dead or wounded on the ground.

All was quiet.

"Sir," ventured Blaine, "we can still make it to the fortress."

"If we do, we'll end up like our missing companies and the Ravelin garrison," replied a panting Duncan. "The ships are our only option."

"At Ravelin there are supplies and a wall, for God's sake!"

"Neither of which helped the garrison all that much!"

"Enough of this," snapped Wallace. "We seem to have fought them off for now. Captain Blaine, have some of your people collect the arrows from any fallen archers and see to our wounded. Redistribute the arrows between two infantry squads — I want that archery unit reformed. Assign a squad to rescue any survivors from the bottom of that pit. Our archers will cover you from here."

As Blaine turned to fulfill her orders, Duncan whispered, "Marshal, we're packed too tightly. Our people don't have enough room to maneuver against grimals."

Barely concealing his spite, Wallace eyed his subordinate. "We'll be under way soon enough, Captain."

A gap opened in the southern defensive line for a rescue team. Medics were out tending to the wounded, and two dozen footmen were being reassigned by their sergeants to the depleted archery unit. While all this happened, the Praetorians remained on high alert. They weren't going to be caught off-guard again.

Duncan watched everything anxiously. "Sir, we have to get out of here."

"Calm yourself, Captain."

Duncan grabbed the marshal by his shoulders and spun him around. "Sir, they're coming back! We need to go now!"

Wallace stared back angrily and freed himself of Duncan's grasp. The marshal was about to order Blaine to restrain the maverick captain when he realized that the warning was too late. Another low rumble sounded, and the ground beneath the northern line collapsed.

With two of the Praetorians' four defensive lines compromised, the battle was rejoined. The grimals danced between the humans with impunity, and the Praetorians were packed so tightly together that there was no room for them to move freely. Soon they regrouped again into squads but the tide had already turned against them.

The grimals brandished formidable weapons: retractable claws in their hands and feet. Combined with their feline quickness and movement, these proved deadlier than the sharpest knife as they tore into the leather armor of their opponents. Perhaps the most disturbing element was the stark silence of the attackers. The only sounds to be heard were shouts from officers and dying humans.

Duncan spied the ring of soldiers that protected the remnant of the archery unit. He fought his way over. All around him were flailing bodies of grimals. It was hard to tell who outnumbered whom. One private caught a leaping attacker on her shield and stabbed upward with her sword, impaling the creature. Just as she extracted her weapon, she was jumped from behind and knocked down. Duncan jabbed a dagger into its back and threw it off, but not before it managed to gouge open the Praetorian's throat. There was nothing Duncan could do.

Marshal Wallace had managed to rally a dozen troops around the standard of Valor's Keep but the grimals fought savagely, using the confusion to a startling advantage. As Wallace felt himself being pressed back, he marveled at the way the attackers managed to keep a battalion of Praetorians completely off-balance. He was unaware of the losses his troops were taking around him. The Praetorship had never lost a battle and it wasn't about to lose now.

Duncan reached the archery squad and grabbed a lieutenant. "Come on, we're leaving," he shouted.

She ordered her troops to follow as Duncan led them to the east side of the road.

"Into the forest," he shouted. "Move!"

The soldiers followed without question. As he turned to call for more troops to retreat, a grimal leaped from the tree above him. It danced away from his sword but he grabbed his dagger and slashed open its belly. It opened its mouth in a silent scream of pain, revealing frightening incisors. It tried to maul his hand but he twisted away and lopped its head off with his sword.

"Let's go, Praetorians," he shouted. "This is Captain Duncan Milius! Fall back to the east perimeter! The east perimeter, into the forest! Fall back!"

Duncan looked back and saw Wallace. Blood spattered the marshal's armor and helmet. With a hoarse battle cry, Wallace leaped into the midst of a group of advancing grimals with his sword arm flailing. He took two out immediately and lopped off the arm of a third before another raked his back with its claws. Wallace roared, spun around and thrust wildly while the grimal nimbly danced out of the way. As it ducked under his next sword stroke and rolled past him, it thrust out its foot and found the open spot in his armor behind his knee. It slashed open his leg with a protruding claw, and Wallace faltered. Duncan tried to fight his way over to his commanding officer as Wallace fought off his attackers from his knees. A grimal slashed his throat open. The standard of Valor's Keep, the honor of which they had all sworn to protect, lay trampled on the ground.

Giving up, Duncan joined the soldiers who were fighting for their lives in the forest. "Northeast, people, move it! Stay away from the road!"

He darted past them and they followed obediently. Even in the thick of battle, with their lives in jeopardy, training overrode their instincts. Duncan looked back and saw a score of Praetorians running at a frenzied pace, weaving around the trees. Behind them, grimals could be seen as dark blurs leaping from one pine to the next in pursuit. The captain spied Sergeant Terrel and two archers. He stopped them and had them fire three rounds at the pursuers before rejoining the flight. Soon, the sounds of battle faded into the distance.

The grimal pursuers quickly gave up the chase. Duncan ordered a halt to the retreat and everyone returned to the road. When they reached the edge of the forest, he stopped them.

"Careful, there's a trap here."

The soldiers shot questioning glances at each other but obeyed nonetheless. They watched their captain step carefully onto the wide path. He surveyed the scene before sprinting to the middle. The others followed. Duncan led them to a large pit that had been cleverly dug in the middle of the road. A taut, thin line of bark extended from the trap to the trees on the west side. The line was coated with an unfamiliar resin that made it tougher than the thickest rope. Inside the pit were the bodies of a dozen Praetorians. They had been slashed and mangled. The fetid stench emanating from the pit indicated that they had been dead for several days.

"They bear the insignia from Captain Alren's company," commented Terrel. "They must have been his scouts sent to warn us."

"We were marching on top of these pits the whole time," remarked a lieutenant. "How could they possibly have known we were coming?"

"They were watching us," replied Duncan, "just like they're watching us right now." The captain made a quick count of the survivors: fifty, maybe sixty soldiers. A dozen seriously wounded, perhaps more. Eight archers but their quivers were nearly empty. He had one lieutenant, three sergeants and Captain Blaine, though she was ready to collapse from a vicious gash in her side.

"We'll bind our wounded and make for the ships. We have to move quickly. It isn't safe here."

Blaine sat down heavily. "We have to go back and finish—"

"There's nothing to finish," interrupted Duncan. "The grimms won't follow us north. We should be okay as long as we keep moving toward the river. Then we'll return to Valandov. For now, rest for a moment."

The Praetorians sat down and tried to catch their breath. No one spoke. The Praetorship had just lost its first battle, and they hadn't even been able to make an honorable fight out of it. Of an entire battalion, little more than a single platoon had survived. The traditional Praetorian stoicism crumbled as the soldiers' faces conveyed their humiliation and dishonor. Everyone wanted to rush back to the fray, but their oath of loyalty demanded total adherence to their superior officers, and since Marshal Wallace was dead and Captain Blaine was barely conscious, that position fell to Duncan.

Duncan himself had no time for misgivings. The realization that he was in command came quickly. He rose and stood over the pit of fallen Praetorians. Quietly, and with due solemnity, he began to chant a morose tune. The soldiers around him perked up and got to their feet. They stood at attention and saluted as Duncan assumed his first role as commander by reciting the funeral dirge.

At journey's end we meet eternal night—
With Honor, Valor and Might.
We defend the Keep against Chaos' shadow
With Honor, Valor and Might.
Whosoever welcomes Eve's cold embrace
With Honor, Valor and Might
Shall prevail in legends of yore retold
With Honor, Valor and Might.
We pass from this age to bequeath to the next
Our Honor, Valor and Might.
May these souls live in death as they did in life—
With Honor, Valor and Might.

They stood there observing a moment of silence. As if snapping out of a trance, Duncan turned to look at his ragtag troop. They looked filthy and utterly downtrodden, as if someone had picked a group of beggars from the street and outfitted them with discarded armor and weapons. They awaited his orders, not caring whether they lived or died.

Duncan spoke hoarsely. "We need to bury these soldiers, but we don't have the time." As if to highlight his point, the breeze carried to them a distant, high-pitched call. The Praetorians looked about nervously, unsure of what to do. They knew the battle was lost, but to leave comrades unburied on the battlefield...

Knowing their thoughts, Duncan continued. "We can't go back and lay hundreds of people to rest. Our primary responsibility is to the living!"

If there was any agreement, it was grudging. More than one fighter interpreted his words as cowardice, including Blaine, but she could think of no other course of action.

"From the sound of those calls, we have about three minutes before they catch up," continued Duncan. He turned to his subordinate. "Lieutenant, organize our medical supplies and redistribute the remaining arrows among four archers. Reassign any extra archers and medics to the infantry."

Thankful to be taking some positive action, the junior officer replied, "Yes, sir." She went about her tasks, and the rest of the troops slumped dejectedly to the ground to take advantage of the short respite.

Duncan surveyed what remained of Wallace's battalion. *They don't trust me*, he realized. *Will they mutiny?*

It was then when he noticed that Sergeant Terrel was missing.

$$* \qquad * \qquad *$$

The remnant of Marshal Wallace's battalion reached the pier three days later. In that time, they had found no evidence of any enemy activity north of the pit trap with the dead Praetorians. From the moment Duncan had led the singing of the funeral dirge, the grimals had left them alone. Duncan ordered the skippers of seven of the galleasses to return to Valandov. His platoon then set out on the remaining ship.

The Praetorians conducted themselves almost in a robotic fashion — they expressed no emotion when carrying out orders. The loss at Ravelin, at once shocking and humiliating, had sapped the joy of performing their duties right out of them. What remained were empty shells. The most debilitating aspect for them was that they were honor bound to avenge their comrades and ensure that they hadn't died in vain, but they were powerless to do anything. Certainly, many felt that they had abandoned their people by retreating and not facing death at their sides. Duncan's argument about living to continue the fight was logical but didn't ease the remorse.

They obeyed Duncan's orders blindly, as if they didn't care whether the next moment brought death or life. Duncan felt as if he had somehow failed in his duty, but he saw no way to raise the morale of his people. He was convinced that had it not been for the Praetorian oath of allegiance, some of these survivors would have mutinied by now.

Duncan shared their grief, but for him there was something much more. He had felt something when he locked eyes with that grimal just before the ambush. He couldn't quite express it, but there had been some kind of rudimentary exchange, a communication of sorts. He knew about the attack before it came.

Then there was Captain Blaine. Despite the injury, her weakness of will had become painfully apparent these last few days. She seemed paralyzed to assume any kind of command ever since Duncan's theory about the grimals was proven correct. He had resorted to treating her like another lieutenant — she deferred to him in every situation.

Which is probably as it should be, he mused. *She should never have been promoted in the first place.*

On the morning of the second day of their journey down river, Blaine awoke Duncan from a fitful sleep.

"Captain Milius, there's something you should see."

"Can't you handle it?" he answered groggily. "This is my first break in twenty hours."

"I'm sorry," replied Blaine. She brushed back a strand of red hair that had fallen over her face and grimaced at the pain in her side. "It's just that I think I know why we haven't seen any grimm activity since the fight."

With a groan, Duncan sat up and dressed himself. He left his quarters and followed Blaine to the ship's bow. A small crowd was gathered here and they stared forlornly ahead. Duncan motioned some of them aside so he could see.

The entire river was blocked. Trees and boulders had been pulled out of the ground and laid across the Saar to form a solid line right across the galleasses' path.

"It doesn't look like we can plow through it," stated a corporal.

"We can put to shore and try to move enough of it to get the ships by," suggested a private.

"Do you have any idea how much that must weigh?"

"If we get everyone to work together, including the crews of all eight ships…"

Duncan closed his eyes and shook his head. His mind flashed back to his childhood, to memories of his birth parents drilling him on the locations of safe paths through the forest. Although many years had passed, he still remembered the network of trails. As Duncan rubbed the scar on his cheek absently, he heard his father's voice — his Teivan father — reiterate lessons he had learned long ago.

Grimals always settle near dependable water sources, he lectured. *Although some roving bands exist, they tend to stay near the rivers and streams that attract larger herbivores and omnivores, which are their main source of food.*

Then why don't we see them crowding along the riverbanks, Duncan remembered asking.

If they stayed too close to the water sources, their prey would pick up their scents, came the answer. *No, grimals are smarter than that. They carry their water back to their settlements, and they set traps out of sight of the water's edge where we won't see them. Knowing grimal habits is the key to knowing how to live with them. You see the damage to those trees, and the way the undersides of the leaves are facing outward? They look natural, don't they?*

Duncan nodded.

They're territorial markers to let other grimal bands know that a clan-group has already claimed the water and food resources in this part of the forest. By recognizing these signs, we know where to cut our trails so we can avoid violent confrontations with them. We may even be able to imitate their markers to tell them where human territory begins and ends.

The debate over how to proceed subsided as the Praetorians and sailors standing with Duncan awaited his response. He knew they were growing impatient, but he had to consider the options. They watched as he wrestled with himself, trying to convince himself of something. Finally, he looked up with a dejected expression. He was about to violate a centuries-old taboo. "Head for the north bank," he sighed. "We'll gather what supplies we can carry. Prepare stretchers for our wounded."

A lieutenant glanced at him. "Sir?"

"You heard me. We're disembarking. There's no way we can get around this blockade. The debris is impossible to move — even with all the crews working together. Whoever did this is bound to return, and we're in no shape to defend ourselves. We'll head north to the Palladum."

"How?" asked Blaine. "The intersection with the Nillus is still a day away. The river is the only way to get there."

Duncan hesitated. "That's not entirely true. There are... Teivan routes."

Blaine and the others around her exchanged mystified glances.

Their commander explained. "We don't have time for my biography. Suffice to say that I'm privy to certain paths through the forest that most Federates aren't aware of. I can guide us safely to the Palladum."

This only increased the unease of the soldiers and sailors within earshot. That he was Teivan was obvious from his accent, but his status as their new commanding officer did nothing to counteract a lifetime of conviction that Teivans were not to be trusted.

"Won't we come across more grimms?" ventured Blaine. "Won't they notice the passage of fifty-six fighters and three hundred sailors?"

"Probably, but they won't bother us. I... that is, Teivans know where the territorial boundaries for all the grimal clans lie, and we know how to avoid them. Our paths are safe for human travel. You have to trust me. Teivans have been living side-by-side with grimals for centuries without trouble."

"Maybe they're trying to force us back on foot since they know they can't ambush us while we're in the middle of the river."

The commander sighed. Wallace would have relieved Blaine if she'd spoken to him this way in front of the common soldiery. Duncan, however, knew that he had to regain the respect of his troops. Besides, there was something to be said for having an informed soldiery. They tended to excel when they understood why they were doing something.

"You're assuming that the grimms are responsible for that blockade," replied Duncan.

"Who else could do it?"

"I don't know. All I can say is that we no longer pose a threat to them so they no longer have any need to pursue us. Why blockade the river anyway? If they wanted to finish us, they had many opportunities to do so before we reached our ships, but they gave up the pursuit. The only major settlement south of us is Ravelin. We can't go east, and west will take us further into the mountains where there's no civilization at all. North is the only direction we can go."

Duncan rubbed the jagged scar on his cheek and looked pensive. "Whoever put up that blockade wants us to think it was the grimals." He snapped out of his reverie. "You all have your orders. Carry them out."

Trustworthy or not, their captain had just issued a command. The Praetorians dispersed. Their ship weighed anchor and they lowered the lifeboats into the water. Blaine set about organizing their supplies and fetching stretchers for the wounded. She also gave instructions for the crews of all eight ships to join them.

In the meantime, Duncan retreated to his quarters, his thoughts still troubled. Someone wanted them to head north and it wasn't the grimals.

*   *   *

The Palladum was the largest and most technologically advanced fortress in the country. It was the Federate's response to incursions from smugglers and militants who used the narrow mouth of the River Nillus to import contraband and to launch raids against Federate outposts. The Palladum was a physical barrier to one of the few accessible entrances to this part of the country and a staging point for sorties against these well-armed factions. Guarding the narrow mouth of the River Nillus, it was a majestic sight.

On both sides of the Nillus, mountains rose to form looming east-west barriers, leaving a gorge between them through which the river flowed. An enormous stone structure five stories high straddled this gorge at its mouth. Beneath it were two portcullises set one hundred meters apart that rested in berths on the river's bottom. When ships required passage, the portcullises were raised out of the water and into the straddling portion of the fortress. A large complex spread up the sides of the gorge containing exercise and training areas, barracks for several regiments of militia soldiers and a company of Praetorians, mess halls, suites for visiting dignitaries, weapons and munitions storehouses, and residences for the attendants of all these military and civilian personnel. The overall population of the Palladum exceeded seven thousand.

At the corners of the exterior walls were short towers that supported short-range catapults. Bastions protruded at regular intervals that featured large ballistae capable of firing spear like ammunition that could pierce the hull of the stoutest frigate. Overall, the Palladum presented the appearance of invulnerability.

The fortress sprawled up the sides of the gorge in squares of ever-decreasing width that culminated in two tall, thin towers that provided advanced warning of anyone who approached by land or by sea. Therefore, Captain Milius' party was spotted well before it arrived at the Palladum's south end.

Next to the southern portcullis were a guardhouse and a gate that was just big enough to accommodate a large wagon. A corporal exited the guardhouse and motioned for Duncan to halt. A pair of archers on top of the roof trained weapons on the captain's beleaguered platoon and its train of weary sailors.

It was mid-afternoon. The sky was overcast and a cool wind blew. Overall, it was a dreary day.

The corporal sized up Duncan's group before addressing the captain. This was the most bedraggled troop of soldiers he had ever seen. One of the officers had a terrible gash in her side and the corporal was surprised to see her standing. About a dozen of them were lying unconscious on stretchers amid stains of blood. There was barely a single soldier who wasn't bandaged. Then there was the armor — every one of them wore a suit that was torn or mangled in several places. And why were they traveling with hundreds of civilians? Perhaps they had to abandon ship somewhere upriver along the Nillus.

"State your business."

"I'm Captain Duncan Milius, senior captain third rank of the Eighteenth Battalion. We seek shelter for these civilians and aid for our wounded en route to our return to Valandov."

The corporal gazed at the newcomer suspiciously. His name was familiar, but few militia soldiers had ever met Duncan Milius. The corporal wasn't even sure what he looked like. Besides, what would he be doing here?

"We haven't received any notice of new Praetorian arrivals, and if you're on your way to Valandov, you're heading in the wrong direction."

Duncan nodded wearily. "We're part of the battle group that was assigned to relieve Fort Ravelin. When we tried to return to our base at Valandov, we discovered that the river was blocked. The Palladum was the only place for us to go. That was eleven days ago."

The corporal stared blankly at him. "Eleven days ago?"

"That's right. Eleven days on foot." Duncan gestured behind him. "Our progress was somewhat slowed by our injured."

The corporal regarded him suspiciously. "Through the forest?"

Duncan glared at the corporal and fought down his mounting frustration. "If we could get our ships around the blockage, we would have used the river to return to Valandov. But we couldn't. So we came here. On foot for eleven days. Through the forest."

The corporal looked past the captain and noted again the haggard appearance of these people. They appeared to have been in a heavy battle, though if they were lying (which was quite possible) it wouldn't be the first time that a militant antigovernment faction attempted to gain illicit entrance to a Federate outpost by posing as wounded soldiers. A base near Torinn was almost overrun recently by such a ruse. The claim of having walked all the way from the Saar didn't make sense either since the only route south from the Palladum was the River Nillus. No, they must have a ship nearby. In the end, the corporal returned to the guardhouse and sent a runner to fetch one of the Praetorian lieutenants.

Presently an officer bearing the symbol of a vulturn's claw over two chevrons emerged from the guardhouse with a squad of soldiers. They all had the emblem of Valor's Keep etched onto their steel breastplates. She saluted and spoke with Duncan for a few moments before signaling to one of the soldiers on top of the gate. She then led the captain and his group inside. The three hundred sailors and attendants were taken to a different part of the fortress.

The Praetorians continued along the lower rampart that faced the river. As they walked, the two officers conversed quietly. "I apologize for the hassle, sir."

Duncan waved off the apology. "That's quite all right, I'm aware of the situation here. Tight security is necessary."

The lieutenant nodded curtly. "How many of you are there, sir?"

Duncan motioned behind them to the fallen Praetorians who were being borne on stretchers. "Sixty-seven, including eleven seriously injured."

The lieutenant pointed to one of the arched bridges. "There's a field hospital across that way. They'll see to the casualties."

Duncan beckoned to Blaine and relayed this information to her. She motioned to the ones who carried the stretchers to follow her to the hospital. Blaine looked like she was ready to collapse. Duncan ordered her to get her own wounds seen to, as well.

"We'll set up the rest of your platoon in the extra barracks," continued the lieutenant. "The civvies will take care of the sailors you brought with you. Captain Marcus has been informed of your arrival. He'll surely want to meet with you. At the moment, he's in his office."

"Very well. Escort my troops to the hospital and inform them to remain there until my return."

"Shall I send someone to take you to the captain?"

"No, thank you, I'll find my way."

"Yes, sir." The lieutenant saluted and Duncan returned it. She then headed up a flight of stairs with the beaten group of soldiers in tow.

Duncan stood there for a moment breathing in the cool mountain air. He folded his arms and leaned into a crenel. A few paces from him, an archer had her sight trained on a passing ship. The captain watched as it slowly passed beneath the bridges and reached the south portcullis. It would be boarded and searched before being given clearance to enter the country.

Duncan closed his eyes and recalled the plan he once saw for this fortress. The last time he was here, the place was still under construction. As he thought about this, Duncan absently rubbed the scar on his left cheek. He had been on leave and had decided to tour the northern regions with his foster-father, Premier Leodore Milius, who was in the midst of an election campaign. They were accompanied by General Cyril Hawkwin, the commander of the national army. Even though Hawkwin was a career militia soldier, his reputation was so great that most

Praetorian officers deferred to him. Hawkwin was largely responsible for pushing Duncan into the Praetorship in the first place.

The captain smiled at this recollection when he suddenly remembered that Jarren had mentioned something about joining Hawkwin's retinue in her last correspondence. Duncan's heart always warmed when he thought about her. It was with a regretful pang that he noted that they were both too invested in their careers. Things could have been very different between them. As it was, they only saw each other a few times each year, though their sense of mutual devotion hadn't dimmed in spite of it. The frequency of their meetings left an enormous ache in him — perhaps that was why he pushed himself so much.

The grating sound of the portcullis lifting brought Duncan back to reality. He had reports to file and a platoon of wayward Praetorians to deal with. Plus, he had to convey the unfortunate news about Ravelin's fall. With a resentful sigh, Duncan continued along the walkway. He passed by two arched bridges before veering off to ascend a stairway on his right. This exited onto a large plateau that was being used to run combat drills. He watched a militia regiment practice the defensive box formation that Marshal Wallace had so stubbornly clung to. He shook his head and continued. Duncan passed by several administrative offices before ducking into a small building with an arched entrance. The standard of Valor's Keep hung limply overhead. There was a door ahead of him and he knocked politely.

"Enter," came the response.

Duncan opened the door and entered. A single window provided light and formed part of the inner defensive wall that backed onto the Palladum's northern flank. There was a large table off to one side with several maps pinned down to it. In the opposite corner, next to the door, was a small desk covered with piles of papers.

Behind these piles sat a man wearing a gray uniform. The likeness of a vulturn clutching a bow with a sword and pike crossed behind it was sewn over his breast. Shoulder epaulets showed two wolvan's teeth above three chevrons — the same rank as Duncan. The man was short and stocky. A tuft of black hair complemented his dark skin. He stood up and extended his hand.

"You must be Captain Duncan Milius. I remember reading about your appointment to Marshal Wallace's battalion in the marshal's last missive. I'm Captain Alhane Marcus. Welcome to the Palladum. Please forgive the disorganization; Marshal Wallace isn't due for his next inspection tour for another two months, so we didn't expect your arrival."

Duncan accepted the handshake and sat down opposite his counterpart. Paperwork, he thought. Duncan suddenly found himself missing his own uniform. Although he disliked the bureaucratic side of a ranking officer's job, he longed for the respite from conflict that it brought. Sometimes the ability to delegate wasn't so bad.

"Thank you," responded Duncan. "The last time I was here was two years ago. The place has changed a great deal. I'm almost tempted to say that it rivals Valor's Keep in its appeal."

Marcus smiled. "Perhaps, but you wouldn't say that if you were stationed here during the winter."

Duncan chuckled. "You're probably right."

"Duncan's a Federate name, isn't it? Central provinces?"

"Yes — Gath, to be specific."

"I'm from Torinn, myself. You don't sound like you're from Gath. Kennedor, perhaps?"

Duncan shook his head and looked away for a second. "I'm Teivan, actually."

Marcus folded his hands together. "Interesting." He leaned forward, assuming a more businesslike tone. "Your armor is slashed open in many places. It looks like you ran into a few grimms on your way over."

"You could say that. My company was stationed in Valandov. We were assigned to the Eighteenth Battalion."

"Ah, Marshal Wallace's own unit. He went with you?"

Duncan nodded.

"The Federate hasn't built any new outposts in this province that I don't know about, has it?"

"No."

"Then you traveled nonstop from Valandov. That's a risky move with the nearest supply depot days away. It practically begs for a grimm attack." Marcus leaned back in his seat and folded his hands behind his head. "So if you were stationed down in Valandov, what are you doing all the way up here? And what happened to the rest of your battalion?"

Duncan inhaled deeply and took a moment to compose his thoughts. He then slowly related the events of the last two weeks.

*

An hour passed. Marcus was shocked at hearing Duncan's story. Neither captain was quite sure what to do next. Obviously, a report would have to be filed, but this was no ordinary report. A priority message would have to be dispatched to Valor's Keep. There would be an investigation and testimony would have to be heard from each of the surviving soldiers. Marshal Wallace was sure to receive a posthumous court-martial. It was decided that Duncan's group would remain at the Palladum until the Keep responded. In the meantime, Marcus begged his counterpart's leave to obtain advice from a higher authority. Duncan didn't bother to ask who it was. Usually, the regional marshal was responsible for such matters but Wallace was dead. Duncan didn't know who would assume this authority and at this point, he didn't care. The last thing he wanted to do was relive the battle again.

Duncan found himself wandering around the vicinity of the extra barracks where his platoon would be staying. He decided to head for the officers' quarters where a change of clothes awaited him. Duncan ran his hand along his tattered armor. He was still dressed in the same outfit that he had been wearing during the battle.

Duncan resolved to find the bathhouse, but first he needed to check on his wounded charges. He jogged down to the lowest level and headed for a nearby bridge. As he did so, off-duty soldiers and civilian attendants looked at him and whispered softly to one another.

The heretical Teivan officer who led his troops through the forest unmolested, mused Duncan sourly. *The rumors are already spreading.*

He mounted the stairs that led to the bridge's walkway and strode briskly along the overpass. It was a narrow path, perhaps two meters wide. He glanced down and noted the long fall to the cold river below. There were four archers on duty here and he brushed past them. He reached the other side and descended the stairs. He was now on the western half of the fortress, the part he was less familiar with. He asked for directions from a passing private and made his way to the field hospital. Once there, he sent the troops who had been treated to the barracks, ordering them to get some sleep. He then entered the hospital.

The place was large and spacious. The common room had about one hundred and fifty beds, a quarter of which were filled with the sick and injured. Duncan approached a nurse and asked her to direct him to his people. She led him to one of the far corners, a spot that had been separated from the rest. Duncan's injured had been transferred from their stretchers into twelve beds, including Blaine, who had stayed behind and was now fast asleep. The captain thanked the nurse and looked at his troops sadly. This wasn't the first time people had been injured or killed under his command, nor would it be the last. Ordering others to their deaths was an unpleasant fact for a military leader that he didn't think he would ever be comfortable doing.

"You're their captain," came a voice from behind.

Duncan wheeled around to find a doctor staring at him. The woman was short and dark-skinned like Marcus. Her long hair was tied into a tight bun that hung at the back of her head.

"Yes," he answered. "How bad are they?"

"They're resting now," she replied. She indicated the patients closest to her. "These six should make a full recovery. They lost a lot of blood, but none of their wounds is life threatening. Whoever administered their first aid did a topnotch job."

"Praetorians are trained to do so in battle. We carry our own medical supplies."

The doctor responded wryly. "So I've heard. This captain should pull through as well, though she has a nasty gash in her side. She won't be up for at least another week. Frankly, I'm surprised she was conscious when she entered the fortress."

"Captain Blaine is a virtuous fighter."

The doctor ignored him. "These others, though, I can't be sure about. The next twenty-four hours are critical. We cleaned up their wounds as best we could, but it may be too much trauma for their bodies to handle. This one's left lung was punctured. We extracted a grimal claw from the wound. He may not live through the night."

She held out the claw and Duncan took it. It was the size of his thumb. It was hard to imagine that such a small weapon could cause so much harm.

"We don't even know his name," stated Duncan somberly.

"Pardon?"

"That corporal who had the claw in his lung. He was part of the scouting party that reported to us about Ravelin. None of us knew his name."

The doctor nodded solemnly and started to walk off. "There's nothing you can do for them now. When they regain consciousness, we'll let them know you were here. You don't look too well yourself. Knowing how to rest and recuperate is as important a virtue as knowing how to fight."

The doctor headed over to her office and sent a nurse out to monitor the patients. Duncan decided not to argue the point with her. He was too tired.

*

He was still holding the grimal claw when he returned to his quarters. He was about to disarm when he noticed a note lying on his pillow summoning him to the east watch tower immediately. He sighed, removed his weapons, rubbed his eyes and left.

The way up to the tower was long and strenuous on the best of days, but for Duncan, every step left a burning sensation in his legs. The doctor was right. He needed to rest. Soon, he promised himself. After this Godforsaken meeting. It was approaching late afternoon and the sun was beginning to set. The temperature was dropping. Duncan's impatience was rising.

He entered the foot of the tower and stared at the long ascent he had yet to make. He estimated that it had to be at least a dozen stories high, though for all he cared it might just as well have been a hundred. Every step reminded him of his promise to seek rest, and his body ached even more as he continued the climb. Why was he hurting so much? He had passed endurance tests as a cadet (never mind what he went through as a Praetorian!) which were far worse than this. Why did his body protest now?

Duncan felt physically and emotionally defeated. He still believed in the Praetorship's integrity, but now there was a scratch on the Keep's armor. Its emblem was tarnished. Perhaps if he'd done more to convince

Wallace of his errors, Duncan wouldn't be here now and seven hundred Praetorians wouldn't have fallen. He berated himself for thinking such thoughts. He wasn't angry with himself. Duncan was angry with his marshal. Wallace's illustrious career was soon to be recorded as having ended with the most astounding loss in the organization's history.

Damn you, Wallace, cursed Duncan. *Why do I have to be the one to tell the world about your dishonor?*

Duncan finally reached the top. The parapet was about four meters square and afforded a spectacular view of the craggy surroundings. Duncan wasn't in the mood for sightseeing, though. He sat down heavily with his back against a crenel.

The two scouts on duty watched his arrival and noticed his rank insignia. "Sir, is there something we can—"

"No, private, thank you," groaned Duncan, "I'm just here to meet someone. I'll be fine. Return to your watch."

They glanced at a third person before complying. Duncan followed their line of sight with his eyes half-shut. He hadn't noticed the presence of this one when he got here. The stranger approached him. A long fur cloak hid an attractive, athletic figure. The stranger was Duncan's height with long dark hair and oak-brown eyes.

The captain felt himself drifting off to sleep. He needed to get back to his quarters!

"Get up, Praetorian!" The woman's voice was sweet but commanding. The scouts looked at each other in dismay. Praetorians generally didn't allow themselves to be addressed in such a fashion. Then again, strange rumors were circulating about the Praetorship lately.

The voice sounded oddly familiar to Duncan. He opened his eyes and stared at the woman's face. His eyes widened and he smiled. "What are you doing here?"

She grinned back. "What do you think?"

He glanced at the scouts who were pretending not to hear. "You're trying to embarrass me," he mumbled.

Jarren Entigen chuckled and knelt beside him. She jerked his chin up and kissed him. Duncan lifted his hand and stroked the back of her head. She pulled back after a moment and put his face in her hands. The impish grin returned.

"That was awful. I think I scraped my chin on your stubble."

"I can't help it. I've been in the field for weeks and—"

"And you couldn't bring a razor?"

Duncan leaned his head against the side of the parapet and stared at her with a futile expression. "You enjoy doing this to me, don't you?"

Jarren held his hands in hers and nodded. "Isn't love wonderful?"

She pulled him up to his feet and they embraced. They held each other closely and kissed again for what seemed to Duncan to be an eternity. The scouts looked away jealously, wondering why they never joined the Praetorship.

*

The lovemaking was tender and carefree, the kind that two people experience after a sweet reunion. Duncan's aches and pains were forgotten. Afterwards, while she dozed lightly in his bed, he made his way to the bathhouse and cleaned himself up. He was amazed at the multiple levels of grime that had accumulated on his body since the battle. Now, for the first time in a long time, he felt refreshed and presentable.

He returned to his quarters to find Jarren awake and waiting for him in bed. He removed his robe and joined her. She sidled up next to him and wrapped her arms around him.

"Mmm, you smell much better. More relaxed, too."

"You seem to have that effect on me."

"And you shaved!" She caressed his smooth cheeks and ran a finger along his scar. "You're starting to look almost human."

Duncan chuckled. "A fine judge you make."

Jarren's left hand retreated from his face and probed beneath the sheets along his naked body. "Careful what you say, I have your most prized possession in my grasp. One false move…"

Duncan appeared unfazed. "Go ahead. I'm a Praetorian. I'm trained to handle anything."

"We'll see about that."

They laughed together and held each other for a long while. The sun had long since set before either of them spoke again.

"My Lady," whispered Duncan. That was his pet name for her. It began as a genuine statement of honor when he first met her. She was a cabinet minister's daughter and he was the head page in the federal parliament — his foster-father's idea of preparing him for future service to his country. Even after they fell in love, he still called her that.

Jarren looked at him impishly. "Yes?"

"I was genuinely surprised to see you up on that parapet. I had no idea you were here."

"Hawkwin decided to begin his inspection tour early. The Palladum's our first stop."

"Where is he now?"

"He left the fortress shortly after noon to make his rounds through some of the nearby frontier outposts. He gave me the rest of the day off and told me that he'd send word of his return. I was quickly growing bored until you arrived. You saved me. You always save me."

"I wish it was intentional. I almost didn't make it here alive."

"I know." Jarren always found it difficult to hear of Duncan's missions. She never knew if their next meeting would be the last. She took a deep breath, fighting back the tears that always came when she considered these thoughts. With a shaky voice she stammered, "I'm sorry I waited so long to find you but I knew you'd be busy. You care too much for your people."

Duncan smiled. He was lucky to find someone who understood so well. As he touched her face, a crack in his Praetorian stoicism appeared in his eyes.

Jarren noticed it right away. "Do you want to talk about it?" she whispered in his ear.

She lifted her head and their eyes locked. Blinking back tears, he recounted the story of the battle. He covered every detail while Jarren lay next to him listening intently. She didn't say a word. She just let him speak and watched as the tension slowly left his body. She knew that he needed this time. He was the sort of person who kept his feelings bottled up. He needed a receptacle, someone who would understand, listen and perhaps even share his burden. She was willing to assume those roles and more if he asked.

Finally, he stopped talking and looked more troubled. "There was one thing I didn't tell Marcus, something that Wallace never understood."

"How you knew about the ambush."

"Yes, that's it exactly." Duncan turned onto his side and propped himself up on one elbow. "I've always been able to assess a combat situation perfectly — I've come to trust my instincts. But this was different. It was a frightening feeling. I could see what they were planning. It was as if I knew their thoughts and they knew mine."

Jarren could see that Duncan sought advice but she didn't know what to say. Her next question was something she dreaded to ask. She spoke with a whisper because she didn't want Duncan to hear the crack in her voice. "Is that why they let you go — because you made contact?"

Duncan looked up at her and stroked her face. She was so beautiful. He choked at the thought of losing her and realized how difficult it was for her to discuss this. "There were settlements in the northern forests hundreds of years before the Federate was even established. In all that time, no one has ever been able to communicate with them. We just assumed that they were a hostile force."

"They are!"

"I know, but we're not hostile by nature so who's to say that they are? In war, the rules change. People are driven to extraordinary actions. Atrocities are committed on all sides, atrocities that defy our nature."

"But the Teivans —" She caught herself too late.

Duncan breathed deeply. "We haven't abandoned humanity, you know that — I'm living proof! So what if we speak a different language or believe in a different religion? These differences are irrelevant! The fact that my people choose to live peacefully in the forest doesn't mean that they collaborate with the enemy. We've had our share of confrontations. It's just that we've figured out how to stay out of the grimals' way."

"I didn't mean it that way. You know that."

"I'm frustrated, that's all. Tired and frustrated."

Jarren drew herself close to him and the two of them lay there together. Duncan whispered "My Lady" softly into her ear and she responded by holding him even tighter.

After a few moments, she broke the silence. "Romi..." Only two people knew his true Teivan name, and she was one of them. He looked at her, and she continued softly. "Why don't you use your birth name? Leave the Federate one behind. It's not who you are."

"You know why."

"You're a ranking officer now. You command your own company! Surely you've earned the respect of your comrades."

Duncan lay there, his disappointment clear on his face. "You should have seen my meeting earlier with Captain Marcus. We were chatting quite nicely until I told him I was Teivan. Then his manner became cold."

"He's just one man. What about the people back at Valandov or your own troops here? You saved their lives."

"I ordered a retreat that led to the first significant loss in the Praetorship's history."

"You know that's not true!"

"That's how they see it. And then I led them on a backwoods trail to the Palladum. I had the courage to lead them through grimal territory on a Teivan path, but not back into battle to avenge the deaths of our own people. I led them through the forest for ten days without incident. It's no wonder they think we're in league with the grimms. To my troops, I'm a Teivan and a coward."

"Romi!"

"It's the truth."

They lapsed back into silence. Jarren tried to think of a way to ease her lover's burden, but there was nothing to do. She nuzzled closer to him, and he embraced her in his arms. They lay there together until the serenity was broken by a loud knock on the door.

With a gentle kiss, Duncan left her and headed for a nearby table where a change of clothes was folded neatly. He pulled on the breeches and slipped the shirt over his head before seeing who was there. He opened the door to find a tall, burly man waiting impatiently. He was an older fellow with a gray mop of hair covering a face that was streaked with lines of experience. He was decked out in armor that was worn and stained from extensive use. His shoulders bore the likeness of a sword in the image of a conifer, with the hilt forming the trunk and the blade forming the conical shape of a pine tree — the crest of the Federated States. Beneath that were two stars with three chevrons.

"Excuse me, but I'm looking for my chief of staff. She's responsible for my scheduling and I'm not entirely sure where I'm supposed to be right now."

Duncan immediately snapped to attention and saluted. "General!"

The commanding officer rolled his eyes. "Duncan, you don't need to do any of that for me! Has the Praetorship sapped all the humor from you?"

The general walked into the room and lifted the captain off his feet with an enormous bear hug. Once he was let go, Duncan leaned against the door to close it while gasping for air. He grinned. "Cyril, Jarren told me you were here, but the Palladum's so big, I didn't know where to start smelling."

General Cyril Hawkwin put his bracer to his nose as Duncan walked past him to the bed. "I just cleaned this last week!"

Duncan lit a lantern and the room was quickly bathed in warm yellow light. "You needed new armor ten years ago! I'm surprised it hasn't started growing its own fungus."

The general folded his arms. "Is that how you address the commander of the Federate armies?"

"I thought you said I didn't have to worry about that."

"I changed my mind," growled Hawkwin.

Duncan sat down on the bed and looked at Jarren fondly. It seemed like they never had enough time. He knew by the way that she returned his gaze that she felt the same way.

He addressed the general. "I assume you've spoken to Captain Marcus?"

"Yes, you and your platoon will remain here until the Grand-General sends word of his decision. You'll be given regular duty shifts, so don't consider it a vacation. Write a full report, and I'll supplement it with testimony from your junior officers. Tomorrow evening, we'll send a priority message to Valor's Keep and find out exactly what they want you to do."

"How long will it take for them to respond?"

"About ten days, perhaps as much as two weeks. It all depends on how quickly the Grand-General and his advisory council react."

The seriousness of the moment was interrupted by a loud rumble from Duncan's belly. Hawkwin and Jarren stared at him incredulously.

"I'm sorry," defended Duncan, "I haven't had a solid meal in a while."

The general headed for the door. "Come, get dressed and we'll go to the mess hall. They're still serving dinner. I gave your troops the next couple of days off, though they're not allowed to leave the fort. It'll be good for them to see you up and about, and they'll likely have many questions that you'll need to answer."

Duncan and Jarren got up. He began to put on his uniform — identical to Marcus' — and she dressed herself while Hawkwin's back was turned.

"Besides," added the general, "you and I have a lot of catching up to do. With your lady's permission, of course."

Jarren smirked and Duncan looked away to hide his sudden blush. They left his quarters and made their way to the nearby mess hall.

*

After dinner, Duncan was summoned to the field hospital. The corporal who had had the grimal claw in his lung was dead.

*   *   *

The heavy smell of impending rain hung in the air. Duncan Milius paced back and forth along the archery range. The platoon under his command was arrayed in a military formation before him. They stood in rows of four fighters. They looked much healthier than when they arrived. The tears and slashes in their armor were patched up and they had obviously benefited from the time off given to them by General Hawkwin. Most of them had come to grips with what had happened and they were now eager to return to the field. They had spent the week drilling and exercising. They were once again the honed warriors who had left Valandov a month ago, though somewhat more humble.

Their new orders had arrived. They were to leave the Palladum and return to Valor's Keep. Duncan moved from one row to the next, inspecting each soldier. Captain Blaine and the only surviving lieutenant stood at the head of the formation. As Duncan walked past, they saluted. He returned it and moved to stand in front of the formation. It was time to address the troops.

"We pause for a moment to remember the courage and valor of our fallen comrades — the seven hundred and thirty-four Praetorians who died at Ravelin and the four who met their fate here." Duncan rested a hand on a small pouch that hung by his side. It held the grimal claw that was extracted from the lung of a dead corporal: a reminder of the changes that needed to be made to the Praetorship, a symbol indicating that after all the training and the drilling, they were still human at the core.

A cold wind whipped across the archery range, an apt complement for the grimness of the moment. It would have made any civilian shiver and huddle for warmth, but these fighters remained where they were, pretending not to notice. Duncan lowered his gaze and closed his eyes. The Grand-General's response came swifter than anyone had expected. Eight days! The captain never realized that carrier birds could fly so fast. In that time, he had come to accept his duty. He would return to the Keep and testify with honesty and integrity. He wanted this episode to end so he could return to regular duty. So did his troops.

Duncan was thankful for Jarren's brief visit. She had left three days ago, and although they were used to being apart for extended periods, he missed her greatly. As much as he wanted her support now, as much as he longed for her advice, he knew that this battle he had to face on his own.

Finally, he lifted his head and finished his address. "Our orders arrived an hour ago. A galleass awaits us. We are to return to Valor's Keep by way of the Rivers Nillus and Saar. Then, it's a long march south from Maribor. We'll travel direct, day and night. You know the drill, you've been through it before. When we reach the Keep, we'll be ordered to participate in Marshal Wallace's court-martial. If any of you have a problem with this, feel free to talk to Captain Blaine or me about it. There will also be counselors available at the Keep.

"I know that this was a first mission for many of you, and I'm sorry that you're being forced to experience the less glorious side of the Praetorship. All I can say is that our task now is to testify truthfully and without reservation — it's the only way to ensure that Ravelin doesn't happen again. Our reputation has been tarnished, but our honor is very much alive. Perhaps it's a worthy lesson to discover that Praetorians are more human than we give ourselves credit. A little humility now and then can be a good thing. We depart in ten minutes. Gather your gear and say your goodbyes. Dismissed."

The troops broke formation and headed back to their barracks. As Captain Duncan Milius turned to walk to his quarters, a fierce chill swept over him. Some unknown awareness at the back of his mind filled him with a profound sense of wrongness. A putrid stench of decay filtered into his nostrils and his mind was invaded with horrible images of destruction and terror. He saw cities lying in ruins. Fields of wheat and orchards burned brightly, their smoke covered the sky. Giant inhuman creatures tore down Gath's walls and pressed inside, devouring everyone in their path. He watched one brute lift up his foster-father and disembowel him, and Duncan's eyes blurred with tears. Another one tore into Jarren, and its maw was drenched in gore and blood from her body. He saw everyone he cared about reduced to bony husks, as if their souls had been violently sucked from them. Valor's Keep, the mightiest fortress in the realm, was swallowed up by the earth.

Then, as quickly as they had come, the dark intrusions were swept aside, leaving Duncan with a disturbing sense of foreboding. He sank to his knees and brought his hands together over his mouth. He was thankful that everyone had left the range so that no one could see him quivering like a frightened child in the middle of the plateau. He had never been more terrified of anything in his life than he was of that vision.

The Circle

The *Explorer* was moored near Longpoint, a lighthouse that jutted out into the middle of the harbor. A sea of merchants and commoners surrounded the dockyard to witness the start of this historic voyage. The people stood quietly and still, as was expected in the Hansic Alliance.

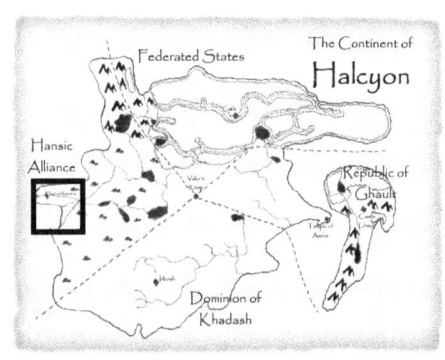

They did so despite the constant sting of light sleet and mist that swirled around the pier. This was winter's last desperate attempt to hold out against spring, and the common folk, unlike the dignitaries below them, shifted their weight from one foot to the other to try to keep warm.

An enormous galleon bobbed in the water before them. Rugen's normally crowded harbor front had been cleared of traffic for this occasion — all the other ships had been moved or rerouted to Lubec, which lay on the opposite shore of the River Odra's mouth.

The galleon's skipper was a retired navy captain who had a handpicked crew with which to explore the unknown waters of the Great Sea. If any land existed beyond the realm of Halcyon, it had been forgotten. If any civilization existed in the midst of the Great Sea, it, too, had passed from memory. They carried enough supplies for a three-month voyage, after which they were to return and report on their findings. The motives were purely economic: the discoverers of any new resources stood to profit tremendously from the monopoly they would gain, as would their patrons.

Behind the crowd, a pair of robed figures stood motionless. Their bodies were completely covered, one in crimson, the other in navy blue. Long cowls hid their faces. Subtle bulges at the chest were all that identified them as women. Except for a map case dangling from the shoulder of the one in blue, the color of their attire was all that distinguished one from the other. They engaged in a silent conversation, nodded and parted ways. The one in crimson was now left alone to watch the proceedings on the pier.

The crashing surf was the only sound to be heard as the captain and her crew stood at attention while the governor inspected them. Forty ceremonial guards from the district garrison waited patiently at the opposite end of the pier. Rivulets of sleet marred the oiled surface of their black, padded leather armor. Their faces stung from the constant pelting of tiny ice pellets, but they pretended not to notice.

The robed figure watched as Governor William Lessander continued with the inspection, studying each sailor's face in turn. The crew arrayed before him consisted of hardened professionals, more than three hundred souls who wore poor masks over their brimming pride. These men and women were being afforded the highest honor possible in the Hanse — short of meeting the chancellor.

The crew members stared straight ahead in a military fashion they had learned during their service in the Hansic armed forces. Such tours of duty, whether in the militia or the navy, were required of every citizen in the realm upon reaching the age of eighteen, and they remained in the service for three years.

Despite the distance, the figure in crimson had no trouble making out Lessander's features, marking him for their encounter later on. A light breeze tousled his jet-black hair while his plain, expressionless features showed no hint of emotion. His eyes were the only crack in his stoic demeanor — eyes that betrayed his intense pride. The governor was dressed in formal garb. His black overcoat and pants were tight and uncomfortable, and they featured a navy-blue sash that ran from shoulder to opposite hip. The district crest was sewn over his heart and he wore a short dagger at his side.

Just as the crimson-robed observer began to grow impatient, the inspection ended. Lessander came about to face the captain. The old sailor was decked out in full naval regalia, a reminder of her esteemed service to her country.

The unseen observer concentrated slightly to augment her hearing. Her instructions were to record every moment of this event for the Inner Membership.

Governor William Lessander spoke formally. "Captain Grayden, I commend you. Yours is the finest crew I've seen in a long time."

"Thank you, sir."

"Do you have any final words to speak on their behalf?"

"No, sir."

A pause. "Very well."

Lessander spun around, marched halfway to the honor guard, and turned to face the crew of the *Explorer*. He looked at the cleric of Samlah who stood nearby. The priest was of medium height, rotund, and his head was shaved according to the demands of his order. A platinum pendant depicting a closed fist hung from his neck. He stepped forward with two acolytes who carried a brazier. They placed it on the dock and the cleric reached into a pouch at his side. He produced a pinch of dust and sprinkled it over the element while the acolytes did their best to shield it from the breeze and the sleet. They lit the brazier and it gave off a strong aroma.

The priest had to raise his voice over the blowing drizzle so everyone could hear him. "We bow our heads in meditation," he called. Everyone present, including the sailors and soldiers at attention, did so and concentrated intensely. "We pray to the Spirits, that in their Games our comrades may find fortune and favor. You follow in the tradition of our ancestors, distant cousins who explored the waters of their own world seeking treasure and glory. Though the full story of their deeds is forever lost to us, Ahenak's Codices tell us that a quest into the unknown is a search for greater understanding. Hear the words that Elren, Bestower of Wisdom, inspired him to write: 'The individual attains Truth by exploring the natural world and applying reason, for only through reason can we unmask the universe.' Godspeed. May Yarmah of the Seas grant you safe passage, may Qedem guide you truly, and may the Spirits in their Forum view you with favor. Amen."

Everyone repeated "Amen" and the acolytes removed the brazier to conclude the proceedings.

Using this as a cue, a military band at the back of the crowd struck up its instruments. The all-brass ensemble played the Hymn to the Hansic League. It was a tribute to the short-lived antecedent to the Hansic Alliance that existed three and-a-half centuries earlier, and it was now the Hanse's national anthem. The hymn had a slow meter and a respectful tone. The people stood quietly at attention, as did the sailors. The militia troops and government officials saluted.

*

Aboard the *Explorer*, muffled sounds of the ceremony penetrated the captain's quarters, where the woman in the navy blue robe sat hunched over a desk. Rifling through the captain's trunk, she removed several large maps. Unslinging her map case, she exchanged the captain's maps with some of her own. Carefully, she placed the maps back in the trunk in exactly the order she found them. After one final cursory glance to make sure nothing was amiss, she stood straight and concentrated. In a moment, she was gone.

*

Back outside, the band had finished playing. Eager to get under way, the captain stepped forward. "Your Honor, we hereby request permission to take our leave of you."

"Permission granted," replied Lessander.

The captain raised her right hand and touched her temple with the tip of her middle finger, a centuries-old naval salute. Lessander returned it and the skipper barked an order to her sailors. The crew boarded the galleon and the captain was heard shouting more commands. The tether lines were hauled in and a hundred oars were broken out. Lessander nodded and signaled to the militia-general.

"Present arms," she cried.

With a single ring, the ceremonial guards drew their swords and saluted the *Explorer*. When the ship pulled away, the general barked, "At ease!" The soldiers sheathed their weapons and the crowd applauded loudly. There was no cheering — such a display would be deemed raucous and inappropriate. The crew of the *Explorer* was being given a hero's sendoff.

*

Still in her place behind the crowd on the pier, the crimson-robed woman turned her head at a slight movement in her periphery. Her companion with the map case had rejoined her. Their unspoken exchange was momentary and their only outward sign of communication was a satisfied nod from the one in crimson. The one in blue had to report back to the Inner Membership. The one in crimson had a meeting to get to.

They parted ways again.

*

On the ship, the navigator set a westward course, beyond the borders of the Hansic Alliance and into uncharted territory. The captain stared back from the navigation deck. She could still hear the applause. The people would remain there until the vessel was out of sight. Then, the governor would dismiss them and they would go about their regular business. She inhaled deeply and scanned the western horizon, eagerly anticipating the task ahead of her.

*

Once the ship disappeared from view, the crowd quieted down and began to disperse. The crimson-robed woman watched Governor Lessander wave absently at the troops on the pier to dismiss them. The regional militia-general who was on hand for the honor guard shouted a command and the soldiers headed for their nearby steeds. Lessander mounted his own animal and the guards formed in around him to escort him to the district keep.

The city of Rugen was built on a steep incline and at its summit lay the home of the governor of the Great Sea District. As they wended their way through the curving streets, merchants and commoners stopped and stared at the escort. Periodically, a break in the tightly packed buildings revealed a glimpse of Lubec, which lay across the River Odra. That city was practically identical to this one and was the seat of power for the regional mayor. They were both densely populated, with two- and three-story buildings crowding the edges of the cobblestone roads. As the main street snaked its way uphill, other arteries branched off at regular intervals. These roads made roughly even circuits around the giant hills upon which the cities were built, giving Rugen and Lubec a layered appearance. Larger intersections featured fountains and small stands of trees, though most of the time the only greenery to be found in either of these cities was in the gardens of the wealthier families who lived near the keeps at the two summits.

The escort continued in silence. Presently they arrived at the keep. It consisted of a large, plain building that functioned as the main audience hall. A single tower stemmed from one end of it, from which an observer could see just past the city and into the surrounding countryside. It also provided a clear view of the River Odra and Lubec on the opposite bank. Three rectangular wings were attached to the main keep, two of which housed the governor's family and his personal guard. The third one included the kitchen and a mess hall. This was all enclosed by a defensive wall that was two stories high. Surrounding the keep were a handful of large stone buildings that were used as offices for the district government. The district's Praetorian garrison was also stationed there in a walled compound of its own.

Two bronze plaques on either side of the arched entrance commemorated the keep's construction. The robed woman kept pace with Lessander's group, all the while keeping her presence secret, her movements feeling like little more than a passing breeze. She glanced at the plaques as she passed by. Written in Old Ghaultic, the one on the left read: "Completed at the behest of Olaf Fenn Brelinner, Patriot and Separatist, first leader of the city-state of the Great Sea, Year 218 After the Appearance." The other plaque was written much later in the Hansic dialect: "Strength of the mind derives from a sense of the just; strength of the flesh, from the unjust."

The robed woman grinned inwardly. *Verse ninety-one from Ahenak's First Codex. What would Olaf Brelinner have thought if he'd known that the words of a man he called 'murderer' would one day greet those who entered his keep?*

Soldiers from the district garrison kept the mob of petitioners at a distance while the governor and his escort dismounted in the keep's courtyard. Their steeds were led away while a frenetic clerk rushed to meet them. A little man with a portly physique, he was huffing from a shortage of breath as he bustled his governor inside to open the legislature.

The unseen woman augmented her hearing again so she could listen to the governor's conversation.

"Sir, representatives from several regions have been awaiting your return."

Lessander's tone barely concealed his annoyance. "Let them wait."

"They're angry, sir."

Lessander stared at him impatiently.

The clerk took a step back. "Very angry."

The militia-general chuckled and led her troops away. The governor walked briskly towards the audience hall with the clerk scurrying along beside him. "We also have important petitions from the masonry, smithy and cobbling guilds. They all seem to be very miffed about the tax issue."

They entered through a side door to avoid the crowd. Lessander was only half-listening as the clerk continued. "There's also this written request for a private audience."

"I don't have time for private audiences."

"It says that it's urgent."

The clerk thrust a sealed envelope at the governor. Lessander broke the seal, removed the letter and scanned its contents. He stopped abruptly.

"What is it?" asked the clerk.

Lessander looked up. "You're not going to believe this."

"Believe what?"

The governor handed him the note. "See what you make of it."

Lessander entered a door on his right and emerged inside the audience hall. It was spacious, comfortably holding the few hundred petitioners with plenty of room to spare. Windows that were two stories tall lined the sides of the chamber, and sconces with torches were attached to the walls between them for occasions when the light outside was insufficient. Today, the windows let pass a dull white light with streaks of sleet, an adequate reflection of the governor's mood. Next to

Lessander was a ceremonial replica of the chancellor's throne from Hansehaven. It bore the crests of each of the five formerly independent city-states that negotiated the creation of the Hansic Alliance two centuries earlier. The Hanse's national crest was displayed above them. An unlit brazier was set beside the right armrest. All this was situated behind a large, raised table. Lessander managed the assembly from here. A dozen meters from the table was a wooden barrier about waist-high.

The robed woman watched discreetly as he moved further into the chamber. A squad of sentries snapped to attention.

Praetorians, mulled the woman, *the impartial observers of our realm.*

There were only a dozen of them, but the woman was confident that they could wipe out Lessander's entire garrison if they wanted to. Their steel armor was heavier than anything found in the Hansic Alliance and they wielded their weapons with deadly efficiency. They were few in number but ferocious in battle, making them the perfect peacekeepers. Every year, thousands of Praetorian hopefuls entered training at Valor's Keep. Very few became cadets. After that, there was a slim chance that they would have what it took to become actual Praetorians.

The clerk had scurried in ahead of Lessander and he now stood at his governor's side. He held the note out to his governor. "In all my years of service, I've never seen the Circle take an interest in local affairs."

"What do you think they want?"

"Damned if I know. Usually they're content with keeping to their tests. I've never heard of them demanding a private audience with anyone outside of the highest government circles."

Lessander considered this for a few moments until the clerk cleared his throat loudly.

Setting aside this unusual request for a private meeting, the governor sighed, "Yes, I know. Bring them in. We'll begin with the regional administrators and guild representatives."

The clerk hurried off to an antechamber while two enormous doors at the far end of the hall opened wide. Commoners started to file in, stopping at the waist-high wall. The clerk led the administrators and guild representatives in from a separate entrance to stand before the governor.

The governor rose and silence quickly descended over the assemblage. Lessander waited until the echoes of their mingled conversations faded away before nodding curtly. An aide entered through the same back door that Lessander had used. She was carrying a scepter that lay on a velvet cushion. A cleric wearing an azure outfit followed her. Unlike her counterpart at the pier, this priestess was old and thin, though she shared the shaved head and the pendant. She reached into a pouch that hung from her sash and sprinkled some incense over the brazier. She then lit it and a sweet fragrance disseminated through the chamber. The cleric's voice resounded clearly.

"We extol the Spirits who dwell in the Forum up on high. May Elren's wisdom prevail as our guiding principle in this, the nineteenth day of L'Xarmonth of the seven hundred and seventieth year After the Appearance, thirty-first day since the election of our governor, William Lessander. May fortune and justice favor him, and let us say, 'Amen.'"

Everyone repeated "Amen". Lessander took the scepter from the waiting clerk and held it aloft. "I hereby declare this day in session."

As he sat, the chamber came abuzz with life.

Three councilors stepped forward. They were dressed in soft brown leathers with heavy wool vests — a stark contrast to the more fashionable black and grays of the city.

"Your Honor," started the one in the middle, "we represent the Rheine area in the Odra's highland region."

Lessander smiled politely and was about ask them to continue when the clerk returned puffing frantically. "Sir, the person who requested the private audience is waiting in the antechamber."

Lessander rose and placed the scepter on his seat. "My apologies, gentlemen and ladies, but this is a pressing matter. We'll deal with your concerns when I return." He stepped down and headed for the antechamber.

The robed woman retreated inside and prepared herself.

Crossing the hall quickly, Lessander entered the antechamber and closed the door behind him, taking care to ensure that the clerk was on the other side. From this room only muffled sounds of the rowdy district assembly could be heard.

The antechamber was about seven meters square with a large window on one wall. The furnishings were soft and velvety. In all, the room presented a decidedly elitist atmosphere, a place where the rich and powerful would feel comfortable waiting for their turn to see the governor. Seated in one of the armchairs was the robed woman. A long cowl hid her face. She motioned to a seat on the opposite end of a low table.

"Sit."

The voice was cracked and barely recognizable as being feminine. Lessander ignored her. "Who are you to pull me away from my legislature? I have important matters that require my personal attention. State your business and be off."

"You may return to your precious legislature once I have gleaned the information I require. Now sit."

She could see that Lessander was losing patience. "I don't have time for your magician's games," he snapped. He grabbed hold of the doorknob and tried to leave the room, but the door was jammed.

"Let me out!"

"Not until you've told me what I need to know." The voice was cold, businesslike.

Lessander glared at her. "I warn you: there is a squad of Praetorians outside this door."

The cloaked woman appeared unfazed. "Shout all you want. They won't hear you."

The governor had had enough. He crossed the room in four paces, repeating his demand in a threatening tone.

"Let me out. Now."

She matched his gaze, rose slowly to her feet, and answered plainly, "No."

A surge of rage swept through him. In a quick motion, he balled his hand into a fist and swung at her with all his strength. Her reaction was just as sudden as his attack. His fist froze ten centimeters from her face and was held there by an invisible, intractable force. The woman appeared unfazed by his fury. He stared wildly at the hand that was suspended in midair. He was unable to move it — the muscles below his elbow were completely stiff and beyond his control, as if they weren't even there any more. He struggled madly, but his hand remained fixed in the position in front of her face. She sat back down, watching with mild amusement as Lessander struggled.

"William Lessander, newly elected governor of the Great Sea District. When we heard of your election, we were somewhat surprised. It appears that the reports of your violent temper were not exaggerated."

His hand was released from its hold, and he stumbled backwards. She motioned to the chair again. "Sit."

The woman drew back her crimson cowl to reveal a gaunt face with sunken eyes and high cheekbones. Her skin looked like it had been pulled tightly over her skull. Her dark hair was long and thin.

"I am called Quinn. I am a tenth-level member of the Circle. We have questions that demand complete answers. Candor is required."

Lessander recognized the title. She could see that although his anger hadn't subsided, he understood that he wasn't leaving this room until he gave her what she wanted. Nursing the hand that was slowly tingling back to life, he sat in the indicated chair.

"Good. I saw that the *Explorer* was put to sea this morning."

"*You* were there?"

Quinn folded her arms. "I was. Where is it headed?"

The governor furrowed his eyebrows. "Why is the Circle interested in this ship?"

Quinn persisted. "Need I remind you of the charter between the Circle and the Commonwealth? We are granted complete autonomy to operate our programs in all the countries, a freedom which includes cooperation from the local and regional authorities."

"What do Hansic economic policies have to do with testing babies?"

"That program is one of many we involve ourselves in. I'm not at liberty to justify my presence here to you or anyone else. The charter renewed by your chancellor compels you cooperate with me. Now answer the question."

Lessander gripped his chair's armrests so tightly that it looked painful. He appeared ready to throttle Quinn, though they both knew he could never get close enough.

"The *Explorer* was headed into the midst of the Great Sea," he said. "This is no secret. Surely you read news pamphlets."

"I need information that isn't printed in the news. I want coordinates."

"There are no specific coordinates. They're supposed to chart a course due west."

"What do they expect to find?"

He eyed Quinn suspiciously. "New fisheries… fresh land to mine for resources… perhaps even a safe passage to Ghault. No one knows for sure. That's why they went out there. To explore. Hence the name of the ship." This was spoken with apparent sarcasm. The Circle member ignored it.

"When do you expect them to return?"

"They carried supplies for a three-month voyage. Why do you need to know all this? What purpose does this information serve?"

Quinn rose and headed for the door. "Thank you for your candor, Governor Lessander. That will be all."

Lessander rose as well. "You know what's out there, don't you? You know what they'll find! Tell me!" He tried to grab her arm but he was thrown back across the room by an invisible force.

Quinn turned to face him. Her expression darkened, revealing her first display of emotion since the start of their encounter. "I would advise that you think again the next time you try to assault me or any other Circle member. I have no issue with death, yours or anyone else's, but to die needlessly would be a waste. As a former military man, I should hope you understand that. Good day, Governor Lessander."

With that, she opened the door and left. As she departed, she heard Lessander's clerk scuttle into the room tittering with excitement.

"Great news, your honor! A dispatch just arrived from Hansehaven. Chancellor Hanser is demanding the presence of all the governors in two weeks."

Quinn paused to listen to the exchange.

Lessander took a deep breath as he picked himself up off the floor. "Why?"

The clerk tittered excitedly. "It's the Kahanne of Assize. She's visiting the Hansic Alliance and they want to receive her with full honors!"

Quinn allowed herself a half-smile. There were very few people on Halcyon she disliked as much as the Chieftain, and the Kahanne was one of them.

*   *

The Circle Enclave was a shadowy place that had earned a unique position in local lore. Children were taught from a young age to believe that if they didn't close the door to their bedrooms, sorcerers from the Enclave would abduct them. It was common to account for inexplicable disappearances as a twisted desire to become a magician by visiting the mysterious Enclave. Even now, nearly three centuries after the Commonwealth constitution made Circle members full citizens of Halcyon, many people still reviled them. The Enclave was a focus for popular mistrust, but to the six thousand men and women who counted themselves a part of the Circle it was a second home.

No one could quite tell exactly where it was. In popular legends, it was "just over those hills" or "out beyond the Great Sea", but its true location was telepathically imprinted on the mind of every Member as part of the induction rite. It could only be reached through what commoners referred to as "magical" means, though such a description was a inaccurate. It only seemed magical because most people lacked the education they needed to understand the true nature of what the Circle called mentallics.

The Enclave was an immense underground complex with no openings to the surface. It was designed very simply, with more than enough room to satisfy the Membership's needs. There were twelve chambers — barracks for the Members, a mess hall and the convocation theater. The theatre was cathedral-like in its proportions and contained small workstations for each Member. They were arranged into ten concentric circles of decreasing diameter, starting with spots for the first-level Members on the outside and ending with a tight ring of six stations on the inside for the tenth-levels. A single place for the Chieftain stood on a dais in the very center. This was where rare meetings were held for the entire membership.

There were no decorations on the walls. Everything about this place espoused functionality over aesthetics, though no one understood why. Some of Halcyon's greatest artisans were Members.

Quinn stood alone in the convocation theater. A dim ball of light floated above and slightly behind her, casting her features in a sinister shadow. It had been four days since the *Explorer's* departure and her aborted conversation with Governor William Lessander. In that time, her suspicions about the coming of the Time of Meeting had mounted. She was now sure that the ancient Enemy was stirring. Would Halcyon survive? Would the Circle survive?

Certainly not under our present leadership!

Quinn stood before the Chieftain's place and stared at it longingly. The whites of her sunken eyes were strangely visible as soft gray spots in the shadow created by the suspended light.

Patience, she cautioned herself. *I must have patience.*

With a flicker of a thought, she levitated into the air and deposited herself on the raised platform. Just as her toes touched stone, a hazy outline took shape next to her. She watched as it coalesced into a human form. Like her, he was cloaked in crimson, but he was tall and gangly. His wispy white hair flowed over his shoulders.

Hello, Quinn. Cain, the Chieftain, stepped forward. His light voice resounded in her head. *A little dim, isn't it?*

He glanced at her ball of light and its radiance increased. Now the entire area was well lit, though the light's radius only covered the first four circles of desks. Quinn could now easily make out his impish expression.

I hope you don't mind, but I added a tinge of yellow to your light, continued Cain. *Your pale white was just a little too depressing.* He tapped his chin. *That reminds me… I always felt that we could use some decorations in here. It all seems sort of…* "Spartan."

This last word was spoken aloud and the sound reverberated through the theater.

I love doing that.

Decorations are a distraction, reprimanded Quinn. *We'll require the undivided attention of every Member when the time comes to enact the Greater Cause.*

Yes, the Greater Cause, agreed Cain. *Too bad we don't know if — well, hello, who have we here?*

Two more hazy forms took shape beside them. One was dressed in the familiar crimson robe. The other newcomer was dressed in tight leather armor. It was stained green and brown so that she looked like a patch of moss. A bow was slung over her shoulder and a quiver with two arrows hung at her side, as did a sword and a dagger. A buckler was strapped to her left forearm. Badges on her shoulder depicted three chevrons beneath the emblem of Valor's Keep. She looked scratched and beaten up.

Cain approached and shook her hand. *Sergeant Terrel.*

Terrel nodded. *Chieftain.*

The remaining four Inner Members materialized before the discussion could continue.

Cain smiled at Terrel. *I apologize for the haste, but, as usual, we don't have much time.*

That's all right, she replied. *Captain Milius didn't see me leave. As far as I know, he thinks I was lost to the grimms in the forest.*

Excellent, let's make this quick. Open your mind to us. Let us see what you saw, hear what you heard.

Terrel nodded and closed her eyes. She concentrated on the events of the last few days. Images of her departure from Valandov with Marshal Wallace's battalion flitted by, followed by memories of Captain Duncan Milius and his disputes with the other senior officers. Terrel probed deeper, reliving the tragic battle with the grimals en route to Ravelin and the order to retreat from the fight. As she focused on these memories, she felt intruding eyes and ears watching and listening from a distance. This was quite unlike the feeling from a joining of minds, in which each participant shared the experiences of the other. That kind of rapport defied description: it was a closeness that was beyond intimacy and transcended sexuality. The connection that the Inner Members opened with her now was of a vastly different nature, more like the uncomfortable feeling she got when someone stood over her shoulder while she read a report, except that when she looked back, no one was there. In a moment, it was over.

Thank you, Terrel, grinned Cain. *We'll reassign you to the Dominion of Khadash. With no armed forces and a minimal presence from the Praetorship, there's little chance of you being recognized.*

The Chieftain addressed one of the other Inner Members. *Reeve, please inform our agent in Irbirah that she's receiving a new assistant. Tell her to use the usual story — the Khadashites who aren't Teivan will be suspicious, but by next week, they won't even remember that Terrel wasn't there to begin with. And get her out of that soldier's uniform!*

Reeve smiled and established a link with the appropriate person. He nodded to Terrel, who prepared herself for transportation.

One last thing, Sergeant, mentioned Cain. *I promise not to read any more reports over your shoulder.*

Terrel grinned at the joke before vanishing from their presence. Reeve concentrated for a moment before nodding affirmatively. *She's there, and our agent is waiting with fresh clothes.*

Good, began Cain. *This is the situation. The* Explorer *was put to sea this week with orders to sail west and find new land or resources or whatever. Failing that, they expect to end up on the east coast of the Isle in Ghault, or, if they're really off course, on the eastern end of Kennedor Province in the Federated States.*

They had no specific heading but carried provisions for three months, added Quinn.

And there's no indication that they really know where they're going? asked Reeve.

Not according to Governor William Lessander, replied Quinn. *He gave me no information beyond what we just told you. I believe that's all he knows.*

Cain nodded. *I agree. I checked our maps and there is a chance that they might miss the Champion's continent entirely. If so, we'll call it a near miss and wait for the Time of Meeting to arrive in another generation.*

Fair enough, replied Reeve, *but let's assume for the moment that the Dark Champion does find the* Explorer. *What then? How do we prevent the Enemy from coming here and destroying us before we're ready?*

Cain looked at Quinn, and she responded. *We've taken steps to ensure that the Champion never finds us. The maps and all the navigational data that the* Explorer *carries have been altered or replaced to conceal the location of the Fingers of Khorshim.*

What good will that do? countered Reeve. *The Enemy knows the geography of this world as well as we do. It knows where the Khorshim are.*

Yes, but if the Explorer *carries no information about them, the Champion won't suspect our presence. It will assume that if we haven't bothered to record their location, we obviously haven't discovered them yet.*

Reeve glanced at the other Inner Members who were listening silently. They gave their assent.

Now that she had gained their approval, Quinn saw an opportunity to nudge the Inner Membership further. She continued speaking matter-of-factly. *We've taken every precaution to ensure our own safety but the mainland is still vulnerable. Since we have no means of tracking the ship without revealing ourselves to the Enemy, we must assume the worst. I recommend that we initiate phase one of the Greater Cause.*

The other Inner Members eyed each other uneasily. This was a situation the Circle had been dreading for centuries, and they, like previous generations, didn't want to be the ones to deal with it.

Cain changed the subject. *There's also the matter of Jehorom Galaddi.*

Quinn turned her back on the group. She was being slapped down, and everyone knew it. *He's a waste of time,* she denounced.

What if he's the one? pressed Reeve. *The Elders did foretell the presence of a savior in their Harbinger.*

He exhibits nothing more than first-level abilities, spat Quinn. *She slowly walked a few steps to her workstation and slumped into the seat.*

Nevertheless, he's worth watching, decided Cain. *Consider his situation: he's Teivan, so from the moment he was born there was a high probability that he'd be a Member someday. Plus, his parents were high up in the breeding program. Who knows what kind of children they were capable of producing?*

We'll never know, will we? argued Quinn. *His parents were killed years ago.*

Yes, but Galaddi survived.

Through no actions of his own! Quinn was becoming angry. The Chieftain was pinning their hopes on conjecture, not evidence. Why couldn't the Inner Members see this? Why was she the only one speaking out against him?

Leaning against his desktop in the center of the convocation hall, Cain exhaled slowly. Quinn didn't know when to give up. *We don't know that. He might have saved himself by using skills on some instinctive level.*

Or it could have been luck. We have to—

"Enough, Quinn!" Cain's bark echoed across the stone chamber. The other Inner Members flinched. Quinn stood her ground, pleased that she had pushed the Chieftain too far.

Cain resumed telepathic conversation. *My decision's been made.* He turned to the rest of the group. *We can't let him return to Valandov with the rest of Marshal Wallace's battle group — we have no one stationed there. Let's divert him to the Palladum.*

My sources inform me that General Hawkwin is due to arrive there in a few days, mentioned one of the other Inner Members.

The Chieftain clapped happily. *Perfect! He'll make sure that Galaddi gets back to Valor's Keep. We won't even have to interfere! He'll do our work for us! We just have to get Galaddi to the Palladum.*

Reeve shook his head. *The River Nillus is the only way to reach the Palladum from Ravelin. When Wallace's battle group returns to their ships, they're going to try to head back to Valandov. For this to work, we'd have to somehow make them want to turn north from the River Saar and head up the Nillus. I don't see a way to do that.*

They were silent for a moment.

What about the Teivan footpaths? ventured one of the other Inner Members. *Duncan Milius is Teivan. He knows where they are and how to use them. We sink the ships and force his battle group to walk to the Palladum.*

What do we do with the sailors? asked Reeve.

Cain interjected. *Let them board their ships and start for Valandov. Before the junction with the Nillus, the River Saar is narrow enough to be easily blocked by us. They'll have no choice but to leave their ships and head north on foot.*

The others nodded. *I'll take care of it,* stated Reeve.

Don't unblock the river until you're absolutely sure they won't come back for anything, instructed Cain.

Reeve smiled and nodded.

What of the Greater Cause? demanded Quinn icily.

It'll wait, replied Cain. *For now, I'll review our file on Jehorom Galaddi. Birth records, lineage... everything. We may need to retest him. In the meantime, return to your posts, and let us pray that the* Explore *does indeed miss its mark.*

Everyone nodded and six bodies grew hazy before gradually disappearing. Only Quinn remained. She dared not vent her anger in the presence of the other Inner Members. But here, alone, she could stew. The Chieftain was making a grave mistake.

*　　*　　*

The Library of the Elders was dark and quiet. It was enormous, containing tens of thousands of volumes. They were stored on rows of shelves that stretched far back into the sanctum, well beyond eyesight. This was a secret place, its existence known to the people of Halcyon through centuries of legend. Only the highest members of the Circle knew its location.

More than three weeks had passed since the decision to send Duncan Milius and his battle group to the Palladum — three weeks since Cain, Quinn and the rest of the Inner Members began a course of action that would affect the future of Halcyon. Cain reflected on this as he strode briskly through the darkness. His long legs carried him swiftly through the chamber. His robe, which would look crimson if this place was lit, flapped lightly as he moved. On either side of him, stacks of shelves reached up to a vaulted ceiling that was so high it was often hidden from view even when there was light. As he walked, he brushed past endless rows of books. The volumes dealt with a diversity of topics, ranging from History, Engineering and Philosophy to Biology, Physics and Mathematics. All of Halcyon's knowledge was stored here, and the Circle had exclusive control over it.

Cain continued walking deeper into the Library. The darkness was no concern for him. If he wished, he could make the place brighter than the brightest day, but for now, he preferred the darkness. The tap of his shoes and the brush of his robe against the shelves echoed in the sanctuary's stillness. Finally, he reached his destination and stopped in the middle of the vast hall. There was no wall to block him, no marker on the floor, just more rows of books goading him onward. He steeled himself for the punishment he knew was coming, the punishment that was inflicted on him every time he tried to pass. He stepped forward and closed his eyes.

With a surge of power, Cain was violently thrown back by an invisible barrier. He landed heavily on the stone floor. He stood up painfully, clenching and unclenching his fists in frustration. This always happened. He had tried to pass by hundreds of times and he was always caught off-guard. The Elders constructed this place and they were the only ones who could cross this point.

They had been dead for centuries.

The Chieftain stared longingly ahead. *We have access to thousands of volumes,* he lamented, *but even more lie just beyond our reach.*

He stood there for several long moments, contemplating the mystery beyond the barrier. What was it that Ahenak wrote in his First Codex? 'Of all the great treasures in the universe, nothing is more valuable than human intellect.' Cain shook his head. The treasure in this place was incalculable, but he would never see any of it in his lifetime.

It was time to get back to work. He knelt to examine the shelf on his left. A ball of dim light popped into existence over his right shoulder. Like the other shelves, this one was crammed with books. He worked his way along the floor and stopped at the wall. He ran his finger delicately along the spines of the last five volumes.

This is all we have left. Soon, there will be nothing more for us.

He stood up and marched back to the aisle, trying to understand why the Elders had sealed away the rest of the Library. What was so important that it had to be locked away like this? And if present generations weren't meant to use it, why wasn't it destroyed or hidden, instead of lying out in plain sight? Obviously, the Elders wanted them to know about it, so there had to be a way to bypass the defenses.

We just have to find it, sighed Cain. *The Elders were as selective in their choices of the kinds of knowledge we're allowed to obtain as the Circle is in the way we ration out what they left for us to see. But the Library's stores will soon run completely dry and the Circle will no longer be able to maintain its control of information. Is this what the Elders intended all along? What will we do when the last books are used up? What will be the Circle's place in Halcyon?*

Cain stood there brooding over these unpleasant thoughts with only the pale ball of light providing illumination. For nearly three hundred years, the Circle had been trying and failing to get past that barrier.

Suddenly, he was wrenched out of his musings as his mind was invaded by a force more powerful than he had ever experienced. It felt as though a chilling wind was sweeping through the Library, filling the Chieftain's head with images of death and decay. The intrusion was terrifying and he felt paralyzed to stop it. He saw the destruction of his people. Valor's Keep… Gath… Hansehaven… Castle Ghault… Irbirah… every settlement in the Commonwealth lay in ruins. A raging firestorm consumed Halcyon. There were terrified screams everywhere. He saw strange creatures of unimaginable size devouring humans, livestock, grimals… anything they could grab. A throaty hiss echoed in his head that slowly grew into malicious laughter. It was a cackle that mocked the Circle, the Commonwealth and all humanity. He saw swarms of the enormous creatures ravaging the countries.

The images disappeared as quickly as they came. Cain shivered and choked. This was the moment he had been dreading all his life.

Within minutes, a new presence filled his mind. A barely effeminate, cracking voice replaced the horrid laughter in his head.

Chieftain?

Cain had barely recovered from the ordeal. He had no desire to deal with her right now. *What is it, Quinn?*

It's here.

A bitter sigh. *I know, I felt it. Send for the others — the hour is upon us. We must join minds and complete the task set out for us by the Elders. We must find the Savior of Order before the Dark Champion engulfs us all.*

What of the Greater Cause? she asked.

Cain put his hand to his forehead and shook his head sadly. The Greater Cause would certainly lead to the destruction of Halcyon, but it may be the only path to salvation. He marveled at Quinn's apparent heartlessness. He felt violated — something had entered his mind illicitly. Every mentallic on Halcyon must have experienced the same effect, yet she took it in stride, as if it was just another daily event! Didn't it occur to her that if the Dark Champion was strong enough to invade Halcyon's most powerful minds, it could certainly run amok over the land with impunity as the vision foretold?

The Chieftain lifted his head and turned around. Quinn was standing behind him. Her cowl was pulled over her face, which was completely hidden from the ball's dim radiance. It was like staring into a dark pit. If he gave his approval to enact the Greater Cause, Halcyon would cease to exist. Humanity would persevere, but what remained would be a mere shadow of what once was. The only way to stop the madness was to find the Savior before the Greater Cause got out of control. Cain inhaled deeply and slowly exhaled. He looked up at Quinn.

Initiate phase one.

Quinn nodded and smiled triumphantly, though her superior couldn't possibly have seen it. Nor could the Chieftain have known about her concern that his conscience might override his judgment. She would have to watchful. She and her superior concentrated as one. Cain's light winked out. Their bodies faded and melded with the darkness until, at last, they disappeared.

THE KAHANNE

The federal parliament in Hansehaven was the oldest and most majestic building in the Hansic Alliance. The main keep was three times larger than the district and municipal keeps in the twin cities of Rugen and Lubec, and it was surrounded by its own

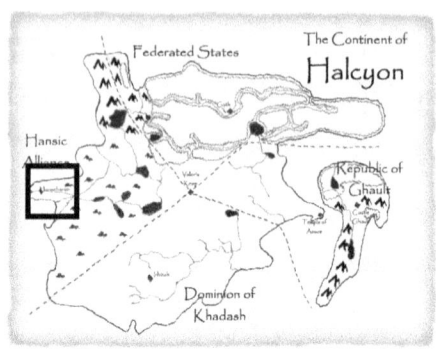

protective wall. Beyond the wall were administrative and financial offices, the national treasury house, and the high courts, not to mention the residences of the top officials who operated these institutions. All this was surrounded by a second wall that was broken up by bastions along the sides and two-story towers at the corners. Numerous spires poked up at the sky from various parts of the complex, a tribute to the ancient city of Halcyon from the Golden Age.

This whole area was situated on an island in the middle of the River Odra. A single bridge extended from its main entrance to the city of Hansehaven, which sprawled along the northern bank. It was second in size only to the combined population of Rugen and Lubec. Most of the people who lived here were connected in some way to the central government, making Hansehaven a city of civil servants.

Unlike most capital cities, which tended to reflect the latest fashions and trends imported by the local aristocracy, Hansehaven, like much of the Hansic Alliance, clung to the past with stubborn determination. It was impossible to tell which buildings were old and which were new because the architectural style hadn't changed in centuries. Music, art, theater — these cultural elements had remained virtually intact since the Great War.

Tradition was at the heart of this day's festivities. Citizens from every part of the Hansic Alliance, along with a contingent from Khadash, had been arriving in the Hansehaven Region for over a week. To accommodate this visit, the day was declared a holiday for Hansehaven. Municipal planners had predicted two hundred thousand visitors, and the local garrison had been supplemented by regiments from other regions as well as an entire Praetorian division to keep the peace. They quickly discovered that it was a conservative estimate.

The visitors and the inhabitants of Hansehaven lined the main street leading to the central cathedral. A dozen militia regiments and four Praetorian battalions were stretched well beyond their capacity to keep the citizenry away from the center of the street. The place was supersaturated with well-wishers and onlookers who wanted to catch a rare glimpse of the Kahanne of Assize.

It was well into midmorning and the crowd was growing restless. The sky was clear, the sun was bright and the temperature was cool but not cold — the perfect day for such an event. In spite of the overwhelming number of people, the noise level of the crowd was surprisingly low. The street wound its way through the city and into the outskirts, and the thick mass of anxious believers followed it the whole way, forming a living buffer between the middle of the road — which was empty — and the businesses and homes which lined its curb.

Soon the blast of a horn was heard in the distance, a trumpet that was echoed by several others. Those at the very edge of the throng were the first to see what the Hansic Alliance had been awaiting for a decade. The Kahanne's entourage slowly crested a hill surrounded by a cloud of Ghaultian militia: the Guardians of Assize. Their polished steel armor gleamed brightly. The ones in front carried twelve standards representing each of the Spirits. They marched slowly and proudly with their eyes trained on the crowd, ready to deal with trouble if it arose. Standing on top of a dozen chariots, over the heads of the surrounding Guardians, were the High Clerics of each Spirit. They were draped in differently colored robes corresponding to their affiliation. These clerics formed a loose circle around a thirteenth chariot, one that was twice the size of each of theirs. It bore a tall platform with an ornate throne. Upon it sat Arlyne Corbonne, representative of the Forum, Kahanne of Assize.

Her dark eyes absorbed everything around her. Her hair was light, though the color was hard to see because it was cut so short that she was almost bald. Arlyne's visage was accentuated by high cheekbones, a small nose and thin lips — a face that would be considered pretty on any other person. She wore a smoke gray robe over a tall, well-developed frame. The neutral color was meant to emphasize the idea that she held no allegiance to any one Spirit. She represented the entire Forum, while each High Cleric represented one Spirit.

Arlyne acknowledged the crowd on either side of her with a nod, a smile, sometimes a wave. Her face and body language expressed the perfect mix of composure, affection, wisdom and charisma. She was the ultimate politician. She could gauge a crowd and present herself as whatever they needed her to be.

Trailing the Kahanne's entourage was a mass of Khadashite pilgrims dressed in frocks of assorted colors that corresponded to the twelve Spiritual orders. They marched in groups according to the orders they supported, and each group was singing a hymn to its own Spirit. What resulted was a cacophony of misbegotten notes and keyless harmonies which completely ruined the atmosphere for the hosting Hansickers, who preferred to view this occasion with due solemnity. It was a testament to the patience of the hosts and the sanctity of the moment that the Khadashites weren't driven from the city.

The Hansickers on either side of the street formed in behind Arlyne's entourage and the trailing Khadashites as they passed by, marching with quietude and dignity. Very soon, the Kahanne had an enormous following, one that stretched back as far as she could see.

Closing her eyes, Arlyne let her senses absorb the smells, sounds, and feel of this city. Every place had a unique character. The foods people ate, the songs they sang, the way they spoke, and how they mourned and celebrated revealed much about how to relate to them. Arlyne always tried to attune herself to the natural rhythms and signals of the places she visited. As Kahanne, she could do nothing less.

Opening her eyes, Arlyne looked around and gazed into the faces of believers. *How far will their faith take them?* she wondered. There were no apparent signs, yet her instincts told her that the Time of Meeting was nearly upon them. Would their faith be strong enough to support them through the inevitable destruction?

As these thoughts crossed her mind, she heard a soft chant. At first, she dismissed it as another Khadashite song and she winced at the possibility of yet another addition to their tumultuous discord. However, as she scanned the crowd lining the street, she noticed scores of mouths moving in synch. It took her a moment to recognize the gentle melody: Elren's Madrigal. Elren was the Spirit of Wisdom, and the hymn was written centuries earlier by a devout follower who likened his reverence for the divinity to the love between two people. It had since become a staple of the daily prayer rituals and it was taught in most schools at the elementary level.

The Hansickers continued to sing, repeating the poem over and over again. Arlyne was spellbound by the crowd's reaction to her (though she realized that it was probably a reaction to the Khadashites as well) and she was held in awe of the emotion of the moment. Few events instilled such an overwhelming response in her. The recitation quickly spread ahead of her entourage so that by the time she rounded a bend or crested a hill, the oncoming bystanders were already chanting. The Khadashites were quickly drowned out, an action that was met by hurt and offended expressions, though most of them abandoned their own singing and chimed in:

My soul is bound to you, my love,
With you, my heart resides.
>*I sacrifice myself to you —*
>*Emotion overrides.*
I therefore pledge my servitude,
My will, you galvanize.
>*I bear this burden like a shield*
>*'Til Chaos is excised.*
With alacrity, I give myself,
In affection, realize
>*Your reverence grants me favor,*
>*My fortune coincides.*
In you, I find my one true faith,
With devotion I reprise —

My soul is bound to you, my love,
With you, my heart resides.

As Arlyne's entourage moved on, more people joined the chanting so that when she finally reached the central cathedral after a long trek through the city, Hansehaven thundered with the religious fervor of hundreds of thousands of voices.

The Kahanne's party stopped at the foot of the steps leading up to the central cathedral, which was the primary shrine for all the Spiritual sects. The entrance consisted of two huge wooden doors that towered over the dignitaries assembled before it. The rest of the building was grandiose and architecturally complex, at least by Hansic standards. To anyone else it would have simply been an outdated, albeit respectable, temple. Its massive brass dome was colored lime green in many places from exposure to the elements. The dome towered over the square, casting much of it in shadow. Like the rest of the buildings in this city, not to mention much of the Hanse, it was designed less for aesthetic pleasure and more for functionality. The only major renovations consisted of repairs to the existing structure. It was never expanded to support the burgeoning population nor updated to suit changing tastes.

Forty-eight steps led up to the entrance, four for each Spirit. From her vantage point on top of the chariot, Arlyne saw that they sported carvings of images that were commonly associated with the divinities. She made out a closed fist for Samlah, wildlife for Rasqu'il, and others. They were designed so that each step comprised one piece of an image. Thus, a viewer looking down at the steps from high up would see twelve large, complete icons leading into the cathedral. A stage with a podium and twelve lit braziers had been erected midway to the top so that Arlyne could easily be viewed by anyone standing within the small square that spread out from the temple. The square was filled with more than fifteen thousand pilgrims with the rest still crammed into the main street. To ensure that everyone would hear the Kahanne's homily, stands were erected intermittently throughout the square and along the winding length of the road. As Arlyne ascended the stairs with the High Clerics in tow, acolytes climbed on top of each stand to act as speakers for the Kahanne. It was their duty to hear what was spoken from the podium and shout it to the next speaker along the line so that the people in between would hear. Due to the city's cramped design, this was the only way to convey these messages to such a large audience since no one wanted to tear down buildings to open up the square.

Chancellor Yarena Hanser, her husband, Lawrence, and the five district governors and their spouses waited patiently on top of the stage. They were decked out in their full dress uniforms — black tunics and breeches with gold baldrics strapped from left shoulder to right hip. In addition, the governors bore their district crests over their hearts while the chancellor displayed emblems with the national standard imprinted upon them. They all sported medals from their militia service, though Governor William Lessander had the most impressive collection. They waited stiffly at attention.

When Arlyne reached their level, Chancellor Yarena Hanser approached her. The chancellor was pale and plain looking, though her expression conveyed the requisite sternness of a Commonwealth leader. The tight outfit betrayed her wiry frame. Since no-one was permitted to approach the Holy Person without consent, she stopped two paces from the Kahanne. Arlyne nodded slightly and beckoned. The chancellor stepped forward, clasped her hands together and bowed her head. When this happened, silence quickly rippled to the back of the crowd so that those who were honored to be standing at the front could actually hear what was being said in hushed tones a dozen meters above them.

"Greetings, Holy One," stated Chancellor Hanser. Her tone, which was normally cool and sharp, expressed a more somber note. She had spent the last few months brushing up on her Ghaultic, which she hadn't spoken since her university days. Although it came back to her quickly during the practice sessions with her tutor, she now felt herself stumbling over the words.

"You may face me," answered Arlyne. Her voice was light and commanding, and her tone reflected Chancellor Hanser's.

The head of state lifted her face to look directly at Arlyne. The chancellor swallowed hard in a dry mouth before speaking. "Holy One, I am Chancellor Yarena Hanser, most humble servant of the Forum." The chancellor gestured to the bureaucrats behind her, who bowed their heads as their names were called out. "May I introduce my husband, Lawrence. Next to him are William Lessander, governor of the Great Sea District; Reginald Clayburgh, governor of the Alpas District; Irene

Hanasser, governor of the Khadashite District; Henry Marchand, governor of the Central Highlands District; and Mina Barranov, governor of the Great Lakes District. On behalf of our people, we welcome the Forum's representative on Halcyon."

The Kahanne smiled slightly. "Your words honor me. I will address the masses now."

Chancellor Hanser stood aside, and with a regal air, Arlyne strode past her and up to the podium. She scanned the crowd. So many people, and not a whisper heard from them! She visited this country all too rarely. Staying mired in the past had its advantages — for one, they never forgot how to treat dignitaries. Arlyne closed her eyes and muttered a silent prayer to the Forum before starting. Every ounce of concentration she had was being devoted to her next words. When she spoke, her voice was clear and resounding. She began with the recitation of the Harbinger which was uttered by the Spirits themselves at the beginning of the Golden Age and which laid out the future history of Halcyon.

"This, it has been given to know: that the realm of Halcyon shall pass through seven ages in its time. Three shall be times of Order, and three shall be times of Chaos, in which land will be laid waste.

"Let it now be known that upon the third coming of Chaos, the bones shall be tossed in a contest of wills to see which shall emerge dominant in the struggle between Order and Chaos and that the victor shall determine the fate of all that is to proceed.

"Everything past, present, and future shall meet at that appointed time to act as witness. Two will enter; one will survive. And the One shall rule them all."

Arlyne paused until the echo of her speakers' voices faded. As well as repeating her words, the speakers were translating the Harbinger into Hansic so that everyone could understand. She continued. "Have we not seen Chaos' visit and revisit? A thousand years ago, our people lived harmoniously, at peace with each other and their environment. That was our Golden Age, a time when science, philosophy and culture flourished." Another pause, and the faint sound of her speakers' voices could be heard. Chancellor Hanser raised her eyebrows slightly and looked at her husband, impressed with the new Kahanne. She had spoken in perfect Hansic with only the slightest hint of an accent.

"Then the forces of Chaos came to scatter us across Halcyon, but we survived. We persevered, though the Assault on Technology ensured that the achievements of the Golden Age were forever lost to us. We turned this Age of Ruin into a benefit and established ourselves throughout the continent. Then, during the Age of Disquiet, we expanded our civilization to the farthest reaches of this continent. Although distrust and fear were pervasive, Chaos was not content. As was foretold by the Harbinger, the Great War came upon us. At this time, the forces of Order would have been destroyed had it not been for the sacrifice of the Elders, whose powers drove Chaos from our world and brought us the Second Harbinger:

"'When it shall come to pass that the Triad of Chaos becomes complete, let it be known that the Savior shall come unto the midst of the darkness, and this one shall wield the Orb.

"'Then shall the appointed time come into being, and then shall all creation stand as witness to the final confrontation between the Savior of Order and the Champion of Chaos. Then, the fate of what has been and what will come shall be made clear, and the One shall rule them all.'"

Another pause. "We are now into the two hundred and ninety-fifth year of the Age of Redemption. We must be wary, for Chaos will return a third time, and I fear that the fated Meeting between our Savior and its Champion draws near. A trial lies ahead, a trial of faith and a test of courage. It may not arrive today or tomorrow, perhaps not even in this generation, but it will come. And we will be ready. We have driven off Chaos twice before and we will do so again, for such is our destiny, even if the Harbinger itself will not reveal the final victor. We therefore pray for ourselves, for our children and for their children, that in their Games the Spirits find favor in us, and let us say, 'Amen.'"

The crowd repeated "Amen". The word slowly rolled back along the main street as successive speakers finished repeating the Kahanne's words. A hushed echo continued to recede in volume for several minutes.

Arlyne paused again and decided to change the tempo. She wanted to end the opening homily on a high note rather than leave them with a sense of foreboding. "It is a great honor to be welcomed to the Hansic Alliance. You are Halcyon's conscience, the instinct that tells us that we cannot know who we are or explore who we might be unless we know who we were. Culture and tradition are unique possessions because present generations are the custodians of a legacy that does not belong to them, but to succeeding generations. We pass on what we have to our descendants trusting not that they will use it and exhaust it, but preserve it for their own children, who will in turn preserve it for theirs. Culture and tradition are antique commodities, for unlike money or titles, they are not meant to be spent, but constantly safeguarded. It is a curious irony that such sentiments are uttered here, in the capital of an economic alliance that values freedom of commerce above all else. Yet, you understand that there are commodities in this world that cannot be traded and with which one cannot negotiate. This is the lesson the Hanse has taught us. This is what you bequeath to your world."

While the speakers finished repeating her words, Arlyne motioned to several attendants. They held up bowls filled with various kinds of incense for each of the twelve braziers. She stepped from one brazier to the next and sprinkled a pinch of each powder into its corresponding flame. A potpourri of odors wafted through the air from the stage, a noxious mixture of smells and scents that forced the hosts to cough lightly. Arlyne returned to the podium and began singing a lighthearted hymn: Forum's Praise. It was traditional to begin such festivities with this piece. After a few seconds, the entire mass of people had chimed in.

Hail the Games of the Forum,
Offer the Spirits' oblation.
Sing to the honor of those who believe
Pray for the favor of Fortune.

> *Sing to L'Xar from birth unto death —*
> *Praise for the one who is Life.*
> *Sing to Elren, whose Wisdom prevails*
> *O'er senselessness, folly and strife.*

Hail Teyull the Protector,
Who heals the sickly and frail.
Hail the Courage of Samlah,
Betrayer of Chaos' veil.

> *Sing to Yarmah, who commands the great Seas,*
> *Who heeds the mariner's call.*
> *Sing for the cradle of Nature —*
> *Rasqu'il, sustainer of all.*

Hail the Earth of Avari,
Riches beyond mortal ken.
Hail the one dubbed Wayfarer:
Qedem, who guides mortal men.
> *Sing to the tempests of Rukh,*
> *Whose Cycles are history's pawn.*
> *Sing to Shakar, Guardian of Souls*
> *Lord of the world beyond.*
Hail the Creatures of Arya,
They respond to the hunter's great shout.
Hail the Spirit whose name is Unknown
Judge of all Games throughout.
> *Bend knee to the Forum! We pray on this day*
> *To Fortune, all give a great cry!*
> *Praise for the One, the One who is King,*
> *Who reigns o'er all from on high.*

With this hymn, Arlyne Corbonne began her first Communion in the Hansic Alliance as Kahanne of Assize.

*   *

Several hours passed. Arlyne, Chancellor Yarena Hanser, her husband Lawrence, the district governors and their spouses, and the High Clerics were lounging in a private sitting room in Hansehaven Castle. The place was comfortable and was furnished to suit the needs of visiting dignitaries. Finely woven tapestries depicting images of the sea and the central highlands covered the cold stone walls, testaments to a mercantile tradition that predated the formation of the Hanse. A soft red carpet was laid over the floor. The aristocrats and religious leaders stood about in small clumps conversing amicably. The informal atmosphere was a welcome break from the morning's arduous service.

Chancellor Hanser, her husband Lawrence, and Arlyne were seated around a short table.

"Holy One," began Chancellor Hanser, "if I may be so bold, I must commend you on your grasp of our dialect. I didn't expect it."

99

Arlyne acknowledged the compliment with a slight nod. "If I am to function as the spiritual leader for all Halcyon, I must communicate in a manner that the masses understand. How else am I to guide them in their efforts to achieve Communion? I am aware that Ghaultic is taught in your schools, but I doubt that it sees everyday use so far from the Ghaultian frontier."

Lawrence mumbled softly into his beard. "I bet the Ghaultians don't extend the same courtesy to us."

The Kahanne cocked her head at him. "You bet correctly."

Chancellor Hanser's eyes flared at her husband, who spluttered, "Forgive me, Holy One, I — I meant no offense. I just —"

A smile played on Arlyne's lips. "No offense was taken. It has been some time since I considered myself Ghaultian." Lawrence breathed easier, though his wife was still angry. The Kahanne continued, pretending not to notice. "As I indicated, I believe that to connect with the… what is the term… ah, common folk, one must speak in a voice they can hear. It is a sharp departure in policy from my predecessor, who maintained that Ghaultic should be universally spoken. Granted, the text of Ahenak's Codices is Old Ghaultic, but its modern derivative should not be considered holy."

The leaders of the Hanse shuddered at the thought of being forced to speak the language of their historic enemy. Nearly six hundred years had passed the first separatists left Ghault, and the use of Ghaultic as a spoken language had been suppressed ever since.

Lawrence was about to mutter another comment but a glance from his wife held him in check. The chancellor decided to change the topic of conversation. "I can't imagine the emotional drain involved in leading a ceremony like we had this morning," she commented.

"One adapts," replied Arlyne.

They were interrupted by a high cleric. He had wispy, thinning brown hair and was clad in the red robes of Rukh. "Holy One, forgive the intrusion," he started in broken Hansic, "but I want to bid you a good night." He turned to his hosts as if he had just noticed them for the first time. "And to you, as well, Chancellor and… uh…" he searched in vain for the right word "… Chancellor's husband."

Lawrence raised a meaty hand to cover his smirk. The chancellor responded in Ghaultic, "Thank you, High Cleric."

The Kahanne nodded slightly and added, "May Rukh lull you to a peaceful rest this night."

"Thank you, Holy One." He bowed his head in the manner that was expected of someone who received the blessing of a Spirit.

The high cleric left and Arlyne returned to their discussion. "When I was an acolyte I found it difficult to envision myself as little more than a minor cleric in the service of the temple at Castle Ghault."

"Speaking of Castle Ghault, how is your father?" inquired Lawrence. "Our last direct correspondence with him had to have been at least two years ago."

Arlyne's tone became slightly cold when she answered. "He is… well, thanks to Teyull." The three of them bowed their heads once in deference to the Spirit she invoked. "We rarely communicate. I try to distance myself from him."

"He is your father," Lawrence pointed out.

Arlyne was pensive for a moment. This was hardly the time to discuss the chilly relationship she had with her father, though she knew it was the subject of numerous rumors. Instead, she replied, "True, but he is also the Padishah of the Republic of Ghault, and as the Kahanne of Assize I must take care not to show any favoritism to him whatsoever. Such a task is already compounded by the fact that Assize is located so deep within the Republic. Often I feel that my administration, far more than previous ones, has taken greater care to ensure the equal treatment of all the countries."

A smile peeked out from under Lawrence's beard. "One adapts."

Arlyne snuck a quick sip from her drink. "Indeed."

"You made some interesting comments about tradition," mentioned the chancellor. "It would seem that our two peoples have more in common than we thought."

Arlyne shrugged. "Perhaps, but you should not dwell on it. My views reflect those of the religious establishment, not Ghaultian politics. Believe me, much goes on in that country to create a sizable gulf between it and everyone else."

"Our Commonwealth ambassador at Valor's Keep has been trying to get his counterpart to open up, but so far he's been unsuccessful." The chancellor frowned. "I would give up my title and land to know what goes on behind that wall."

Arlyne allowed herself a mild chuckle. "The Republic sealed itself behind that barrier decades ago. Since then, no one has been able to export any substantial information, and those of us who have passes to travel abroad are sworn to speak nothing of what we know. Imagine that! I, the representative of the Forum, must yield to their earthly authority!"

"Is there nothing you can do?"

"My fa— that is, the Padishah does it to put me in my place, but he knows he cannot win should I choose to challenge him. Frankly, I have not the time for such political games. For others, though, the consequences of noncompliance can be deadly."

The chancellor appeared unfazed by this statement. Lawrence gaped. "Surely they can't threaten the Holy Person," he whispered. "You are a citizen of every nation!"

"They have informants," Arlyne replied simply. She flicked her eyes in the direction of her chief steward, who waited patiently in case anyone required his services. Chancellor Hanser and her husband sucked in their breath, wondering if there was anything they could do but knowing that the steward's superiors would learn quickly if anything untoward happened to him. Arlyne, though, didn't appear bothered. "Do not be disturbed by this revelation. Remember that this is a way of life in the Republic. Those who are born into it seldom give it a second thought. I am the first Ghaultian in a hundred years to attain this office. My predecessors from the Dominion of Khadash and the Hansic Alliance dealt with it accordingly, so why not me?"

Chancellor Hanser decided to change the subject before someone overheard them. "Holy One, your entourage leaves tomorrow morning. Are you sure you can't extend your stay? Visits from the Kahanne of Assize are so rare."

"Regrettably, I cannot. Rukh has made this journey long and arduous — his Elements have not granted us speedy passage. The annual tribute must be made to the Forum in five months and I have yet to visit Irbirah."

"That should be an experience," muttered Lawrence.

"Khadashites have a unique world view," replied Arlyne. "I look forward to the visit. Unfortunately, Qedem ensures that a convoy such as mine does not move as quickly as I would like — slower now, without Rukh's approval — and the travel time takes its toll."

Chancellor Hanser nodded in understanding. "I presume, then, that you won't be stopping by the Federate."

Arlyne shook her head. "Many of my predecessors have tried and failed to make inroads into that country. The one remaining temple to the Forum lies in Kennedor, but that has more to do with its status as a former duchy of Ghault than any national policy emanating from Gath. We cannot force them into accepting the Spirits. For now, it is enough that they recognize the One True Deity. The truth will win out on its own. It just takes time.

"For similar reasons I have decided to skirt Valor's Keep. My presence there would merely complicate the diplomatic schism between the Republic and the rest of the Commonwealth. In any event, the Grand-General would certainly oppose any visit."

"The Praetorship is godless," cursed Lawrence. The chancellor looked at him sharply.

Arlyne took the comment in stride. "Perhaps, but that is a burden they alone must bear. It is for the Unknown to judge."

There was a moment of silence between them during which they overheard snippets of other conversations. Finally, the chancellor spoke up. Her expression was troubled.

"Holy One, I must admit that I feel somewhat disturbed by your warning about the coming of the Time of Meeting. Is it really upon us?"

Arlyne answered carefully. "There have been no overt signs, but my instinct tells me that Samlah cannot force the Champion of Chaos to remain idle for long. The Circle's representative to the Commonwealth Council agrees that the Dark Champion is stirring."

At the mention of the Circle they shifted uncomfortably, recalling Governor Lessander's report about his encounter with Quinn and the Circle's inexplicable interest in the *Explorer*.

Sensing their feelings, the Kahanne spoke carefully. "Granted, the Circle has yet to earn the trust of the people of Halcyon, but should the Time of Meeting truly be upon us, we will look to them for aid. Perhaps it is merely ill fortune that my feelings coincide with the departure of your *Explorer* ship from Rugen, but a part of me dreads what Yarmah may reveal in the vastness of the Great Sea. No one has ever ventured out there. Let us pray that we can contain whatever they bring back."

This led to a disquieting moment when no one spoke. After a short while, the Kahanne rose. The chancellor and her husband followed.

"Chancellor, I must take my leave of you. I am weary from the day's events. With your permission, I will retreat to my quarters."

Yarena and Lawrence Hanser bowed their heads and Arlyne acknowledged the ritual with a slight nod. As she strode regally to the door, the others in the room bowed their heads as well. She turned back to them and uttered a blessing, calling upon the Spirit of Souls to guard them in their sleep: "May Shakar watch over you."

Once she was gone, the conversations resumed. The leaders of the Hanse sat back down and eyed each other worriedly.

*　　　*　　　*

It had already been a long and exhausting trip but it was far from over. More than a week had passed since the Kahanne's visit to Hansehaven and her conversation with Yarena and Lawrence Hanser. As her carriage bumped lightly on the road, Arlye smiled at the memory of their discussion of politics and religion, and at Lawrence's indignation when she told them about Ghault's spies and informants in her retinue. Following that, Arlyne quickly

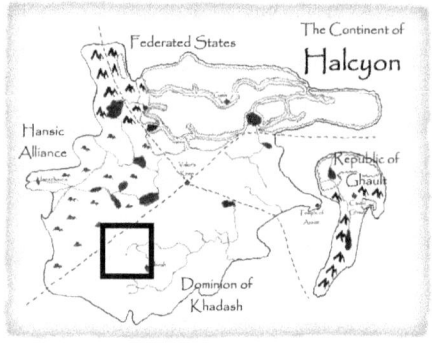

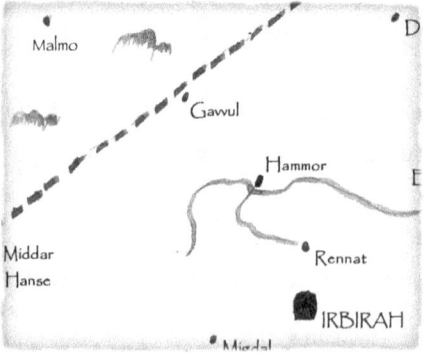

discovered that the mild annoyance she felt over the presence of the relatively small number of Khadashite pilgrims in the capital of the Hanse was a mere prelude to what awaited her in the Dominion of Khadash.

The population of Khadash was scattered throughout the country in small farming villages and hamlets. Large towns were found only at the intersections of major trade routes. The capital, Irbirah, was the only real city. Thus, Arlyne was constantly passing through one tiny settlement after another, and with every new village came new pilgrims.

She had never experienced anything quite like it. Usually, when she came to a town, people from all over the region would come to see her. After sitting through one or two Communion services, they would go home. Instead, these Khadashites followed her everywhere, starting with the ones she met in Hansehaven. They formed one gigantic caravan, stretching beyond eyesight along the road. They brought along their own pack animals, tents and supplies, and they seemed to leave only when their food ran out. At night, they camped en masse on vacant land or even in the woods. Entire families would gather around one of the hundreds of campfires and sing songs to the Forum accompanied by instruments of every sort. Some of the tunes were traditional, but many more were unfamiliar even to the Khadashite members of the Kahanne's entourage. Looking back on the trip, Arlyne admitted to herself that in spite of their peculiarities, no one derived more joy from worshipping the Forum than the people of Khadash.

Yet they had liabilities, too. Chief among them was the absence of an organized militia. This left border patrols to the Praetorship, a fact that the other countries resented since, indirectly, they were paying for Khadash's defense. Arlyne knew that this view was somewhat limited. Since Khadash had no natural enemies like grimals, antigovernment militants or criminal guilds, and since it had no history of factionalism, there was no need for a national defense force to keep everything together. If her reports were accurate, there were fewer Praetorians stationed here than in any other country. Of course, this disparity tended to make meetings with the Commonwealth Council arduous even at the best of times, though no one denied that Khadashites made up a significant chunk of the Praetorship's ranks.

Arlyne rested her forehead in her hand as she reflected on all this. There were times during her visit when she struggled to contain herself. When she felt herself about to burst, she was never sure if she was going to laugh or weep. To say that Khadashites were strange was an understatement. Arlyne preferred to see them as unique. Non-Khadashite colleagues who visited this country with the previous Kahanne spoke as if it was an ordeal. Hers began at Hansehaven when the mass of Khadashite pilgrims met her at the entrance to the city. They followed her along the River Odra and through the Central Highlands. They never seemed to tire of singing and dancing and it was only with the greatest difficulty that Arlyne kept her composure when she asked them to stop so that she and the clerics in her company could meditate in peace.

The foothills along the boundary between the Hanse and Khadash constituted the only unguarded border in Halcyon. At the time, Arlyne wasn't even aware that she had entered Khadash until she noticed that the foothills were receding and that the line of pilgrims behind her was growing. By the second week after her departure from Hansehaven, she was sure that there were more people trailing her entourage than she had seen in the entire city of Hansehaven that day she had led the service. The presence of such a multitude would have been invigorating had it occurred anywhere else. Here, with thousands of people shouting, singing and dancing to their own tunes and rhythms, she felt like leaving her post and running home. Five days ago, she was ready to concoct an excuse to head back to the shelter of the high walls surrounding Ghault when an acolyte presented her with a pair of earplugs that she knew she would cherish forever. Yet, despite her irritation, Arlyne was proud that the people of Khadash served the Forum. They needed their Kahanne.

They were ten days away from Irbirah when they stopped in the town of Gavvul which lay in the foothills of the county of Middest. Arlyne looked about curiously. There was no uniform architectural style. Some buildings appeared to have been constructed in the most haphazard manner possible while others were exquisitely designed. The Kahanne's caravan reached the local Temple to the Forum. A crowd of thousands waited outside as she and the high clerics in her company entered the temple to pay homage to the Forum. This moment of fervent prayer, which comprised the core of the worship service, always inspired the Khadashites to quiet down. Arlyne still didn't understand why. They were loud and boisterous for everything else. Nevertheless, when the Kahanne and her clerics entered the temple, all became silent.

It was a simple building that comfortably seated about two hundred people. The vaulted ceiling was low and narrow and the dome, which was situated above the altar at the far end, was puny in comparison to the others they had seen in this country. The outer layer of plaster that weatherproofed the walls was cracked and flaking. This was obviously a relatively poor town, one in which the common folk had sacrificed a great deal to have a temple. Arlyne was suddenly ashamed of her attitude to these people. True, they were different and sometimes offensive, but they were also dedicated. Arlyne felt as if she had suddenly been humbled, and she could tell as she glanced at her companions that they felt the same way.

The Kahanne approached the altar followed by the twelve representatives of the Spirits. She sprinkled a fine white powder over the elements of the braziers that rested on top of the altars and lit them. They gave off a mixture of aromas that would have made any other person sick, but these religious leaders were quite used to the smell.

"Extol the Spirits who dwell on high, sing songs of praise to the Forum. We offer a sacrifice of fire and fragrance so that You, in Your eternal dwelling place, may find favor within us, Your most humble servants. We appeal to the Spirits so that their Games bestow Fortune upon the good people of Gavvul, that they may live in health and peace."

"Amen." The high clerics' chorus echoed through the small temple and it was heard clearly by the throng outside. The people used it as a cue to restart their singing and chanting. The high clerics hung their heads and looked at one another with exasperation. The incense was wasted here. There could be no Communion with all that noise.

There was a raucous cheer when Arlyne and the high clerics exited. Gavvul's elected town priest approached them and the crowd quieted down. He remained standing several paces away from Arlyne. His head was bowed and his hands were clasped within the long sleeves of his robe. Arlyne was impressed. This was a rare Khadashite priest who was aware of the proper protocols.

"You may approach."

As the local priest complied, he lifted his gaze to meet the Kahanne's eyes. He struggled with his Ghaultic as he said, "As the duly elected religious leader of Gavvul, I want to thank you for addressing the Forum on our behalf."

Arlyne smiled slightly and nodded. He knew that she spoke Hansic but he tried to address her in her native language instead. She was impressed again. The high clerics behind her exhaled thankfully. He didn't address her as "Holy One" but that was okay. He hadn't made any serious blunders. Yet.

The priest grinned widely back at her and extended his hand.

Arlyne heard some of the high clerics gasp. This was but another in a long line of ritual missteps from the Khadashites, though it was the first time that someone offered to touch the Holy Person. Everyone waited for a few tense moments to see what the Kahanne would do. She blinked several times as she stared at the extended hand. There were whispers from the crowd. It was time for her to do what she did best. It was time for her to be who they needed her to be.

She grasped the offered hand and shook it vigorously. "The pleasure was mine," she replied in Hansic, "though it is I who should be thanking you for your hospitality."

The crowd cheered more loudly than ever before. The priest held his hand up and gazed at it as if admiring a blessed icon. He stepped back into the crowd and was swarmed by people who wanted to experience the Holy Person by touching his hand. The high clerics and the entourage from Assize were unable to hide their shock. Some of them swooned. Arlyne stepped forward and waved, an action that brought even more cheers her way. She smiled warmly at them, though her mind raced to find a way to explain her behavior to her colleagues.

Arlyne stood alone in front of the throng absorbing the adulation. The high clerics and the local priest looked on from the stairs leading to the temple. Suddenly, and without warning, the Kahanne's body convulsed and she fell to her knees. The cheering was quickly replaced by an uneasy silence as her attendants rushed to her side.

Arlyne looked around but everything faded from view. A vicious cackle filled her head and her mind was invaded by horrible images. She saw creatures of unthinkable size ravaging the Temple of Assize. They swarmed around it and tore down its walls, causing the roof to collapse and crush people to death. The survivors were hauled out of the wreckage by the creatures and devoured alive. There were screams all around her and her body grew cold. She doubled over and vomited from the overwhelming stench of burning flesh and decay. She witnessed the destruction of everything she cherished: the priesthood, friends and family, her colleagues.

Everything lay in ruins.

The silence was broken by several cries for help from the crowd. A handful of people in the audience had also collapsed.

As suddenly as they had come, the intrusions in Arlyne's mind were swept aside. When she opened her eyes she saw attendants standing around her. Glancing between their legs, she saw the shocked and concerned faces of worshippers. She looked up and noticed that the high cleric of Samlah was supporting her head.

Arlyne sat up. "How long was I incapacitated?"

"About ten seconds, Holy One."

The Kahanne looked about and saw a woman near the front of the crowd slowly get to her feet who apparently experienced the same phenomenon. Arlyne tried to pick others out of the audience who saw the vision, but it was difficult to see from her vantage point. Even though she was deeply shaken, her mind was already analyzing what just happened.

I must contact the Circle immediately, she decided.

Arlyne waved off her attendants. "Prepare the transports and inform Irbirah that we must regretfully cancel our visit," she ordered groggily. Her companions were stunned. First, she was shaking hands with commoners, and now she was canceling engagements! Perhaps she had taken ill from whatever had caused her to faint.

The Kahanne sensed their apprehension but decided that there would be time to explain her actions later. "Obey my commands," she barked. The attendants and servants scurried off to prepare the carriages.

Arlyne beckoned to the high clerics while the Khadashites looked on with dismay. "We must return to Assize immediately," she instructed.

"Why?" asked one.

Arlyne inhaled deeply and looked at the high clerics of Rasqu'il and L'Xar. They made no visible movements, but she read the approval in their eyes.

"It's finally here. We knew it was coming — the Harbinger predicted it a thousand years ago. I cannot be sure until I investigate further, but I believe I have just been contacted by the Champion of Chaos."

Four Months
Before the Time of Meeting

- Almost two months after the *Explorer's* departure from Lubec in the Hansic Alliance

- Almost two months after Cain announced that a Teivan, Jehorom Galaddi, might be the Savior of Order

- Almost two months after Cain, Quinn and the other Inner Members discussed their plans for preparing for the Dark Champion's return to Halcyon

- Almost six weeks after Captain Duncan Milius and his group arrived at the Palladum

- Almost five weeks after Cain, Quinn, Kahanne Arlyne Corbonne, Captain Duncan Milius, and every Circle Member experienced the Dark Champion's visions of destruction

COURT MARTIAL

The vulturn was the largest predatory bird in Halcyon. It used cunning and stealth as well as brute force to bring down its prey. When hunting, it stood motionless on a branch so that its brown feathers melded with the color of the bark around it. By the time its target realized its

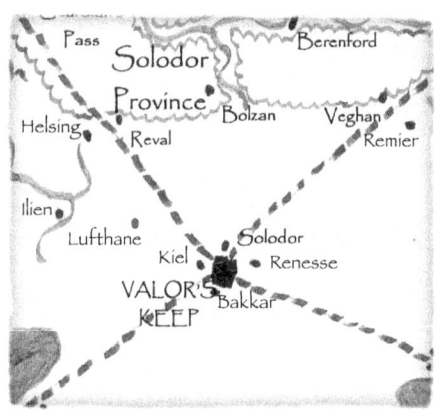

presence it was too late. It could swoop down from the trees and pluck a large rodent from the ground with its powerful talons. Sometimes a vulturn could be spotted catching smaller birds right out of the air. On rare occasions, vulturns had been known to skim the surface of a river and snatch fish out of the water. Vulturns were graceful and elegant yet dangerous and lethal. They used a variety of deadly methods to achieve their objectives, and thus they were chosen to be the symbol of the Praetorship.

A vulturn clutching a bow in its talons with a sword and a pike crossed behind it: this was the Praetorian standard that appeared on every uniform, in every camp, and which accompanied the Praetorship into battle. Its likeness was depicted on a hundred standards that adorned the outer walls of Valor's Keep, the Praetorship's stronghold. That this place was called a keep was a misnomer. The outer wall boxed in an area that was large enough to accommodate a small city.

Duncan Milius' weary platoon approached the north gate. They had marched nonstop from Bolzan, where they had disembarked from their galleasses at the end of the River Saar. They hadn't even paused in Solodor for a rest. It was more than three weeks since they set out from the Palladum and everyone, especially Duncan, wanted to get the proceedings here over with quickly so they could return to regular duty.

The gatehouse had a small portal built into the heavy doors to allow for convenient passage to those on foot. Duncan's group stopped a dozen meters before the sealed north gate and waited as three Praetorians approached them from the portal. The guards had their swords drawn and their shields raised in a non-provocative yet defensive posture. Their steel armor gleamed dully as the sun hid behind a thick sheet of clouds. A pair of archers on top of the gatehouse had weapons trained on the newcomers.

The sergeant stepped forward, leaving the two privates a few paces behind. He studied the newcomers and noticed the ragged condition of their armor — the patches and stitch lines were quite visible. These troops had obviously seen a lot of action. Rumors were just reaching them now about a rout of Praetorian forces in the Federated States. Supposedly, it had something to do with misinformation and an alliance between Teivan extremists and a grimal tribe. Perhaps these were the survivors. The sergeant shrugged. He found the rumors hard to believe. What kind of person — even a Teivan — would want to deal with grimms anyway? The stories of a Praetorian failure were probably concocted by a local militia unit.

The sergeant stopped a couple of meters away from Duncan and noted the rank insignia on his shoulders. This had to be him.

"State your business."

"Senior Captain Third Rank Duncan Milius, commander of the remnant of the eighteenth Federate battalion."

The sergeant and his two privates sheathed their weapons immediately, snapped to attention and saluted. The archers on top of the wall let down their guard.

"Sir!"

"At ease, sergeant."

The soldiers dropped their salutes and relaxed. "Thank you, sir. We've been expecting you. The privates will lead your troops to their barracks. If you'll follow me, the Grand-General ordered that you and Captain Eliss Blaine be taken to him right away."

"Very well."

Duncan looked back at Blaine, who nodded at him. She turned back and called for the Lieutenant.

"Yes, sir?"

"Follow these privates to your barracks. Remain there until you receive further instructions from either Captain Milius or me, or a ranking officer. Understood?"

"Yes, sir."

"On your way, then."

The lieutenant and the rest of the troops followed the two privates through the portal. The sergeant led Blaine and Duncan through a moment later.

"This way, sirs. The Grand-General ordered me to bring you to his study."

The sergeant led the two captains inside. Duncan always felt overwhelmed whenever he was here. The place was so enormous that it was easy to forget they were inside a fortress. They walked past several training grounds where cadet hopefuls were being introduced to the Praetorship's basic training course. Duncan chuckled at the memory. Nothing in all his time with the Federate militia prepared him for what he endured as a cadet here at the Keep. Of a recruitment unit of two hundred, only a handful stayed on to join the Praetorship's ranks.

The sergeant led them to a large administrative complex. They entered the unremarkable wood structure and ascended a flight of stairs to the second level. At the end of the hallway, the sergeant held open a door for them.

"Sirs, if you please. The Grand-General will be along shortly."

Duncan and Blaine entered and dismissed the sergeant.

Duncan looked around. The study was bright and well furnished. There was a large window on one side to allow the sun to filter in. On days like today when the sky was cloudy, several lanterns sufficed.

Duncan and Blaine stood at ease in the middle. It was improper to sit until their commanding officer permitted them to do so, and since he hadn't arrived, they waited patiently. They had exchanged little more than a few words to each other since their arrival — they were too wrapped up in their own thoughts. Neither of them knew what kind of reaction to expect from the Grand-General. Blaine had never even met him. All she knew of Grand-General Bowen were stories about his sternness and abrasiveness. Duncan, on the other hand, knew better. He had personal dealings with the Grand-General on two occasions, one of which resulted in his promotion to junior lieutenant first rank a mere seventeen months after his cadet service.

The captains scanned their surroundings. Blaine recognized the thick rug that covered the stone floor. She had seen a similar design in a gallery in Bakkar, where she grew up. It was a hodgepodge of streaks, wavy lines and blotches. The realization came suddenly that she wasn't staring at a rug, but at a wall tapestry. She smiled to herself — it was probably for the better that the Grand-General had chosen to cover it up with furniture instead of throwing it out. At least this way he wouldn't offend Khadashite sensibilities.

Duncan was busy admiring the wall hangings that decorated the room. There was a commemoration of the siege of Mildurn, which took place two hundred and fifty years ago when Federate forces relieved a provincial outpost in the Alpas Mountains that was under grimal attack. Nearly two thousand militia troops died that day, but the mission was successful. It was a pivotal moment in the history of the Federate because it led to the induction of the province of Valandov into the federation.

There was another tapestry depicting a landscape with a city of exquisite beauty — marble buildings with gold-trimmed roofs and shining spires. A rising sun cast an elegant yellow hue over everything. It was an awe-inspiring sight unlike anything he had ever seen before.

"It's an artist's rendition of the Golden Age." The voice that came from the door was soft, belying one of the keenest strategic minds in Halcyon.

The captains snapped to attention. "Sir!"

Grand-General Dorian Bowen strode into the study. He wasn't an imposing man like General Hawkwin, but his otherwise average build was toughened by decades of hardened military service. He took a seat in front of the hanging that had caught Duncan's attention.

"It was a gift from Padishah Cedric IV Deis upon my instatement as Grand-General. But that one behind you is even more impressive."

The captains turned around. Before them was an exquisite oil painting. Lush greenery framed the foreground of a scene featuring a rich forest that spread through a valley. There were rolling mountains in the background. This was all silhouetted against a sky bright with swirling colors that melted into each other. "This one came to me by way of the former Khadashite premier. The Creation of the Universe."

"Ganeden," murmured Duncan, using the Teivan word.

Bowen nodded approvingly. "You know the myth."

"The One True Deity created the universe in six days."

"Very good, Captain." He pointed to Blaine. "Why do you think I keep it here?"

She glanced at Duncan, her gray eyes questing for an answer. Nothing was forthcoming.

Disappointed, the Grand-General turned to Duncan. The captain thought for a moment before clearing his throat.

"It's a myth from the ancient world, before our people came to Halcyon. Before the Golden Age."

"And…?"

"And all that knowledge is gone. All the history, all the achievements… Demeter Ahenak made sure of it. Six hundred years ago, he made sure that the only writings people studied were his own Codices. He destroyed all the rest. Because of him, all we have left are vague stories."

"So why do I keep a picture of Creation in my study?"

"It's a reminder of the past, of what was lost during the Age of Ruin. It reminds us that the Praetorship exists to prevent such a thing from happening again."

Bowen addressed Blaine. "Do you see, Captain? History tells us why we're here. It's because of History that we do the things that we do. That's why it's a required course for our cadets. It's a relationship I expect all of my officers to understand."

He motioned to the chairs in front of his desk. "Please, sit."

Duncan and Blaine did as they were told. Bowen stood back up, removed his weapons belt and placed it on a hook near the door. He then resumed his place opposite the junior officers. "You'll find that I don't stand on formalities when I'm meeting my officers privately in my own study."

The Grand-General eyed them critically while they shifted nervously. He took a deep breath before beginning. "Several weeks ago I received a report from one of the most respected commanders in

Halcyon. In it, General Cyril Hawkwin informed me that not only did I lose nearly an entire battalion of troops, but that the battle itself was lost. In addition, he reported the following acts: ignorance on the part of the commanding officer, insubordination on the part of a senior officer —" at this pronouncement Duncan averted his gaze "— and the order to retreat from combat."

Bowen stood back up and faced the wall behind him. When he spoke, he sounded angry and ashamed. "Insubordination… ignorance… retreat… These words are are utterly foreign to this organization!" He stood there for a few moments with his back to them. Duncan and Blaine gripped their seats nervously. Neither dared speak. Finally, the Grand-General turned around. His expression was cold and hard. "Does either of you deny these charges?"

Blaine shook her head somberly. "No, sir."

Duncan squeezed his eyes shut and bowed his head. "No, sir."

"This is the first incident of its kind in three hundred years. I've consulted with my advisory council and we've reached a unanimous decision. I will head up this investigation personally. Officials from the military court are interviewing your troops as we speak. Nothing has been determined yet. No blame has been laid, no punishment meted out. My council and I will interview each of you privately and at length. As of now, you're ordered to say nothing of what transpired at Ravelin. You're not to discuss the issues at hand with each other, with your platoon or with anyone else. Failure to comply will result in court-martial and imprisonment. Do you understand these terms?"

Blaine nodded solemnly. "Yes, sir."

Duncan hadn't shifted his gaze. "Yes, sir."

"Good. Do you have anything to say off the record before I begin? If you do, this is your only chance. You will be held accountable for your actions and your testimony from this point on."

Blaine shook her head again. "No, sir."

Grand-General Bowen looked at Duncan, waiting for a response. The captain's hand absently grabbed a hold of the pouch at his side that held the claw from a grimal that killed a Praetorian — a reminder of what went wrong at Ravelin.

If I fail them now, they'll have died for nothing.

He then thought of Jarren. How he wanted her at his side. He only wished that he could express half as much confidence in himself as she expressed in him. Finally, after taking a deep breath, he answered.

"No, sir."

This was it. The most critical moment in his life had begun. He opened his eyes and looked directly at the Grand-General for the first time, facing the challenge with uncertain courage.

*   *   *

Three days passed. Duncan and Blaine weren't permitted to even see their troops, let alone talk with them. The captains were housed in opposite ends of the Keep to prevent them from making contact. Their platoon had been restricted to its barracks and two training fields. They ate at different times than everyone else and they were kept under constant surveillance by court officials. Twenty-four hour personal escorts were assigned to Blaine and Duncan who ensured that while the captains were granted leave to roam the Keep at will, they made no contact, casual or otherwise, with anyone else. A blanket of secrecy covered the whole affair to the point where Grand-General Bowen contemplated issuing a general order prohibiting all public discussions of the event. His advisory council convinced him otherwise, pointing out that it was impossible to police the conversations of tens of thousands of people.

By the time Duncan received his summons to attend court on the afternoon of the third day, he could no longer stand it. The atmosphere around him was suffocating. No one who saw him was sure whether to view him as the man who saved a platoon of soldiers from certain death or the man who disobeyed orders and fled while his comrades fought and died.

He donned his uniform. It was a smoke gray outfit with a black weapons belt and boots to match. The crest of the Praetorship was sewn on the breast over his heart. Opposite the vulturn emblem were the medals and honors he had attained in his short career. With a dry cloth, he gave them one last polish: awards for gallantry and valor in battle, awards for tactical ingenuity, and awards for achieving his ranks faster than anyone else in the history of the Praetorship. Awards that could be stripped from him today.

He exited his quarters and met up with his escort. They mounted their steeds and trotted off to the courthouse, which was located near the center of the Keep. They threw cloaks over their uniforms to shield them from the light drizzle. The sky had been overcast ever since Duncan's arrival and now the weather had taken a turn for the worse. As they rode they passed by large, muddy archery ranges and training fields. Proctors had their cadets out in full force despite the rain and they stopped their exercises momentarily to watch him pass by. It seemed as if everyone in Valor's Keep knew about what was happening. In spite of the Grand-General's gag order, word had gotten out.

Oddly enough, Duncan wasn't nervous. An eerie quietude had descended over him. He thought of the soldiers who died at Ravelin. He thought of Jarren, whom he knew would support him regardless of the day's outcome. He steeled himself for the worst. This was the moment of decision.

They reached the courthouse and dismounted. A private led their animals away while they entered. It was an unremarkable building that consisted of one giant room. At the front was a small stage with a long table and high chairs. Directly in front of those were two desks with accompanying seats. The rest of the room was filled with benches to accommodate about a hundred and fifty onlookers. This day, the gallery was full. Duncan's escort led him in from the back of the room and the assembly quieted down. As the captain walked past, he noticed that his entire platoon was present, as were several ranking officers from the Praetorian corps as well as the Federate ambassador to the Commonwealth, his staff and the six provincial consuls.

Duncan's escort led him to one of the desks and told him to sit. After a moment, Blaine entered with her escort and was told to sit at the other desk. The room grew completely silent as Grand-General Bowen entered with his four-member advisory council of senior generals in tow. The Praetorians in the gallery saluted while the commanders took their places on the stage. Bowen acknowledged the salute and ordered Duncan and Blaine to rise.

"Senior Captain First Rank Elliss Blaine, I'll deal with you first since yours is the less complicated case. You have been absolved of all complicity in this matter."

There was a noticeable sigh from her as Bowen continued. There was no reaction from the people in the gallery, who appeared to have been expecting this judgment.

"This court martial has determined that you were following your orders and serving the best interests of your battalion. The fact that Marshal Wallace was proven wrong does not make your initial actions against Captain Milius wrong as well. You and the surviving members of the eighteenth Federate battalion are to be reassigned for active duty in the Federated States at the earliest possible convenience."

There were nods of approval and smiles of satisfaction at this pronouncement. This was what the troops had been hoping for.

The Grand-General now directed his attention to Duncan. "Senior Captain Third Rank Duncan Milius, your fate is a somewhat more complicated matter. As a ranking officer, it was your duty to ensure that Marshal Wallace was acting in the best interests of his battalion. Any disagreements that you had with him should have been made in private. As much as it was your duty to keep your commanding officer in line, it was also your duty — and his as well — to present a united front to the soldiers. I'm sure you'll agree that there is a need for the soldiery to see that their command-level staff agree on policies that affect them. To do otherwise would be a negative influence and a detriment to morale."

"I agree, sir."

"I hoped you would. This breakdown in communication between you was partly responsible for the deaths of some seven hundred Praetorians, warriors for whom there can be no honorable burial, fighters for whom there can be no adequate memorial. It is the belief of this court martial that Senior Marshal Second Rank Corinn Wallace acted with malice and prejudice toward Captain Duncan Milius, particularly in the matter of Captain Milius' background as a Teivan."

There were murmurs of surprise from the gallery. The captain looked sharply at his Grand-General, who didn't seem to notice. Duncan had hoped to avoid making his background an issue but he saw that it hardly mattered any more.

Bowen called for order before continuing. "This charge implicates Captain Blaine as well, though she made the correct choice in obeying the orders of her commanding officer. No one here is a seer or a prophet. You were proven right, Captain Milius, but you could just have easily been proven wrong. Marshal Wallace behaved negligently by ignoring the advice of a ranking officer whose prowess and analytical skill have been demonstrated time and again. It is the judgment of this court martial that Marshal Corinn Wallace be posthumously relieved of command."

This was also met with approval from the gallery. There could be no other judgment for someone who led his troops to disaster.

Bowen cleared his throat before continuing. Duncan noticed his hesitation, and the mood in the room became more anxious. "It is also the judgment of this court martial that Captain Duncan Milius acted in the best interests of his troops when he ordered the retreat —" more murmurs "— and that his behavior was consistent with the best interests of the Praetorship."

Duncan noted the disapproving glances directed at the Grand-General and himself. Bowen stood up and everyone tensed. "Does anyone here question this judgment?"

There was dead silence in the room.

"Because if you do, you're missing a basic lesson here, a lesson paid for in blood, and you do not deserve to call yourself Praetorian!" He paused deliberately before continuing. "Prowess means nothing if your life is wasted on a lost cause. Where's the honor in that?"

Bowen sat back down slowly, and he rested his hands on the desk in front of him. "Marshal Wallace should have known that the tide had turned against him, as any sensible commander would have in his place, but he was blind to that possibility because of the pride of Valor's Keep. Captain Milius made the impossible choice that his commanding officer refused to consider. Is that not the mark of a competent officer? Is that not the mark of a good leader?"

Bowen's challenging tone silenced the opposition for now, but Duncan knew that there were many people in the room who weren't convinced.

The Grand-General straightened up and finished his remarks. "It's a worthy lesson to understand that sometimes the most important part of knowing when to fight is knowing when not to fight, and the price of this lesson is a black mark that will tarnish the Praetorship's honor for a long time to come. Do you agree with these statements, Captain Milius?"

"I do."

"Do either of you have anything to add?"

The captains glanced at each other. "No, sir."

"Very well."

Bowen paused for a moment as he considered his next words. Grinning slightly in a way that almost seemed mischievous, he indicated one of the officers at the end of the table. "As you know, General Leyva is the commander-in-chief of our forces in the Federate. General, I believe we now have two command-level positions open, do we not?"

"Yes, sir," acknowledged Leyva. "Marshal Reghan in Torinn Province has had to resign her commission due to a serious illness. That, along with Marshal Wallace's death, leaves two openings for regional commanders in Torinn and Valandov."

"Thank you, General." With his elbows on the desk in front of him, Bowen clasped his hands. His advisory council watched him with knowing expressions, though two of them clearly disapproved of what was coming.

"Our resources are strained to their limits and we need the best people in positions of authority. Therefore, effective immediately, I hereby promote Captain Duncan Milius to the commission of junior marshal third rank. This promotion is conditional — *Marshal* Milius will have to submit weekly reports to the provincial governor as well as to General Leyva. Do you accept these conditions?"

There was complete silence from the gallery. The Grand-General was promoting a man — a Teivan — who ordered a retreat! Duncan himself was barely able to contain his shock. He expected reassignment or at best a commendation. But this?

"Yes, sir," he stammered.

Bowen smiled. "Good. You will assume command of the Praetorian forces in Valandov Province. Your knack for innovation and your leadership qualities — not to mention your experience with Federate politics and grimals, and your heritage as a Teivan — make you the perfect candidate for this post. Your first mission is to finish what you started. You're going back to Ravelin, and this time you're going to finish the job."

More silence. Bowen had presided over many courts martial in his career but he had never experienced anything like this until now. The tension was electrifying.

The Grand-General's face darkened, and he looked directly at his new marshal. "Duncan Milius, this was not an unanimous decision. There are those who value a man who knows when to back down, but there are others who see cowardice in people who are unwilling to take risks. You will be judged by your conduct over the next few months. You have much to prove."

Bowen's gaze swept across the court room. He lingered on the faces of the soldiers who survived Ravelin with Duncan.

"Our new marshal leaves in the morning with a detachment of fresh troops," announced the Grand-General. "If anyone in this room cares to join him, stand now."

The survivors of Wallace's battalion needed no prompting. Every one of them stood up. Looking back at them, Duncan was overcome with pride. He looked sideways at Captain Blaine who was also on her feet. She smiled at him and nodded.

Bowen's eyes gleamed. "Considering the circumstances surrounding this case and in deference to our fallen comrades — for whom we are still mourning — we will forego the traditional promotion ceremony."

He rose, and everyone followed suit. "We observe a moment of silence in their memory."

It was a long, disquieting moment. Finally, the Grand-General looked up.

"This court is dismissed," he declared softly.

The buzz of two dozen conversations immediately filled the room. The Federate ambassador, Blaine and a number of other people including two generals approached Duncan to congratulate him. He shook hands and thanked them all, though his mind was a whirlwind. He absently rubbed the scar that ran the length of his left cheek. Jarren and his foster-father were going to be proud.

CARAVAN

Kahanne Arlyne Corbonne dozed lightly in her carriage as she traveled from Murky Lake to the border crossing at Gossamyr. She had attended the previous Kahanne on his tour through the Hansic Alliance and the western provinces of the Federated States, so she was used to long, overland

travel. Yet despite her previous experiences, Arlyne found this trip especially trying. Feeling the need for fresh air, she opened a window and poked her head out. As she did so, she heard a raucous cheer from the trailing Khadashites. With a sigh, Arlyne summoned one of the Guardians of Assize, her personal sentries. He bowed his head toward her as he kept pace with the carriage's movement.

"How long until we reach the border?" asked Arlyne.

"We should arrive within the hour, Holy One."

Arlyne surveyed the landscape. It boasted no remarkable features — there were flat wheat fields everywhere she looked. Perhaps it was no wonder that the inhabitants developed an eccentric lifestyle. They had to make up for an otherwise dull country.

She returned her attention to the guard who was still marching with his eyes to the ground. "Very well. You may resume your duty."

"Thank you, Holy One."

Arlyne retreated inside the carriage and the sentry stepped back into the defensive line the Guardians of Assize had formed around the Kahanne's vehicle.

One hour, she mused. *One more hour.*

She found herself thinking about her truncated visit to this country. She had never been forced to cancel an engagement until now, but the vision from the Dark Champion a month ago had caused her to do so. The bouncing carriage lolled her back to sleep again.

*

The carriage halted, snapping the Kahanne awake. She looked out through a side window and saw a dark stone wall stretching across the horizon. Ahead of her was a large, heavily patrolled gate. It was a bright day, though the ground was damp from a recent shower. A cool easterly breeze was blowing. Arlyne could hardly believe that a whole hour had passed. They had reached the border to the Republic of Ghault.

There were six high clerical carriages ahead of hers and six following behind, not to mention the sizable company of attendants and Guardians. Arlyne estimated that it would take hours to process so many papers, yet somehow they managed to move more quickly than she expected. The Ghaultian border patrol must have been alerted to their arrival. Even so, it was still forty-five minutes before Arlyne's own carriage made it to the gate. Soon there was a polite rap on the window next to her. She opened it and found herself staring at a border sentry who was averting his gaze. He had a short crop of brown hair, a thin neck and a gaunt face with a goatee and mustache. A tight navy blue uniform showed through his black leather armor. His headgear was tucked carefully under his left arm to avoid ruffling a short red plume. Judging by the pips on his collar, he was the regimental commander from the Ghaultian border town of Neufort.

He took three steps back and bowed. He was obviously terrified. "I beg your forgiveness, Holy One, but I'm bound by His Grace's regulations to inspect all incoming vehicles."

Arlyne paused for several moments before responding. Could this man be serious? "Do you know who I am?" she demanded.

Only a handful of people in the world were granted the honor of being spoken to by the Kahanne of Assize, but no one had ever offended her. The commander sank to his knees. "Please, forgive me, Holy One, but I have no choice! The command comes from the Padishah's own office!"

She didn't really have a choice. Not even the Kahanne of Assize was above Ghaultian law. Besides, if this officer disobeyed his orders, he would most certainly be dishonorably discharged or even imprisoned, and they would simply find someone else to do the job.

"You may conduct your search," she growled.

With his eyes still averted, the commander got to his feet, approached her carriage and opened her door personally. She stepped out and glanced around. They had stopped right in front of the gate's huge wooden doors, which were opened wide. The wall itself was two stories high and was well patrolled. It featured a wide walkway with high crenellations. Additional archers had been positioned along both sides of the gatehouse to watch the mass of pilgrims who were being forcibly held back by a line of spearmen. Two squads of Praetorians were also present to make sure that the spearmen didn't get overzealous in their efforts to keep the Khadashites at bay. The gatehouse itself was two meters higher than the wall. This defense ran the length of Ghault's boundaries with Khadash and the Federate — a total of more than fifteen hundred kilometers. Its ten-year construction had nearly bankrupted the country.

Arlyne looked ahead and watched as members of her entourage were searched one at a time by sentries wearing the same navy blue uniforms. After a few minutes, the commander emerged from her carriage. He still kept his eyes averted and his head bowed.

"Holy One, again I beg forgiveness for this intrusion. You may pass."

Arlyne strode regally back to her vehicle. "May the Spirits bestow fortune upon you," she intoned.

"Thank you, Holy One."

She entered, shut the door and sat down heavily. She found these border crossings very trying. She would have to bring the issue up again with the Padishah's officials. What kind of contraband would servants of the Forum be smuggling into the Republic of Ghault? Did the office of Kahanne mean nothing? This was the Padishah's way of reminding the Kahanne to keep her place, though she suspected that there was something personal in this, too. She shook her head sadly. She had been away from the royal court ever since her induction as a full cleric of Rasqu'il. How long ago was that? Twenty years? Twenty-five? Yet, despite her isolation from courtly life, she felt uneasy about the political future of her country. Unsettling rumors crisscrossed the land, rumors that had even made their way into the halls of the Temple of Assize. Could it be true that two of the dukes were building a private army? Could the stories of breakthroughs in armament technology be valid? And all this at a time when the Champion of Chaos had announced its presence to the world. She wasn't sure of anything any more.

Her carriage pulled away and her eyes strayed to the window next to her. As she passed beneath the gatehouse, she noticed one of her attendants being led to a door inside the wall by a soldier with a district crest on her shoulder. Arlyne noted that it was the attendant whom she had pointed out to Chancellor Hanser as being an agent for one of Ghault's covert intelligence networks. Feeling drained, Arlyne sat back in her seat, wondering what he was reporting about.

ONE MONTH
BEFORE THE TIME OF MEETING

- More than five months after the *Explorer's* departure from Lubec in the Hansic Alliance

- More than five months after Cain announced that a Teivan, Jehorom Galaddi, might be the Savior of Order

- Almost five months after Cain, Quinn, Kahanne Arlyne Corbonne, Captain Duncan Milius, and every Circle Member experienced the Dark Champion's visions of destruction

- Fourteen weeks since Kahanne Arlyne Corbonne's return to the Republic of Ghault from Khadash

- Almost fourteen weeks after Captain Duncan Milius' promotion to marshal and his reassignment to Valandov Province in the Federated States

The middle of the second month of summer was a time of feasting and thanksgiving, for this was when, according to the Codices, the Spirits first made themselves known to the people of Halcyon at the end of the Golden Age. This was a time of

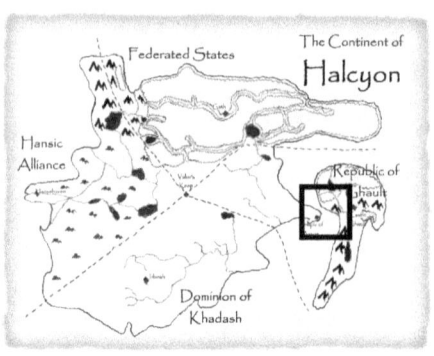

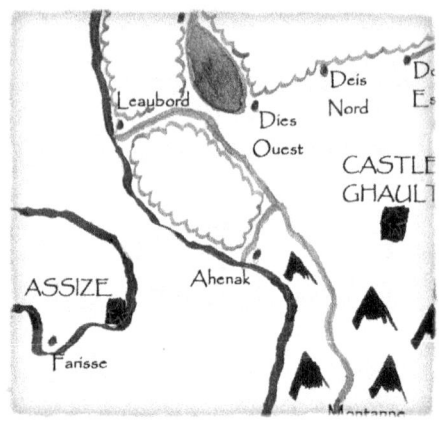

pilgrimage to the Temple of Assize, which lay deep inside Ghaultian territory. Security was a serious concern, and the Republic's militia was out in force to keep the peace and ensure that no one wandered into restricted areas. There were tens of thousands of pilgrims, and the security officials kept a meticulous watch. Suspected spies were detained and possibly jailed, though most of the time they were brought to the nearest border crossing and forced to leave.

The religious establishment was always displeased with such policies. It maintained that most of those being detained were innocent, and indeed, they were. It was a poorly kept secret that the militia had a quota of people who needed to be ejected from the country. This way, they could keep the number of unwanted visitors to a minimum. Unfortunately, this contradicted the Kahanne's belief that the Temple of Assize should be accessible to everyone. Years earlier, when the Republic of Ghault sealed itself behind its extensive border wall, one of the concessions the Padishah made to the Commonwealth was to allow safe passage for a certain number of pilgrims each year. Moving the Temple out of Ghault was impossible since it was built on the very spot where the Spirits first made themselves known, so the religious leadership had to yield to the political leadership.

"What will you tell the people today?"

Arlyne glanced at her companion: Yair, High Cleric of Samlah, a longtime friend and confidante. Yair had been one of her key sponsors in her bid to achieve the position of Kahanne. Arlyne smiled for a moment and looked away. "I have not yet decided."

"Not decided?" Yair leaned forward in her seat and rested an arm on the table in front of her. "You are about to lead a festival service!"

The two women were sitting in an antechamber off to the side of Assize's main cathedral, waiting for their cues to enter. The muffled sound of thousands of hushed voices reached them through the closed door.

"There are the words that I write and there are the words in my heart. They are not always the same thing."

"You are still troubled by the event in Gavvul."

Arlyne nodded. She had been in constant contact throughout all of spring and the first half of summer with her own people and with the Circle, and after all that time no one had come up with an explanation for what had transpired that day nearly four months ago. Arlyne still shivered when she reflected on it. She had been leading Communion in the local temple to the Forum when the Dark Champion invaded her thoughts with images of death and destruction.

"I have meditated at great length on it," she responded. "I have consulted with the heads of our Spiritual orders, as you well know. I have discussed the matter at length with the Circle."

Yair regarded her Kahanne curiously. "The Circle? I was unaware of this."

"I have my contacts." Arlyne sat down opposite the High Cleric. "The Circle calls it a 'mentallic surge'."

"Do they?"

The Kahanne paused for a moment, her expression saddened. "The phenomenon was experienced by every mentallic on Halcyon, from first-levels to tenth-levels. It manifested for everyone at exactly the same moment as a vivid dream. The common features of these visions involved the destruction of the people and objects the individual held most dear. The feelings of horror and terror were palatable."

Yair's chair creaked under her weight as she leaned back. Arlyne had never spoken about what she saw that day.

The Kahanne continued. "What is most disturbing is that until now, it was assumed that only high-level Members were capable of capturing that kind of visual, olfactory and sensory detail. The fact that the every Member received it suggests that we are dealing with a phenomenon so powerful that it has not been found on Halcyon since the time of the Elders."

"But you are not a Circle Member. How is it that such a thing could affect you?"

Arlyne hesitated for a moment as she considered how to respond. She shrugged. "I am the Kahanne. It is only logical that I should be a target for any attack."

"Then the Circle agrees with us that the Dark Champion was responsible."

The Kahanne nodded solemnly.

"What does the Circle intend to do now?"

Arlyne folded her arms across her chest and shook her head. "We have spent the last four months waiting for something to happen. The Circle expects some sort of attack against the continent, though they refuse to comment on precisely where that attack will come from or in what form. I am convinced it is somehow connected to the *Explorer*'s departure from Rugen in the early spring, but I have no proof for this suspicion since no Circle Member will respond to my speculation. But, like the Circle and the Ghaultian dukes, we have informers of our own. We are aware of the Inner Membership's visit with Governor William Lessander the day the *Explorer* set out more than five months ago."

Yair smiled. She remembered reading the same report.

Arlyne continued. "So, was the mentallic surge a premonition — a message sent by the Dark Champion to instill a sense of fear?"

"If fear was the goal, why did the Enemy not choose a form of communication that the general public could hear?"

"Indeed." Arlyne breathed deeply. "If mentallics were its sole targets, they obviously pose the most dangerous threat to the Champion. Therefore, the Champion is undaunted by any civilian institution or army, even the Praetorship. It also suggests that the Savior of Order must be a Circle Member."

The Kahanne rose and gestured to the closed door. "So now you see: there are the words I have written for today's festivities, and there are the words in my heart I know I must speak."

Arlyne sighed heavily and tried to clear her mind. She hadn't slept well since the mentallic surge violated her all those weeks ago. She was finding it increasingly difficult to concentrate, especially on occasions like this.

I must be strong, she told herself. *We must all be strong.*

There was a window in the antechamber and she peered outside. From here, she could see much of the sprawling complex that was Assize. Her quarters, and those of the clerics and acolytes who lived here permanently, were located in a wing that abutted the great Temple. She could see one of the long walls of the towering structure — an architectural marvel. Massive stained-glass windows were set into recesses every two meters, and between them arched buttresses stretched to the ground to help distribute the weight of the domed roof. The Temple was built between the cracked remnants of two gigantic spires. Their precision and smoothness testified to the lost technology of the Golden Age. Far in the distance, Arlyne made out the clerical seminary and three more broken spires. The foundations of every building in Assize incorporated remains from the Golden City of Halcyon.

The enormous square between the seminary and the Temple was filled with pilgrims who were here to celebrate the Epiphany. The worshippers were ready.

"It is time for me to take my place."

Yair stood up and brushed past her Kahanne. As she opened the door, the low rumble of thousands of quiet conversations filled the antechamber. Arlyne peeked past her. The cathedral in the Temple of Assize was completely full. Thousands more were gathered outside to hear the Kahanne's words through the mouths of her speakers. The cathedral was the largest building of its kind in Halcyon. Two gigantic pillars marked its entrance. The vaulted ceiling was eight stories high and was buttressed by an array of tall, thin columns with wide arches spanning the distance between them. The ceiling was beautifully decorated with icons depicting the twelve Spirits wearing the colors of their respective orders, each standing in the midst of its associated symbol. Sunlight filtering in from the entrance, the skylights and the stained-glass windows that adorned the walls cast the immense chamber in a bright, warm hue. This day, the sky was cloudless.

The altar at the far end from the entrance was located on top of a raised portion of the floor. An orchestra pit was positioned next to this. It was filled with musicians from every corner of the continent, even the Federate — Kennedor Province was the only part of that country which still openly supported the Forum.

"I look forward to hearing your words, Holy One."

Yair slipped out, leaving Arlyne alone with her thoughts.

The worshippers grew silent as the string section began to play a slow yet pleasant tune. It was a fugal arrangement that began with a four-bar refrain. Each time it repeated, a new section chimed in with a variation on the original theme. Soon the horns and woodwinds had joined in with the strings to produce an oratorio that was as complex as it was enchanting. The members of the congregation were captivated as they allowed the music's eloquence to flow through them. It was soothing and inspiring all at once.

The Kahanne used this as a backdrop for her entrance. Striding in from the antechamber, she slowly ascended the steps to the altar. She was accompanied by a number of her closest acolytes as well as three of the twelve high clerics — the rest were running services in their own dioceses. She exchanged a quick glance with Yair before continuing.

Arlyne wore a long gray robe with voluminous sleeves. Her head was freshly shaved for the occasion. She stood alone in front of the altar and waited as the echo of the oratorio's last refrain faded away. Soon there was nothing but silence in the cathedral. She took a short moment to scan the crowd. She was always amazed at the overwhelming number of people the Temple could accommodate. She nodded her head slightly — a cue for the conductor. He raised his baton and motioned for the orchestra to begin. This was the signal for the congregation to rise. The orchestra played a two-bar introduction to a familiar festival hymn. At the beginning of the third bar, the congregation chimed in.

Let all exalt the One Most High, to whom our praise is due.
Creation is His testament, humanity His glory.
In one day, He made heaven, on that day He made earth.
From nothingness, He fashioned them, to nothingness they return.

He left His Spirits as guides through our travails:
Our Father, our King, who made us in His image.
Our Father our King, who gave us knowledge of good and evil.
Our Father our King, who fashions Order from Chaos.
Our Father our King, who set us apart from the creatures of the earth.
Let all exalt the One Most High, to whom our praise is due.

The string section played on a higher key to allow the congregation to participate in a choral harmony of sorts. The swelling voices and their symphonic accompaniment created a sound that could not be heard anywhere else on the continent. It was a thunderous tumult of devotion that was part of a religious tradition that had shaped civilization on Halcyon for nearly eight hundred years.

Soon the orchestra brought the hymn to a dramatic close and the congregation sat back down. Although the opening prayer was finished, its echo hung in the air for a few more minutes. Arlyne waited for the sound of shuffling feet to disappear before beginning. Her voice carried solidly to the back of the cathedral.

"We give thanks to the One Most High for fashioning the universe and making us who we are. We give thanks to the One Most High for creating the Forum and the Spirits to watch over us and care for us. May their fortune favor us through the impending hour of Chaos, and may they take notice of this day's Communion."

"Amen." The congregation's response reverberated loudly. Arlyne turned away to light the first of twelve braziers that was positioned behind her. As she did so, the room darkened as the bright sky became shrouded under a cloak of black storm clouds. There were a few whispers from the crowd as people wondered how a storm front could move in so quickly.

An incredible peal of thunder caused everything to shake. The thousands of pilgrims who stood outside grew frightened and panicky, all the while staring fearfully at the Spirits-cursed change in weather. This sparked some surprised murmurs from the congregation that now sat nervously inside the Temple. Arlyne shot a glance back at the assemblage and the whispers immediately stopped. She was about to admonish the crowd — the first time she or any of her predecessors ever had to do such a thing — when her attention was drawn to the main entrance to the cathedral.

A powerful wind blasted through the ranks of scared pilgrims and into the Temple of Assize, throwing some people into the seats in front of them. Great fingers of pink lightning burst from one cloud to another directly over the temple roof, occasionally reaching down to strike the building. The unnatural lightning was visible through the Temple's skylights, and the phenomenon caused the panic from the pilgrims outside to spread quickly inside. One bolt struck glass and a skylight shattered, sending razor-sharp fragments raining down on dozens of people. They tried to scramble out of the way but they only succeeded in adding more confusion to the fray.

The powerful gales continued to blow inside and they seemed to be aimed directly at Arlyne. Terrified worshippers looked on with trepidation as their Kahanne was pinned to the altar by the wind. It quickly became so dark in the cathedral that no one could see clearly between the strobe-like bursts of pink lightning. Suddenly, two sconces latched to the wall just above the altar lit themselves. The lightning stopped abruptly so that the only light in the chamber emanated from the pair of torches. Yelps of pain and sobs were heard from every part of the cathedral, while clerics and acolytes tried to calm people's nerves. The wind died down and Arlyne could move again. She stood in front of the torches that had lit themselves and called for attention.

Most people did as she asked but they didn't focus on their Kahanne. They looked on in shock as the tongues of flame from the torches grew to enormous lengths, stretching into the vastness of the sanctum. The crowd was ominously silent. Arlyne was transfixed by the winding strands of fire. Slowly twisting, turning, and intertwining, the tongues of flame formed the fiery shape of a gigantic serpent's head. Casting the entire cathedral in a bright orange glow, it hung suspended in the air above the congregation. Its jaw moved, and a throaty hiss was heard throughout the surrounding countryside.

"Hear me now, mortal denizens of Halcyon! Hearken to the voice of the Champion of Chaos — the Triad is now at hand. Let the bones be tossed so the One may rule eternally."

Wrenching her gaze from the fiery head, Arlyne looked behind it to the Cathedral's main entrance. She stared uncomprehending at a massive shape framed in the doorway. It was silhouetted by the lightning flashing behind it, and it was impossible to make out any features other than its head, limbs, and hulking body. Its mass filled the entire entrance.

With a sudden blinding flash, the flames dissipated and the hulking body in the entrance vanished. The storm outside dispersed as quickly as it had come, leaving only black scorch marks and thousands of hysterical citizens as proof that anything had happened at all. The sun emerged to shine as brightly as before, lighting up the Temple's interior with warmth and beauty. A stunned Kahanne dropped to her knees before the altar, her body trembling.

After a few moments, Arlyne had calmed herself enough to look up at the terrified faces of the high clerics and her acolytes. Ignoring them, she squeezed her eyes tightly together and focused her mind on one single thought. She knew that those watching her would think that she was attempting to Commune. Perhaps this was best, for instead of contacting the Spirits Arlyne had a more mundane concern. In a powerful burst they could not ignore, the Kahanne of Assize sent a message to the Circle's Inner Membership.

The Dark Champion is on its way. The Time of Meeting is upon us.

Opening her eyes, Arlyne rose to her feet. Ignoring the terrorized civilians in the Temple, she looked with resolve at the clerics and acolytes around her.

"Prepare my transport and gather the necessary supplies. I must depart for Valor's Keep. Now."

FLIGHT

The convocation theater was full. Free-floating balls of light provided ample illumination for the six thousand Members. Despite the large number of people, it seemed as if they were only taking up a small portion of the enormous chamber even though there wasn't a vacant seat to be found. They sat behind desks that were arranged into concentric circles which decreased in circumference from a thousand seats in the outermost ring to just six in the innermost one. The people were dressed in robes that bore the colors of their levels. Underneath, many of them wore their civilian clothing. For some, not even the families of these Members were aware of their double lives.

It took days to transport everyone to the Circle Enclave for a convocation, and as a result, convocations were only held twice a year. This was their first-ever emergency gathering, and the unease was palpable.

The Members sat in their places listening calmly to their Chieftain's pronouncement. He stood on a dais in the very center of the circles surrounded by the other six Inner Members. Apart from the odd shifting or coughing, there was not a sound to be heard in the theater. Cain's voice echoed clearly in their heads.

Cain gave them his customary greeting and paused. He gazed for a long moment at his fellow Members. Sorrow and worry were etched onto his face. Cain sighed. It was time.

I don't know how to put this delicately, so I'll just say it. We've managed to confirm what many of you already know. The Champion of Chaos made itself known to the world a week ago at the Temple of Assize.

There was astonishment from the handful who hadn't yet heard the news. Worried murmurs escaped from many lower level Members for whom telepathy wasn't a routine form of communication.

The details of the event are irrelevant for the moment, he continued. *What's important is the fact that unlike last spring's mentallic surge, the Dark Champion manifested itself physically in one of the few places it knew people would take notice. It obviously chose Assize because of the symbolic nature of the site — the spot where the Harbinger was first uttered is now the same spot where its last prophecy came true.*

Cain let this information sink in while he scanned the crowd. He detected much apprehension, but he needed to be forthcoming. They had to know what was coming.

You're all being placed on high alert, he continued. *When the Enemy arrives, you'll be summoned to Valor's Keep. Obviously, there isn't enough room for everyone in our tower, so we'll work something out with the Grand-General. Our task will be to provide whatever aid we can for the Praetorship until we're ready to initiate phase two of the Greater Cause, though I pray that this won't become necessary.*

The Members were visibly uncomfortable at the thought of this possibility. Although most of the first-levels were successfully linked, phase one was still proceeding very slowly. It had been more than four months since Cain had authorized Quinn to begin her work on it. The intricate network of links required for the psychic nexus had to be painstakingly built one mind at a time. This was further complicated by the fact that each mind had to be in exactly the right place in the network, connected to precisely the right people. One mistake would cause an imbalance that could permanently damage everyone in the nexus. This sent a collective shiver through the Membership.

Cain studied Quinn. She wanted to accelerate the Greater Cause while he searched frantically for the Savior of Order. He recalled the day so many weeks ago – had it really been more than four months? – when the Dark Champion invaded his mind with images of death and destruction. He had been in the Library attempting to break the Elders' invisible barrier as he had done countless times before. The Enemy had violated his mind that day. The memory of that violation was as vivid now as when it had just happened, just as he knew it was for every Circle Member. Yet Quinn seemed immune to its effects. The ensuing argument with her had been less than cordial, and Cain was sure that if it wasn't for his mentallic superiority, she would have deposed him long ago.

The Chieftain brushed this aside and finished what would likely be remembered as the briefest address in the Circle's history. *Let's take a break. Get up, walk around and stretch. In thirty minutes, report to your supervising eighth- and ninth-level Members. They'll provide you with detailed briefings and instructions on our plans as we move forward. Following that, we'll conclude this emergency convocation. First- and Second-Level Members will remain to work with Quinn and her team on the first phase of the Greater Cause. Everyone else will be free to leave. As usual, supervisors will see to the teleportation of those who cannot do so themselves. Be ready to move to the Keep when the call comes. That's all.*

What followed would have been an eerie sight for any non-mentallic. The people in the theater rose from their seats and mingled as they would if this was an ordinary gathering, but they engaged in hundreds of conversations without uttering a single word. There was the presence of typical hand gestures and body language to accompany the dialogue, but nothing was spoken out loud. Apart from the occasional chuckle or cough, the only sounds to be heard in the convocation theater were moving chairs, rustling clothes and shuffling feet.

The number of people gradually diminished as more of them were teleported away or they left for other chambers in the Enclave. Eventually, the Inner Circle, two green-robed sixth-levels and a blue-robed eighth-level gathered in a secluded corner of the convocation theatre.

I'd say that went rather well, stated Reeve. He pulled up a chair and settled his bulk into it.

As well as anyone can expect, added Phylar, one of the other Inner Members. *I suspect that the reality of the situation won't hit them until they have to move to Valor's Keep.*

Enough chitchat, interrupted Cain. *Let's get this over with so we can get back to business.*

The other four Inner Members approached and took seats.

We have updates from our head operatives in the Republic of Ghault and the Federated States, continued the Chieftain.

The three Lesser Members approached and pulled back their cowls. The eighth-level was a man whose armor showed plainly through his robe. The sixth-levels were a man and a woman, both of whom appeared to be of noble stature.

The program of destabilization in the Republic has been accelerated, stated the noble. *We've made sure that a number of rumors have been brought to the Grand-General's attention over the last few months. When news of his reaction makes its way to Castle Ghault, it will serve to increase anxieties.*

Dukes Robert du Dijinn and Cecil du Langue have been pushed into becoming the major players, added the woman. *Neither Castle Ghault nor the dukes are fully aware of the technological advances of the other. When the Padishah discovers the scope of his own ignorance, it should be too late. The dukes will already have made their move.*

What of the animosity we wanted to foster? asked one Inner Member.

It's worked better than any of us imagined, replied the woman. *The dukes are ready to kill the Padishah right now.*

You have to rein them in, warned Cain. *We can't have them make any move before we're ready. Instigate some setbacks in their weapons development programs — that should keep their emotions under wrap for a few months. We can't have open warfare until Jehorom Galaddi is in place.*

The sixth-levels nodded.

Good, off you go.

The sixth-levels concentrated. After a moment, their bodies started to fade as their constituent particles broke apart for reassembly elsewhere. The Chieftain turned to the eighth-level and motioned for him to begin his report.

Jehorom Galaddi has met with moderate success in his new post. It's only been four months since his arrival and it took him a while to adjust.

Reeve rubbed his eyes. *This is all fine and well, but has he exhibited any more unusual behavior?*

Not to my knowledge.

Cain nodded. *Thank you, that'll be all. Return to your garrison.*

Yes, Chieftain. The eighth-level concentrated slightly, and his body faded away as the other two had. In a moment, he was completely gone.

Reeve inhaled deeply and studied the other Inner Members. They didn't look very optimistic about the coming Chaos. He glanced at Cain. *What if we're wrong about Galaddi?*

We're not.

Are you sure? asked Phylar. *The Circle has been breeding Teivans since it was established, but so far, we haven't produced anyone with more than tenth-level abilities.*

You're forgetting something, replied Cain. *Remember that day when I contacted Terrel while she was en route to Ravelin? It was about five and a half months ago when she was our agent with Marshal Corinn Wallace's battalion in Valandov Province.*

The others nodded. *That was right before the battle, before we rerouted Duncan Milius to the Palladum,* clarified Reeve.

Right, confirmed Cain. *When I contacted her, I told her that I secretly sat in on Marshal Wallace's strategy session. What I didn't tell her was that I was also there to scan Galaddi.*

And?

Cain threw his arms up. *And nothing! I couldn't get through. I'm always able to tell when a person has no mentallic capabilities because my scan comes out negative. The opposite holds true with a person who possesses such abilities, but with Galaddi, I got neither a positive nor a negative response.*

That means nothing, rebuked Quinn.

It means that his mind has a natural defense mechanism that blocks any scanning attempt. I felt him pushing me back!

Quinn was incredulous. *You're pinning the salvation of Halcyon on a hunch?*

I'm doing no such thing, replied Cain angrily. *The Harbingers foretell the coming of a Savior to combat the Champion!*

What if the Circle itself is the Savior of Order? demanded Quinn harshly.

Cain was growing frustrated with his subordinate. *It's always a possibility, which is why I've given approval for the first two phases of the Greater Cause. While you initiate that program, I'll research our only other likely candidate.*

Cain noticed Quinn's look of disgust. Had he been speaking out loud he would have been shouting. He pointed an accusing finger at her. *What if you're the one who's wrong? What then? The Time of Meeting will come upon us, the Dark Champion will destroy Halcyon and the Savior with it, and the world will be ruled for eternity by the forces of Chaos! You may want to gamble with our fates, but I don't see a second chance for us! We must exhaust all other options before choosing a final course of action.*

Quinn looked away. She was unable to hide this much rage from the others. *As you wish.*

The Chieftain shook his head. Somehow, he had to make her understand. *We all have jobs to do. Let's pray that we find our answers before it's too late.*

The Inner Members nodded their agreement before teleporting themselves away. Only Quinn remained. She needed some time to clear her head. She had to find support. Phylar was sure to back her up, but Reeve would undoubtedly support the Chieftain. That left the other three. She had to bring them all on side before making any kind of move, and she had to secure it before the Chieftain's policies destroyed them all.

*　　　*　　　*

The capital of the Dominion of Khadash was located in the center of a river basin that formed the country's economic hub. The national legislature was the city's focal point. Unlike the government facilities in the other countries, Irbirah's legislature boasted a simple yet elegant

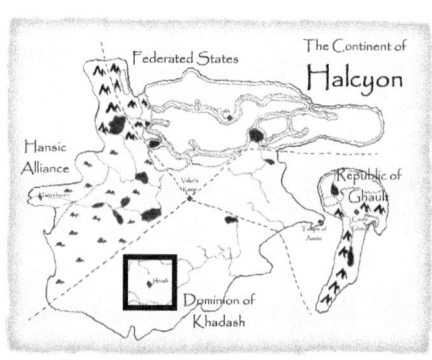

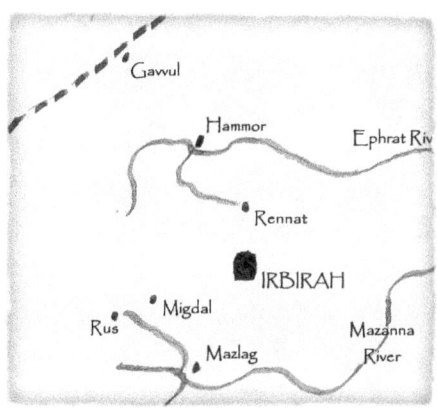

design. The complex looked like a large, decorated stone block with evenly spaced oblong windows marking the offices of the parliamentarians. At the center of the complex, under a sharply peaked roof, was the legislative assembly.

The premier's office was located in the middle of a long corridor that led to the offices of his cabinet ministers. They comprised the top floor of the three-story administrative wing.

Warm browns and greens colored the office of Premier Glendon Fortinbras. The floor was softly carpeted, the furniture antique. Behind the desk sat a dark, heavyset man wearing a thick, red velvet overcoat and brown leather pants. As he rifled through some paperwork, he ran his fingers over a head that once sported a mop of curly black hair. Although he'd been bald for twenty years, it was a habit he'd been unable to break. The faded blue light of false dawn penetrated the curtain covering the window. The room was brightly lit by the glow from four lanterns.

The air across from Fortinbras became distorted, and when he looked up, he found the Circle Chieftain standing before him. Fortinbras was unfazed by the sudden visit. Getting back to his work, he pointed at a chair.

"Have a seat, Cain, I'll be right with you." The voice was a rumbling basso that seemed to fill the room even when used quietly.

The Chieftain pulled his crimson robes around him and sat in the indicated chair. "It's still the last day of the Epiphany. Shouldn't you be at home with Shani and Dannia?"

"I had some work to catch up on before the legislature resumes tomorrow. This bill has to be passed by the middle of next week." Sighing, he put down what he was doing. He smiled at his guest. "This could take a while. Why don't you tell me what you need."

Cain smiled back. "You look tired."

Fortinbras chuckled. "It's not easy running a country. You should try it."

"No thanks, I have my own problems."

"I'm sure. Have you met with the Membership yet?"

"We adjourned three hours ago. I've spent the last little while tracking you down."

Fortinbras put an elbow on the desk and rested his chin in his hand. "Are you initiating the Greater Cause?"

Cain nodded. "We'll be getting ready for phase two soon."

The premier of Khadash exhaled deeply. He sat back, folding his arms over his generous belly. "So you're taking this, ah… event… at Assize seriously?"

A glance at the Chieftain gave him his answer.

"What do you need me to do?" asked Fortinbras nervously.

"We need to make preparations. Start importing as much dry foodstuffs as you can. Direct the farming communities in Khadash's heartland to send their surpluses to the three coastal towns. When the warehouses fill up, we'll start shipping everything to the Khorshim."

Fortinbras fought down his fear. "Are we in full evacuation mode?"

"Not yet. I want the supplies to be in place ahead of the people."

"That's sensible." A thought occurred to the premier. "How can we be sure the Khorshim will be safe?"

Cain sat back in his chair wearily. "You remember when the *Explorer* set out from Rugen?"

"Of course, that was almost six months ago. What of it?"

"Right before they put to sea — during the ceremony on the pier, actually — I had Quinn replace the navigation charts with maps that omitted the Fingers of Khorshim."

Fortinbras was skeptical. "And you think *that* will stop the Enemy from finding us there?"

The Chieftain shook his head. "Nothing is certain, but if our maps don't include the Khorshim, it stands to reason that the Dark Champion will assume we don't know about them."

"That's a very tenuous assumption."

"It's better than nothing. What choice do we have? We're in no shape to resist the Enemy directly. Not without the Savior."

The premier drew another long breath. "Fine. I'll dissolve Parliament and send the politicians back to their constituents to organize everything. What of the surpluses from the border communities?"

"Tell them to gather their supplies, but don't send them south just yet. If my guess is right, we'll need to restock Valor's Keep. I'm not prepared to abandon the rest of Halcyon entirely."

Fortinbras nodded in agreement. "Nor am I." A thought occurred to him. "We're going to need other supplies than just food. Tar, coal, metal. Things we can't produce ourselves." His expression darkened. "I think I'll have to visit the Hansic Alliance."

"It won't be that bad." Cain looked up. "Why don't you take Dannia with you? I'm sure she'd enjoy the trip."

The premier considered this. "Enjoy it — no. The outside world is no place for us, never has been. She knows that, but it will do her some good to experience another culture, even one that rejects us. She's turning nineteen, can you believe it?"

The Chieftain chuckled and shook his head. He made a motion in the air with his hands. "I remember when she was this big."

Fortinbras smiled at the fond memory. "You know, she always liked you."

"Take her with you," pressed Cain. "Governor William Lessander of the Great Sea District is still unattached. Quinn tells me he's quite dashing."

The premier laughed. "Quinn's about as cold as they come! Besides, aren't you worried about tainting our bloodlines?"

Cain rose to leave. "A little shakeup now and then couldn't hurt."

"I'd rather she stuck to her own kind."

The Chieftain shrugged.

Fortinbras folded his hands together on his desk and gazed up at Cain shrewdly. "There wouldn't be any ulterior motive in your push to have my daughter join me, would there?"

Looking back, Cain smiled weakly. "And that would be...?"

"Well, let's see. She's a recent inductee to the Circle, has been waiting for her first assignment as an agent..."

"No," answered Cain quickly, "that wasn't my first thought, though it wouldn't hurt to have someone with you who can communicate with us instantly."

"Not your first thought?"

The Chieftain sighed. "Fine, maybe it was. But if something happens on your journey, something that requires our attention, we can respond immediately if she's there."

"Right." Fortinbras got up and walked past his desk to see the Chieftain off. Dannia's safety wasn't what bothered him — he knew his daughter was safe in the Circle's care. His mood became somber again. "Tell me the truth, my friend. Will we survive?"

"Your trip to the Hanse, or the Time of Meeting?"

"You know what I mean."

Cain looked directly into Fortinbras' eyes. The premier saw the worry and uncertainty. After a moment of silence, the Chieftain answered.

"I don't know."

Fortinbras returned to his desk. By the time he sat back down, Cain was gone.

*   *   *

The Library of the Elders was dark and still, just as it always was. The endless rows of bookshelves looked like they hadn't been disturbed in centuries. No one knew how far back the enormous hall extended, but each set of shelves was tall enough to touch the ceiling, which was always hidden from view.

A ball of radiance appeared at the front of the sanctum, illuminating a large desk. A body materialized before it. Appearing at first as a hazy form, it gradually coalesced and came into focus. Satisfied that his transportation was successful, Cain spun around with great purpose and marched along the center aisle, passing row after row of books. The ball followed him overhead, lighting up each row in turn and returning it to the darkness when it passed.

After a while, Cain found what he was looking for. He stopped and turned to make his way along a shelf. Almost as an afterthought, his body left the ground. The radiance followed him until he could see the faint outline of the ceiling. He selected a book and floated back to the main aisle.

He looked back toward the desk, but hesitated. Instead, he gazed longingly ahead into the darkness. He had done this a thousand times, and he would do it a thousand more. There had to be a way in! The Elders wouldn't have left all those books in plain sight if there wasn't a way in!

He forgot that he was still a few meters in the air. He moved forward, bracing himself for the impact. A surge of energy engulfed him and threw him violently backwards. He plummeted to the floor and landed heavily. The light winked out.

Stupid, stupid, stupid! He tried to sit up but couldn't move his legs. Suppressing the pain, he concentrated on his back, and his skin peeled away in his mind's eye. He saw his spine and his nervous system. He saw the shattered vertebrae and the severed nerve connections. Carefully, he pushed the bones together and sealed the fractures. He repaired the damaged cells and restarted them. Slowly, he moved his legs and stood up. The healing process lasted a split second.

You'll be no good to the Savior of Order if you kill yourself here, he reprimanded himself. With a sizzle, the light returned and he recovered the book. He hurried back to the desk to study it.

RAVELIN

Jarren Entigen slept peacefully, dimly aware of the hand gently shaking her shoulder. Clinging stubbornly to her slumber, she moaned her objections as a familiar voice attempted to rouse her.

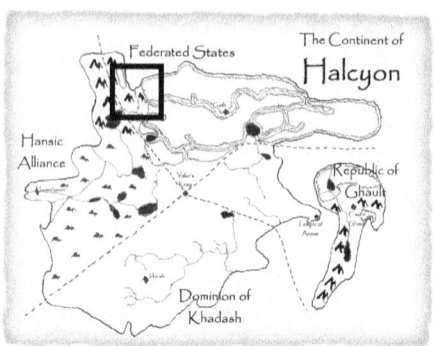

"It's time to wake up."

"Mmmm..."

"You're going to miss breakfast."

"What time is it...?"

"Almost 6:30."

Opening one eye, she strained to look over her shoulder at a grinning face. Behind the mischievous expression, she saw the tenderness in his eyes and felt his devotion to her. A scar cut across the side of his face, the residue of a killer's knife. Tracing the line with her finger, she murmured, "You go. I'll catch up with you later."

Duncan Milius stood up and shook his head. "Nope. Cyril will be there and he'll start his inspection right after." He slipped his pants on and grabbed a pair of socks. "You know how these things go. The chief-of-staff to the commander of the Federate militia can't be late."

"I'll call in sick and send my assistant."

"You don't have an assistant."

"Grr. It's too early. Tell him that if he doesn't give me my beauty rest, you'll demote him to refuse duty after you make Grand-General."

Duncan chuckled. "That's a good one. I'll pass it on." He pulled his shirt on.

Turning onto her back, Jarren folded her hands behind her head and regarded him impishly. "You look better without all that on, you know."

He shook his head and smiled.

"Honestly," she continued. "I'd be happy to help, if you want."

She pawed at him with her foot. Grabbing her by the ankle, he started to massage her.

She moaned happily and stared up at the ceiling. Although they were in a military building, the personal quarters of the garrison commander felt surprisingly warm. A mix of wood and stone, it doubled as Duncan's living space and office. Large regional maps hung on the walls, and the round table where he met in strategy sessions with his senior officers was cluttered with pieces representing military units that looked like they were borrowed from a board game. Apart from this, everything else in the room was clean and organized. Although he had been the commander here for three months, he had only lately begun to add personal touches to his quarters.

Enjoying her foot massage, Jarren purred, "This is nice, Romi."

She knew he found her hard to resist when she used his Teivan nickname. Pleasantly, he replied, "Is it? What about this?" Taking hold of both feet in his hands, he started pulling.

Jarren yelped. "Don't you dare!"

Duncan chuckled and released her. Walking around the bed, he bent down and kissed her. "Breakfast is in ten minutes."

"Ten?! Make it twenty."

"Fifteen. See you soon."

Grabbing the jacket to his uniform, he headed out. With a groan, she pulled the bedding over her head and curled into a ball.

*

When Jarren arrived for breakfast, Duncan was still greeting his troops. She watched from the back of the mess hall as he made his rounds of the platoons. The camaraderie was genuine, and she noted that he made sure to greet everyone regardless of rank or position. As she saw their warm responses to him, she felt intense pride for her lover. By the time Jarren had her tray of food and joined Duncan at the officers' table, he was already deeply in conversation with General Cyril Hawkwin. At her approach, the burly commander of the Federate armies rose.

"Welcome to breakfast. I'm surprised you made it."

Jarren smirked and sat down. Eying Duncan, she replied, "I have a good alarm system."

"No doubt."

The general returned to his seat. Digging into her meal, Jarren glanced at Duncan. "So, do you know all their names yet?"

"Not quite, but I'm working on it."

Hawkwin grinned. "Duncan and I were just talking about how he's settled into his new job. 'Marshal Milius' — it has a nice ring."

Duncan snuck a sip of his drink. "The paperwork's a killer."

One of Duncan's captains who was sitting nearby chuckled at this. Duncan exchanged glances with him as his mood darkened. "But starting tomorrow, I'll be getting a break from it."

The others at the table nodded solemnly as they finished their meals. Jarren shuddered inwardly. She was used to having him leave for risky missions, but this was the first time she was present for his departure. On top of this was her anxiety over the nature of this particular assignment: his return to Ravelin, the place where Marshall Corinn Wallace had led his own battalion to a stunning defeat — a first for the Praetorship, and a battle from which Duncan had barely escaped alive. Jarren knew that the other survivors of Ravelin were here in this very mess hall preparing for their own return. She wondered what they were thinking. Were they looking for vengeance? Justice? Or did they want to ensure that their comrades hadn't died in vain?

The fully reconstituted Eighteenth Battalion had spent the last three months training for this mission, and Duncan had been the architect. After today's inspection from General Hawkwin, they would set out. Jarren expected to feel overwhelmed with anxiety this morning. Yet, as she reflected on the reactions of the troops when Duncan greeted them, she saw only admiration and respect, and the marshal's own confidence was palpable. They trusted him completely, and so did she.

Duncan finished his plate and stretched. He glanced at her and caught her expression.

"What is it?" he asked softly.

Jarren shrugged. "Nothing."

Smiling grimly, she returned to her half-eaten breakfast.

*

Hawkwin, Duncan and Jarren began the inspection tour later that morning. The bright mood in the mess hall was now replaced by a strong sense of urgency. Valandov's Praetorian compound, which housed a battalion of nearly eight hundred troops — plus their support staff and other non-Praetorian personnel — was emptying out. Each of the battalion's sixteen platoons was responsible for carrying its own armaments, food, water, medical supplies and camping gear.

Jarren watched with interest as soldiers hurried back and forth gathering what they needed and relaying information. All around them, sergeants and officers barked commands to their juniors, ordering them to secure their packs and weapons, but what stood out the most for Jarren was the organization and precision.

"Do you train for this, too?" she asked absently.

"Absolutely," replied Duncan. "The Praetorship has drills for everything. We'll be fully equipped with the boats loaded by lunchtime."

"Contrast that with life in the militia," quipped Hawkwin. "It takes us a bit longer to mobilize."

Jarren smirked, recalling her own mandatory militia service many years earlier. "Yes, I remember." She addressed Duncan again. "If you'll be ready by lunchtime, why wait until tomorrow to leave?"

"I've given the troops the afternoon and evening off."

"You let them know in Valandov to expect your people, right?" asked Hawkwin.

The marshal nodded. "Oh, yes."

Jarren walked next to him. In an undertone that only he could hear, she demurred, "There wouldn't be any other reason you might have delayed your departure, would there?"

Feigning ignorance, he replied, "Now what would that be?"

By now they were exiting the Praetorian compound and entering the city of Valandov itself. It was large, with more than one hundred thousand people living within its walls — and even more in the outlying farming villages. It was in defense of these villages that the majority of the local militia spent its time. Apart from policing duties, they fended off periodic incursions from grimal bands. The base for Valandov's regiment was next to the Praetorian compound and they shared many training facilities.

In an almost comical mirror of the hustle in the Praetorian compound, the shops and taverns out here on the road to the dockyard buzzed with life as local businesses prepared for an influx of off-duty Praetorians.

"It looks like it's going to be a productive afternoon," commented Hawkwin.

"And evening," added Jarren playfully.

Duncan smiled and winked at her. "They'll have a week on the river to recover."

She laughed.

The orderly thumping sound of a marching troop interrupted them. A fully armed and equipped Praetorian platoon jogged past, their huge backpacks bouncing in time. Jarren saw that the soldiers carried their own food packs, bedroll, and basic medical kit along with their standard array of tough leather armor and weaponry. People in the street made way for them as they headed down to the dockyard.

"How much do those things weigh?" wondered Jarren.

"Enough," replied Duncan. "They'll unload them onto the ships, but once we arrive we'll all be carrying packs just like that all day long."

"Don't you bring along supply wagons?"

"Not for this mission."

She looked at him quizzically.

Duncan eyed Hawkwin as he responded. "I won't repeat Wallace's mistakes. We need to be mobile — quick and light. Each of us will carry our own supplies for a week. When we reopen the fort, we'll send word to the ships and restock it."

"He'll also send word to us," added Hawkwin. "Once Ravelin is secure, we'll send a regiment of the national militia to staff it along with one of Duncan's companies. Then we can reopen the trade route into the Hanse." Hawkwin sighed. This mission was considered a top priority by Premier Leodore Milius — a longtime friend of the general's and foster-father to the young marshal now standing with him. Hawkwin had no illusions about the extreme danger facing his friend's son.

Soon they reached the dockyard where nine galleasses bearing the standard of Valor's Keep were tethered along with a host of commercial vessels. The platoon that had jogged past them was unloading its packs.

Jarren gaped at the tall-masted ships. Sailors crawled all over the rigging and the hulls, preparing the ships to transport Duncan's unit.

"What does a mission like this cost?" she marveled.

Duncan shrugged. "For us, it's mostly free."

"Excuse me?"

Hawkwin chuckled. "The Praetorship pays for the salaries and equipment for its own troops whether they're on assignment or not. Everything else — food, accommodation, these ships and their crew — all that is borne by the national treasury."

Jarren shook her head. "Isn't that a bit one-sided?"

"That depends on your perspective," replied Hawkwin. "Ravelin was more than just a frontier post. It guarded one of the only overland trade routes between Valandov Province and the Hanse's Alpas District. Without the Ravelin garrison to keep the pass open, the economies on both sides of the border have been shattered. The financial benefit of reopening that trade route more than offsets the cost of this mission."

"Then shouldn't the Hansic Alliance help pay for it?"

Hawkwin coughed uncomfortably. "That's a political question. I don't do politics."

Duncan smiled, but he quickly hid it when he glanced at Jarren. Her gaze had returned to the galleasses arrayed before them, concern etched onto her face.

"So there won't be any backup from the Hanse?" she asked.

"Ravelin's in Federate territory."

She turned to Hawkwin. "And you'll be here, waiting for news from Duncan?"

"That's right."

"But Valandov is a week away. If Duncan needs help..."

Duncan and Hawkwin exchanged knowing glances.

"This is a Praetorian fight," replied Duncan carefully. "The general and I agree that sending more troops poses an unnecessary risk."

"What if you need help?" she repeated, more sternly this time.

Duncan placed his hands gently on her shoulders and held her gaze. "We won't."

"You did last time."

"I wasn't in charge last time."

The image of Duncan's arrival at the Palladum half a year ago came suddenly to Jarren. She remembered the torn and bloody appearance of his group and Duncan's own exhaustion. She recalled his frightening account of the battle at Ravelin, of the savagery of the grimals, and of Marshal Corinn Wallace's complete failure. She knew about all of his missions, but that was the first time she had ever truly felt that she had come close to losing him.

Jarren looked away from Duncan, afraid that he might read some of these thoughts in her eyes. As she turned to head back to the road into the city, she saw a group of uniformed men carrying heavy packs board one of the galleasses. She could see strange tools and devices protruding from the tops of the packs.

"Who are they?" she asked. "They aren't Praetorian, and they don't look like members of the sailing crew."

Duncan hesitated. "They're... part of the plan."

"You mean your battle plan?"

"Yes."

She looked squarely at Hawkwin. "I thought this was a Praetorian mission."

"It is. Those people have certain specialities. It's an interesting plan. No-one's ever tried anything like it before."

Hands on her hips, Jarren stood angrily before them. "An *interesting* plan? You're gambling lives on an *interesting* plan?"

Duncan stepped forward. "Jarren, it will work. Trust me. I'll be back in three weeks at the most. I'll tell you all about it then."

"Why don't you tell me now."

Duncan reached out for her and held her close. They stood together for a moment in the midst of the bustling activity on the pier. Whispering softly in her ear, he replied, "Because you'd kill me."

Smiling ruefully and shaking her head, she clasped his hand as they walked back into the city, with General Cyril Hawkwin following discreetly behind.

*　　　*　　　*

The following morning, Duncan's unit set out. General Hawkwin saw them off at the pier, as did several of Valandov's notables and politicians. The marshal needed no reminding about the importance of this mission, though they impressed it upon him anyway. He nodded and smiled, giving them what he hoped was enough assurance to calm their worries.

Jarren was absent, though Duncan was hardly surprised. They had said everything they needed to last night. He formed a mental picture of her and hung onto it for as long as he could. Long, dark hair framing a soft, oval face... almond-shaped eyes the color of oak... thin, inviting lips... In all their years together, she had never come to see him off on any of his missions and he preferred it that way. From this moment on, every moment and every thought had to be focussed on his duty.

After a quick inspection and a ceremony that was thankfully short, Hawkwin dismissed them to their ships. Within a half-hour, all nine galleasses were on their way.

The week went by slowly. With a platoon of troops, a full crew, and all the food and supplies necessary for the mission, each galleass was cramped. Praetorians who were accustomed to a daily regimen of training and patrol found themselves with little to do and no space to stretch out. Duncan's officers did their best to keep the soldiers fresh and busy, but it proved impossible to stave off the tedium of sailing upriver for days on end.

When the thickness of the leafy forest started to give way to the alpines of the Alpas Mountains, everyone knew that their destination was near, and they all agreed that their last morning on the river couldn't come quickly enough. Duncan awoke before the rest of his troops and stared out at the shoreline in the distance from the aft deck of his galleass. Rather than dwelling on the coming mission, he found himself reflecting on the journey he had made along this very route five months ago. At the time, the first spring thaw was just underway. Now, in the foothills of the mountains, the first chills of autumn were just setting in.

Back then, Duncan remembered very dreary weather, but today, the river reflected the sky's brightness. It was an uplifting feeling, and he sighed as he scanned the shoreline in the distance. Thinking back five months, Duncan remembered watching a faunn take a long drink from the river's edge. He had been on wakeup call that morning, and he used the tranquillity as an excuse to wake the soldiery in person rather than with a bugle. This set the whole unit behind schedule by several minutes, and Duncan smiled as he recalled Marshal Wallace's angry reaction.

Now Duncan was the marshal, and he concerned himself with different priorities. As far as he knew, he was the first Teivan to achieve a senior rank in any military force on Halcyon. As such, he succeeded best when he merged his military and Teivan training. He prepared himself to enter the forest in which he was raised and to guide his troops to victory. He closed his eyes and breathed deeply, and his mind calmed. After a moment, he opened his eyes scanned the shoreline.

A flash of movement caught his attention and he turned to see Captain Eliss Blaine join him. She was Wallace's first officer five months ago. Now, she was Duncan's. In the short time she had served under him, she had proven herself to be a far more capable officer than Duncan had expected.

"Faraway thoughts?" she asked quietly.

Duncan rubbed the jagged scar on his cheek absently. "Not what you'd think," he replied. "I was just reflecting on our last trip out here."

"So was I."

They leaned on the aft rail together in silence, as if observing a moment of remembrance for their fallen comrades. Out of an entire company of troops, barely a single platoon had survived. Duncan contemplated this. More than seven hundred Praetorians dead, and the survivors — every one of them — were with him on this mission.

As if sharing his thoughts, Blaine asked, "Sir, what do you expect to encounter on the road?"

The marshal continued to stare at the shoreline. "Remains of our old supply trains? Rotting corpses? No, I doubt it very much. Remember the reports we reviewed from our first march on Ravelin. Wallace's scouts found a deserted fortress. No-one knows what grimals do with the dead, but they certainly don't leave bodies lying around."

Blaine nodded, then followed Duncan's line of sight. "You seem to be looking for something."

Her marshal smiled and cocked his head. "I suppose I am, in a way. It's just past dawn. At this time, larger animals like the faunn usually drink their days' fill before a quick feed."

"And...?"

Duncan sighed and looked at her. "And there's a curious absence of wildlife."

Blaine looked back at the shoreline, but having grown up in a city all her life, she wasn't sure what to look for. Sensing her confusion, Duncan supplied an answer.

"There could be grimal hunting bands prowling about, or a vulturn or some other predator looking for a last-minute kill. Or it might be nothing."

"But if there are grimal hunters, won't they see us?"

Duncan nodded. "Yep."

Blaine looked curiously at him. "Doesn't that concern you? If they know we're coming, they'll set their defenses."

"Of course it concerns me, but there's nothing we can do about it. As for their defenses, you've reviewed our strategy. They can't rely on their traps this time. The advantage will be ours. In any event, by the time we debark and head out, they'll know we're here."

"Let's hope they've relaxed their guard after five months. Maybe they think we aren't coming back."

"I don't think so. Grimals are smart — very smart. Ravelin wasn't just some random outpost. They successfully overwhelmed a fully staffed fortress. No-one gives up that kind of investment without a fight."

"Or two fights."

"Indeed."

Duncan looked upriver and saw the pier in the distance. He turned to Blaine. "It's time. Wake the troops. It's dry rations this morning and a quick debarkation. I want us marching south within the hour."

*

Our defensive lines are down!

Duncan watched grimals dance between his people with impunity. The Praetorians were packed so tightly together that there was no room for them to move freely. They quickly regrouped into squads, but the tide had already turned against them.

We need our archers!

Duncan fought his way over to the ring of soldiers that protected the remnant of the archery unit. All around him were flailing bodies of grimals and humans. Right ahead of him, a private caught a leaping attacker on her shield and stabbed upward with her sword, impaling the creature. As she extracted her weapon, she was jumped from behind and knocked down. Duncan jabbed his dagger into its back and threw it off, but it had sunk its claws into her throat. With no time to think, Duncan darted away.

I have to take control!

Duncan reached the archery squad and grabbed a lieutenant. "Come on, we're leaving!"

Duncan led them to the east side of the road.

"Into the forest!" he shouted. "Move!"

A grimal jumped from the tree above him before he could save more of his troops. It danced sideways from his sword but he grabbed his dagger and slashed open its belly. It opened its mouth in a silent scream of pain, revealing frightening incisors. It tried to maul his hand but he twisted away and lopped its head off with his sword.

"Let's go, Praetorians," he shouted. "This is Captain Duncan Milius! Fall back to the east perimeter! The east perimeter, into the forest! Fall back!"

Duncan looked back and saw Marshal Wallace falter. Surrounded by the bodies of grimals and humans, he fell prone to his knees. Duncan tried to fight his way over to his commander. A grimal slashed Wallace's throat open. The standard of Valor's Keep, the honor of which they had all sworn to protect, lay trampled on the ground.

With a hoarse cry, Duncan gave up. "Northeast, people, move it! Stay away from the road!"

He darted past them and they followed obediently. Looking back, Duncan saw a score of Praetorians running at a frenzied pace, weaving around the trees. Behind them, grimals looked like dark blurs leaping from one pine to the next in pursuit. Duncan ordered his archers to fire three rounds at the pursuers before rejoining the flight. Soon, the sounds of battle faded into the distance...

*

That battle felt like a lifetime ago. Now, he was in command, supervising the debarkation of his troops in their mission to retake Fort

Ravelin and restore the Praetorship's honor. The battle plan was his this time. Failure or success now fell on him.

Taking a deep breath, Duncan remembered how he was drawn to the grimals right before the battle, how he *knew* their intentions, and how he *knew* how to escape. Duncan was counting on this strange intuition to carry him through his return to Ravelin. He never explained this to Jarren — she wouldn't believe him, nor would she forgive him for betting his life on such a reckless hunch.

But he *knew*, and his troops believed it.

Captain Blaine moved to stand beside him, her large pack slung over one shoulder. The foredeck of their ship bobbed lightly as they stood on it.

"I wish we had a topographical map," she muttered. "Taking the high ground is fine in theory, but you need to know where the high ground is!"

Duncan smiled. "True enough. I guess we'll just have to make one as we go." He pointed south to the Alpas Mountains in the distance, where Ravelin was located. "Besides, we're in the foothills now. The closer we get to those, the higher the elevation."

Blaine nodded. "True enough."

The pier at the start of the road to Ravelin was much smaller than Valandov's dockyard. It was able to accommodate only two galleasses at once. The ships were forced to maneuver around one another to access the pier. The last of the galleasses — Duncan's ship — was now in position. He looked on proudly as three of the four squads debarked and jogged to their assigned positions on the road.

"They're ready for this," murmured Blaine, as if reading his thoughts. "You've trained them well. We've all been briefed. We know our jobs. The troops believe in you."

Duncan eyed her curiously, unsure how to respond.

Belief in a Teivan, he marveled.

"Assemble the senior staff," he replied. "Let's get this mission underway."

Blaine saluted and headed off.

Duncan headed below. From this point on, he had to make sure that he was no longer seen from the shore. He headed aft to his quarters, which doubled as a makeshift war room. He passed through the sailors' quarters, and the few who weren't on duty scrambled out of their hammocks to salute him. Duncan had long ago given up on trying to explain that he wasn't their commanding officer, but the ship's skipper insisted that Duncan let them show their respect. Returning their salutes, the marshal left them to their rest.

Presently, Blaine arrived with the other three captains and took their places. After a week on the river, they had learned to ignore the ship's constant bobbing.

"The debarkation went well," stated Duncan.

"Yes, sir," answered Blaine. "No problems to report."

The commander nodded. "And the squads that are still on the ships...?"

Captain Muryn responded. "In their quarters on the lower decks, as ordered. Each ship has one squad remaining."

"Excellent." Duncan studied Muryn. A squat, broad man with brooding features, he was the officer left in charge of Valandov's garrison when Wallace left to relieve Ravelin. Had Duncan not been promoted, Muryn would probably have been given Wallace's command. In the short time they had served together, Duncan had been impressed by his professionalism and insight.

The marshal addressed his first officer. "Captain Blaine, you'll move out with the troops along the road as soon as possible."

"Yes, sir."

"You were here last time, you know what to expect. You know what grimal traps can do."

The others noticed the unspoken understanding that passed between Duncan and Blaine. Duncan thought for a moment about the non-Praetorians that Jarren saw boarding one of their ships at Valandov, the people who carried the strange implements.

"Follow your guides, listen to their advice. Let your sappers do their work and protect them at all costs. Our success — and your lives — depend on it."

"I've given Captain Lewellyn direct responsibility over them," she replied.

Duncan turned to Lewellyn. "Excellent." He addressed Lewellyn and Blaine. "Take your time. The grimals will expect our return along the road — they'll have reset their traps and maybe even made some new ones. Don't take any unnecessary risks, and whatever you do, stay out of the large defensive formations that did us in last time. The keys to success against grimals are maneuvers in squads and platoons."

"We know, sir. You prepared us for this."

Duncan smiled grimly. "I know." He leaned in close, holding his two captains with his gaze. He spoke slowly and emphatically, and his Teivan accent became more pronounced. "I want to greet all of my troops when we meet up. Do you understand?"

Blaine and Lewellyn returned his gaze with steely determination. "You will, sir. All of us."

The marshal nodded solemnly. "You're dismissed. We'll see you in a few days."

Blaine and Lewellyn rose, saluted, and left. Duncan turned to Muryn. "Your lieutenants are ready?"

"Yes, sir. As I said, one squad remains below deck on each ship. If the grimals are watching, it will look to them as if the ships have completely emptied."

"Good. Have the ships' captains send word: the remaining troops are confined to quarters. The order is to rest. We have a long night ahead of us."

Muryn stood up. "We do indeed, sir."

Duncan rose, as well. "I'll inform the captains to anchor the galleasses in the middle of the river."

Muryn nodded. "Good idea." The captain saluted, and Duncan returned it. "See you at midnight, sir."

*

The full moon lit up a cloudy sky. A cool breeze sent light waves across the river as each galleass lowered a skiff to the water. Nine skiffs — each carrying a full squad of troops — detached from their transports and rowed away. Avoiding the pier, they landed several hundred meters downriver and waded ashore. Without a word or a signal to one another, the squads spread out along the shoreline and quietly entered the forest. Illuminated only by the moonlight, they sprinted up the steep hill that rose from the water's edge. When they reached the top, the troops fanned out to form a wide defensive line while Duncan, Captain Muryn, and their two platoon lieutenants met in the middle. They pulled binoculars from their packs and formed a semicircle.

"Scan for the highest ground," murmured Duncan.

"There," pointed a lieutenant.

"Another to our south, directly ahead," added Muryn.

"Lieutenant Salles?" asked Duncan.

"Nothing I can see to the east, sir."

Duncan scanned the field of view. "Very well," he concluded. "Captain Muryn, take your platoon to the rise on the west and establish your perimeter. I'll lead my group south. Take your time and watch for trip wires. Follow your sappers. Move when they move, stop when they stop. You will protect them at all costs. And for all our sakes, keep it quiet."

The marshal paused for a moment and cocked his head. He closed his eyes and absorbed his surroundings. The chirps of insects and the flaps of tiny wings were all around. His Teivan senses came alive.

"Do you hear all that?" he whispered. Now they were all listening intently, and the forest's nighttime sounds seemed to amplify. "It's when that goes quiet that we need to be really worried," continued the marshal. "Dismissed."

The officers nodded and headed off. Duncan and Salles returned to their platoon. At a few hand gestures from the marshal and the lieutenant, the squad sergeants redeployed their troops. Four of the strange soldiers that Jarren had noticed back in Valandov went to work. Using specialized lenses, they squatted down and moved ahead slowly, scanning the forest floor methodically. The Praetorians around them formed a tight defensive pattern — the ones in front with their swords in hand searched the woods ahead of them for signs of the enemy, while archers behind them scoured the treetops. The troops were alert, seeking all around them for signs of movement.

Before long, they had reached the top of the southern rise. From here, they saw that the forest leveled out before sloping down into a ravine. The ground then rose up into a small ridge before disappearing into the darkness. Duncan felt rather than heard Muryn's platoon reach its destination. He motioned to his aide, who lit a small covered lantern.

"Corporal, report our status," murmured Duncan.

Removing one side of the hood, the corporal flashed a series of signals to the adjacent hill. A series of flashes came back to them.

"They're fine, Marshal. No enemy contact."

Duncan nodded. "Good. What do they see?"

The corporal sent another series of flashes, then waited for the response. They communicated this way for several minutes before the corporal answered.

"They see the same ravine and ridge as we do. There doesn't seem to be a way around."

Duncan considered this. Unlike humans, who preferred to live up high where they could see their surroundings, grimals thrived in the deep ravines and crevasses of the Federate's forests. The ravines were where the animals they hunted came to drink, and traversing these ravines was dangerous for humans during the daytime, let alone at night.

Most humans, Duncan corrected himself. Teivans knew how to avoid interaction with grimals. Duncan had done so hundreds of times as a child — his parents drilled it into him because they knew that his survival might one day depend it.

Maybe today, he mulled.

Then again, grimals didn't live in *every* ravine...

*

Captain Eliss Blaine tugged her helmet off and ran a hand through red curls that were cropped short to the Praetorian standard. Her troops marched quickly and quietly south. It had been almost a full day since they debarked from the galleasses. In that time, there had been no signs of grimal activity. Their camp on the road last night also passed without incident. Yet, she felt a growing anxiety. They were getting close to the spot where Wallace's battle group was ambushed all those months ago. Not that she could easily tell from her surroundings, she thought caustically. To her, every part of the forest looked like every other part. A whistle sounded from the front of her battle group's formation, and the troops came to an immediate stop. Pulling her helmet on tight, she jogged ahead to the scouting team that had made the call.

Blaine's troops marched in three separate units. Two platoons under Captain Lewellyn's command had assumed scouting positions along the forest's edge on either side of the main road, with the main force following thirty meters behind. The scouting groups were being directed by specialists using the same scanning tools as the ones traveling with Duncan. It was one of these specialists who had whistled the stop.

"Report."

The platoon on the eastern side of the road opened its formation to allow Captain Blaine through. They immediately resumed their defensive posture, scanning the forest for signs of danger.

The scout who had raised the alarm was crouched on the ground by the forest's edge. He beckoned to the captain.

"A tripwire, sir, cleverly hidden, just like Marshal Milius described."

Blaine bent down to examine the thin, taut line of resin-coated bark that stretched virtually unseen across the roadway. The two platoons on scouting duty, she noted, had halted within meters of it.

"Any idea what it does?" she asked.

"No, sir, but you can see where it extends into those brambles. I suspect the mechanism to spring the trap is hidden in there."

Blaine stared at it for a moment, and then something Duncan had once said about underbrush clicked in her memory.

"It's the underbrush," she murmured.

"Sir?"

"Our training with Marshal Milius. Remember what he said about this part of the forest? Mostly pines with minimal underbrush."

The scout shook his head in amazement. "The grimms are using the brambles to cover the mechanisms for their traps. We need to stay on the alert for more of these signs. How does the Marshal know all this?"

Blaine shrugged. "He's Teivan. They all do."

"What do we do? With a group our size, someone's bound to trip it."

"Captain Blaine?"

"Yes, Sergeant?"

"The western scout unit reports that the other end of the tripwire is secured to a tree by the road. There appears to be no mechanism of any kind."

"Ask Captain Lewellyn if they see any patches of brambles or other underbrush."

"Sir?"

"Just do it."

With a shrug, the sergeant hurried off.

Nodding her head toward the bramble patch, Blaine drew her sword and advanced into the forest with the scout following behind. The troops around her tensed and readied themselves, making sure to give a wide berth to the thin, dangerous line that stretched across the road.

"Don't touch it," warned the scout.

Nodding curtly, Blaine inched as close as she dared and peered into the brush. "I can see an apparatus of some sort," she reported. "There's a small crisscrossing network of lines that extends into a hole in the ground."

She moved aside so the scout could take a look. After a moment, she asked, "What do you think? Can we cut it?"

The scout shook his head. "This is more intricate than I imagined. I don't know what will happen if we tamper with it."

Blaine smiled slightly. "That's not exactly true. We do know one thing."

The sergeant who had made the first report called in to her from the forest's edge. "Sir, Captain Lewellyn reports no underbrush of any kind."

Blaine and the scout exchanged glances. "I didn't think they would. Order the two scouting parties into the forest, and tell our main force to stay back. We're springing a trap."

"Yes, sir."

As the sergeant darted off, the scout asked, "Are you sure about this?"

Blaine nodded. "I don't want it behind us if we have to fall back, and if we ever hope to reopen this road, we need to find these things and disarm them."

The sergeant returned again. "The units are ready."

The captain stood up and kicked at the wire.

Blaine and the others felt the ground tremble as a deep rumble sounded from the road. Several moments passed as the noise faded away and everyone tensed for the attack they were sure was coming.

Nothing.

Tentatively, the two scout groups returned to the road to find a wide pit several meters deep. Blaine shivered at the memory of the last time she saw something like this. Looking into it, she half-expected to find the rotted remains of her fallen comrades, but the pit was thankfully empty.

Captain Lewellyn approached her from the western scout group. "There's no hint of grimal movement."

Blaine gestured to the sprung trap. "Well, if they didn't know we were here before, they probably know now."

"We should redeploy the main force to move around it."

"No," objected Blaine. "Last time, they attacked right in the middle of our redeployment. They caught us out of position and off-balance. Not again. Break out some axes and take down a few trees. We'll use the trunks as a makeshift bridge."

"Yes, sir."

The two commanders headed off to spread the order.

*

The rest of the day passed with no sign of grimal activity. Towards evening, the scout groups announced the discovery of another tripwire.

"We should spring it like we did the last one," suggested Blaine.

Lewellyn nodded. "I agree."

Blaine addressed their lieutenants. "When that's done, scout ahead about fifty meters. You should find another trap."

Lewellyn looked at her quizzically. "How do you know that?"

Blaine sighed. "If it was here before, it's probably still here now." She looked carefully at their surroundings. "This is it. This is where we were ambushed the first time. Two pit traps — the one we just found, and the next one — took out two of our defensive lines. The grimms swept in during the confusion and overwhelmed us."

Lewellyn looked about anxiously. By now, they didn't need the marshal's Teivan senses to tell them that they were being watched.

Sharing his thoughts, Blaine continued. "We'll lose the daylight soon. We should spring these traps quickly, lay down our bridges and make camp. I don't want to be caught between two gaping pits when the attack comes. Not again."

Lewellyn nodded his agreement and issued the orders. Within minutes, the chops of axes on wood echoed around them. They were soon drowned out by a pair of low rumbles. Before long, the first tree trunks were being laid across the pits. By the time twilight took hold, both pit traps were behind them and they were making camp.

The two captains sat together in the center of the formation with their aides. As she munched absently on her dry rations, Blaine looked around proudly. Torches were pitched into the ground around the camp's perimeter, but there were no fires within the camp itself — mobility was key to defending against grimms, and campfires got in the way. Each platoon was responsible for keeping its section of the perimeter lit, and although the extra light would provide only scant seconds of warning, that was all the Praetorians needed to be on their feet with weapons in hand. They had spent months training for this mission. They were ready.

The troops clustered together in squads. Between the perimeter torches and the noise from dozens of quiet conversations, Blaine had no doubt that the grimms had to be aware of their location. But would it be enough?

"Do you think they'll come tonight?"

Blaine considered this question. She regarded the corporal who asked it. The young man was two years into his field service. Like her, he was a survivor of Marshal Wallace's battalion, and, like her, he chose to forego extended leave to return to Ravelin. He knew as well as she did that the grimms would come when they felt the humans were most vulnerable — when their guard was down.

It was well into the early hours of the next morning when the answer came. The pitch that the Federates used to fuel their torches burned for almost the full night. The perimeter flames began to sputter just as the faint predawn light touched the sky.

"For the valor of the Keep!"

The Praetorian battle cry echoed throughout the camp, accompanied by the blare of horns. Blaine had thrown off her bedroll and was ready for battle before she even realized what was happening. Without a word, she and Lewellyn divided the defense between them. He took command of the western front while she darted to the east.

Masses of dark blurs flew from the trees on either side of the road to attack the waking camp. The outmost defensive lines were quickly overwhelmed, but the Praetorians were better prepared than they were under Marshal Wallace. Having learned from their previous experience, they had spent the last few weeks drilling for many situations — including this one.

"Keep to your squads!" shouted Blaine. "Cover each other! Archers, look to the treetops! Pikes, to the tree-line!"

Her commands were hardly needed. The platoon and squad commanders had tight control over their troops. The grimals were attacking in two waves. The first was a frontal assault on the ground, but other groups were leaping over the pikes to land catlike behind the front line. A second line of infantry armed with short swords engaged these grimals before they could finish the pikes from the back. Within minutes the archery unit was fully formed and organized, and they started picking off grimals as they leaped from the tree cover.

The grimals' feline agility was difficult to counter, and the razor claws on their hands and feet slashed and cut as if from nowhere. But what the Praetorians lacked in speed they made up for in discipline. Under Wallace's command, the battle was quickly reduced to a bloody melee, but now the humans kept to their defensive patterns. Blaine watched as her troops resisted the urge to follow the grimals into individual combat. The grimals danced and tumbled around her troops as they did before, but instead of allowing themselves to be pulled free of their formations, the Praetorians stood firm, forcing the grimals to come to them. The squads on the ends slowly pinched inward, giving the Praetorian lines an almost semicircular shape. It would quickly become impossible for the grimals to deftly dance free of one human without moving into the range of someone else.

Blaine noted with pride that her troops were forcing the grimals back, but sneaking a look behind her, she saw that Lewellyn's force was having significant trouble. There seemed to be twice as many attackers on his side than hers.

Darting forward with her reserve force, she shouted at the squad commanders in front of her.

"Reinforce the western line!"

They obeyed without hesitation, and three dozen Praetorians wheeled around and sprinted for Lewellyn's position.

Blaine scarcely had time to consider the significance of her move. The grimals were fighting more ferociously on the western side of the road than on the eastern side, where she was. Yet Marshal Milius was somewhere deep in the forest on *her* side.

Had he made a mistake?

A short horn blast sounded clearly behind her. She turned back and saw that Lewellyn was still hard-pressed in spite of the reinforcements she had sent. She ordered the squads on the ends that were pinching in to press forward so she could tighten her lines. She then sent another squad west.

Or maybe they *are* drawing us away from something, she mused.

There was no time to consider this further as she raised her shield to defend a grimal attack. Its claws skittered away and she stabbed forward, catching its side as it leaped away. As it fell, it twisted around in a way no human could and slashed with its foot, slicing into Blaine's shield arm with a claw. It followed through and rolled toward the center of battle, eying her venomously. Roaring in pain and anger, Blaine resisted the urge to follow it, knowing that if it didn't succumb its wound it would fall prey to one of her flanking squads.

She shouted a command, and the squads in the middle of her formation pressed their advantage. The semicircle had now tightened to the point where she could see the entire battle in her periphery. The grimals were confined to the center, with the Praetorian formation having effectively eliminated the advantage of the enemy's agility.

As before, the grimals were almost completely silent. Even their cries of pain were oddly muted, making it simple for the humans to hear what was going on around them. Blaine didn't have to look behind her to know what was happening. Thinning her own line a bit, she sent Lewellyn more reinforcements.

Then everything stopped.

As one, the grimals pulled back. They crouched to the ground and cocked their heads as if listening for something, though Blaine could hear nothing. Then, with an eeriness that would haunt Blaine long after the battle's end, the grimals' eyes narrowed, they hissed forcefully, and darted into the forest. Some of the troops around her cheered, though most were dumbfounded.

More shouts behind them caused her to turn around. The grimals who were keeping Lewellyn's force at bay were fleeing into the forest and scrambling to the treetops. Leaping from top to top, the grimals cleared the Praetorians' wide formation and sprinted across the road. Taking advantage of the flight, the archery unit fired indiscriminately, taking down grimals as they passed. In a moment, it was over.

Lewellyn, panting and bleeding, ran up to Blaine.

"Captain Blaine, is it done?"

Blaine thought for a quick moment. The grimals had heard something. Something that called to them.

The marshal!

Hurrying forward, Blaine started shouting commands.

"Attack formations! Squad by squad! Pikes in front, swords behind! Archers to me! Pursue the enemy!"

Lewellyn touched her shoulder. "Into the forest?"

She nodded. "Into the forest. Leave a detachment of medics to deal with the wounded. We'll bury our dead afterwards."

Blaine held Lewellyn's gaze. "This is it."

The Praetorians reformed into attack lines. At a nod from her commander, one of Blaine's aides put a horn to her lips and blasted a long clear note. With a series of hoarse cries, they stormed the forest. Within minutes, they heard another horn blast from somewhere ahead of them.

*　　　*

An eerie silence filled the forest. A place that should have been teeming with life felt dead. For what seemed the umpteenth time, Duncan scanned his surroundings, noting the stark absence of wildlife. The troops around him felt it, too. It was a suffocating feeling that weighed on all of them.

After nearly two days of slinking through the forest, they had met with nothing, but any doubts that Captain Muryn and the rest of the unit harbored about Duncan's theory were evaporating quickly. None of them had ever felt anything so oppressive.

"Report," whispered the marshal.

"The squads are in position, as usual," replied Muryn.

Duncan looked around. "There's nothing usual about any of this. You don't need to be a Teivan to know there's something wrong."

The captain nodded. "Whereabouts do you think we are?"

Duncan took a deep breath as he considered the question. It was dawn right now, and his troops were positioned on top of three rises with deep creeks between them. They had spent the last two days alternating travel and rest every two hours in a constant push south through the uneven foothills.

"If the maps we've been making of the terrain are accurate, we should be roughly parallel to the spot where Marshal Wallace's battalion was ambushed."

"And parallel to our main force," added Muryn.

"Right."

The two senior officers stood near the middle of the central rise. "It's getting light," said Duncan. "Let's look around."

Duncan and Muryn pulled binoculars from their packs. Scouts in all three attack groups were doing the same. Almost immediately, they noticed a dark shady haze in the distance rising from the forest floor.

"What is that?" wondered the captain.

The scouts saw the same thing. They all looked to their marshal for an answer. Duncan studied it for a moment longer before slowly lowering the binoculars, his gaze locked on the horizon.

"I have no idea," he murmured.

Muryn exchanged concerned looks with the troops who were with them. "But sir, your Teivan..."

"There's no Teivan tradition or folk tale I can think of to explain *that*," replied Duncan.

They were interrupted by the echo of distant shouts. The Praetorians were momentarily distracted; apart from their own hushed conversations, these were the only sounds to be heard in the forest's uncanny stillness.

"It's Captain Blaine's group — it has to be!" exclaimed one of the sergeants.

"Man your positions!" hissed the marshal. The troops around him immediately snapped their attention back to their posts. Duncan motioned angrily to the units on the other two rises. "And make sure they're focused, too!"

Muryn immediately summoned two runners and sent them off.

"What do we do?" asked the captain.

Duncan didn't answer immediately. He raised his binoculars again, his attention focused on the horizon. The light was growing steadily, and it was now possible to make out what seemed to be an earthen wall of some kind. The distant echoes were growing frequent.

"It's begun," muttered Duncan. He packed his binoculars away. "Redeploy into two groups. Muryn, take your command east and follow the top of that ridge. I'll lead my group parallel with yours on the other side of that ravine, over there. We stay in constant sight of one another."

"Yes, sir!"

"And Muryn — tell your squad commanders that we move with speed. Whatever that is out there, we need to reach it while the grimals are engaged with our forces on the main road. Understood?"

"What about our sappers? Do we still scan for traps?"

"No time. We'll have to risk it."

Muryn saluted. "See you soon, sir."

Duncan returned it. Muryn darted off while the marshal barked commands to the troops around him. Within minutes, the group on the central rise was redistributed to the other two units.

They moved out, jogging at an easy pace.

"Weapons out!" shouted the marshal.

Both units obeyed immediately.

Ahead of them, the ravine turned sharply to the east. Duncan's group assumed a defensive posture at the bend, lining the top with archers, while Muryn's group stormed down the other edge of the ravine to cross to Duncan's side. By now, the hazy earthwork they had spotted from afar was close enough to make out. It occupied what seemed to be a wide hillock that covered the entire field of view ahead of them. Duncan reached for his binoculars and took a quick look.

"That makes no sense," he muttered. "It isn't supposed to exist."

It was indeed an earthen wall, but unlike most human constructions, this one looked natural, as if the forest floor had somehow bent itself upward. It didn't look very high and it had no uniform shape — it wove around the trees and rocks that stood in its path, often incorporating them into its structure. But what struck the marshal was behind the wall. Thick, dark clumps attached to the trees, some of them very high up, with the blurs of jumping grimals moving between them. There weren't very many, Duncan noted, but they had no way of knowing the extent of this... what was this? Duncan lowered his binoculars for a moment as he realized why his battle group had been able to move this far into the forest unmolested.

Another trap!

Duncan raised the binoculars again, and this time he focused on a lone grimal perched on top of the earthwork. It seemed to stare right back at him. It narrowed its eyes and half-opened its mouth. The marshal could practically hear the feline hiss escape its maw. Duncan was suddenly overcome with a momentary quake of fear. Dropping the binoculars, he nearly doubled over. It passed almost immediately. When he picked the binoculars up and looked back, the grimal was gone.

Muryn's unit had finished crossing the ravine. They were now all together in one single battle group. From here, the ground sloped upward to the earthwork. Duncan was reminded of the drills they practiced regularly about storming a fortified position on an elevation, but in those drills, the defenders didn't come at you from the treetops...

The marshal repacked his binoculars. At that moment, a horn echoed faintly from the west.

Duncan didn't hesitate. Trap or not, it was time to finish what they'd started. Drawing his sword, he cried, "For the valor of the Keep!"

The forest reverberated with his troops' response. They formed their battle lines and charged up the slope. Duncan looked up and saw the familiar blurs, but there were very few of them. The archery unit went to work and some of the blurs were brought down.

"They're keeping their distance," remarked one of his lieutenants.

"Of course," replied Duncan. "Captain Blaine is doing her job." He pointed to the sergeant of his guard. "Tell them where we are!"

The sergeant put a horn to her lips and returned Blaine's call.

The earthwork was now directly ahead. The first infantry lines were now facing resistance, but the defenders were badly outnumbered. The grimals pulled back again. Duncan was now only a few dozen meters from the earthwork. He could see that it was barely three meters high.

Pointing at the top of the barrier, he shouted, "Get us up there!"

The sergeant closest to him ordered her squad forward to boost the marshal's group up. The top of the earthwork was just wide enough to walk on. Duncan took the lead and he was up in an instant. Seemingly from nowhere, a grimal lunged at him, forcing him to roll backwards. His pack dug into the top of the earthwork, and when he tried to twist away from the attack he tumbled to the ground, losing his weapon. The grimal slashed at him repeatedly, and as he dodged around he loosened the pack on his back. Feigning a stab with his dagger, he unhooked one of his shoulder straps and swung the heavy pack around, catching his enemy by surprise. He knocked the grimal over and lunged forward, burying the knife in its side. When Duncan spun around to retrieve his sword, he realized that he had tumbled *inside* the earthwork. His guard had now jumped down to form a protective semicircle around him, but the rest of their unit was still on the other side of the earthwork.

Half a dozen grimals eyed them venomously from nearby treetops, keeping their distance. Duncan spied several more behind them, swinging heavily between the boughs with dark bundles under their arms. Squinting, Duncan caught a fleeting sight of two miniature, feline eyes staring out at him from within the bundles.

Then he understood. Two of Duncan's guards unslung their bows, but he waved them off.

"No — fall back."

"Sir?"

"You heard me. Fall back to the other side of the wall. Keep your guard up, but make no offensive moves."

Taking the lead again, Duncan scrambled up the tree next to him and swung himself to the top of the earthwork. Unslinging his own bow, he held the grimals back while the rest of his squad followed him. Then he noticed that the eerie silence had descended on them again. He turned to the west — toward the road — and his heart sunk.

The forest was alive with a swarm of dark blurs, and they were moving towards them faster than Duncan thought possible.

Below him, Captain Muryn was already organizing defensive lines in a pattern they had practiced dozens of times before departing Valandov. An archery unit three lines thick pulled back on their bowstrings and let a volley fly. Half the arrows ricocheted off the pine trees, but many hit their marks. By the time the first grimal bodies hit the ground, the archers had reloaded their weapons to fire again.

Duncan reached for his binoculars before remembering that his pack was still on the forest floor inside the wall. Even without it, though, he could see that the grimals were returning in force.

Returning from the road...

He watched one grimal high in the treetops arch its back and hiss a challenge at him, but as it lunged forward it faltered, an arrow notched in its back.

"Sergeant, your scope!"

"Sir!" His squad commander handed the device over and he peered through it. The forest floor receded from the hillock all around them, but despite the uneven terrain he saw a flash of metal in the growing morning light.

"Sound the horn again!"

The sergeant grabbed the horn that was slung over her shoulder and put it to her lips. It blared loudly and clearly across the forest, and it was answered quickly by a similar blast from the west.

Blaine!

The grimals reached the infantry lines, but instead of engaging them, they pulled back and scrambled southward, obeying commands only they could hear.

"They're trying to surround us," shouted the sergeant.

"I don't think so," replied Duncan. "Look."

The grimals clung to the trees, trying to achieve adequate cover as they were pressed by Praetorian forces from two sides. By now the battle groups could see each other and they started shouting commands back and forth to coordinate their movements.

"Captain Blaine!"

"We're here, sir! The grimms are pulling south!"

Duncan nodded. "My guard and I are on top of the earthwork. Swing your unit south in an attack formation. Three lines deep, archers ready — but *do not engage*. Muryn, secure the north perimeter!"

"Yes, sir!"

"Captain Lewellyn!"

"Here, sir!"

"Hold your position between Muryn and Blaine. Do not engage the enemy without my command!"

Duncan stole a quick glance toward the shelters inside the earthwork. There was no more movement. Whatever lived here was gone.

Long moments passed. As if frozen in time, the opposing grimal and Praetorian forces eyed each other warily, neither side prepared to resume hostilities.

Reaching a decision, Duncan squeezed past the corporal who was protecting his front side.

"Sir..."

"Not now, corporal."

Duncan put a hand to his side before realizing that his sword was on the ground near his pack. Leaning his bow against the tree next to him, he drew his dagger, held it up deliberately, and placed it carefully on the ground by his feet. The marshal walked out slowly with his hands outstretched, alone and unarmed. A host of grimals watched him intently, seemingly unsure of what to do. Before long, a grimal dropped down from a tree ahead of him, landing softly on the top of the earthwork. Duncan studied it, but it was impossible to tell if this was the same one he saw through the binoculars before the battle. He stopped less than a dozen meters away, and he realized that this was the closest he had ever been to one of these feral creatures without a weapon in his hand. It crouched down, poised to strike, never taking its yellow slit-eyes off him. They stared at one another for what seemed a lifetime, though it was probably only a minute or two. Duncan felt something — an exchange of sorts. A rudimentary understanding, though he had no way to process it right now.

They held each other's gaze for a moment longer. Then the grimal jumped back up the tree and scrambled inside the earthwork, followed by the rest of the grimals.

"Archers at the ready," called one of the lieutenants.

"No," barked the marshal. "Do not fire at them, do not engage them in any way! Hold your positions. Captains, to me!"

Duncan jumped down and waited a minute for Blaine, Lewellyn, and Muryn to join him.

"What just happened, sir?" asked Blaine.

"I'm not exactly sure," replied Duncan.

"Is it victory?"

Duncan looked back at the retreating grimals. They all appeared to be inside the earthen wall. "A small victory — for now. Pull all our forces back to the road."

"We have injured there," said Lewellyn, "and dead."

Duncan nodded. "Make camp on the road. Full defensive formations, as before. Tend to the wounded. Bury our dead along the sides of the road."

"Sir?"

"Along the sides, Captain, with grave markers — enough for *all* of our fallen comrades."

The captains nodded solemnly.

"We'll camp for the day and resume our journey to Ravelin with all speed in the morning," continued Duncan. "Dismissed."

The captains saluted and headed off to disperse their units. Duncan's guard formed around him as he headed toward the road. Descending the slope, he looked back at the grimal fortification and reflected on what he had seen behind it, wondering at the significance of what they had found today.

*   *

General Cyril Hawkwin shook his head in amazement. He had read Duncan's report several times, but now, to hear it again in person, he was still amazed.

"A village?"

Duncan shrugged.

"A grimal village?"

"Maybe not a village in our sense of it, but for them, yes."

Hawkwin gave his younger friend a sideways glance. "What does that mean, exactly?"

Duncan shrugged again. "I'm not sure, but they now know that we know they're there."

"And you're sure they've left for good?"

Duncan shook his head. "Not at all. There was no indication of surrender. It was more like resignation. I don't think they were expecting us to find them that way. They'll test us, Cyril, and we always need to be ready. I have no doubt of their ability to cut off Ravelin again if they detect even the slightest weakness. But now, at least, they know that we can set traps, too."

The general sighed. "I suppose that'll have to do. I'll inform the premier that he'll have to strengthen the garrison from now on."

"And you'll need scouts," added Duncan, "good ones. Scouts who know how to sweep the road for traps. We can't be sure that we found all of them."

Hawkwin nodded and took another deep breath. He and Duncan were standing on top of a narrow bridge that spanned the distance between Ravelin's twin watch towers. From here, one could see the road carve a line north through the rolling forest to the pier at the River Saar, which was now clogged with Duncan's nine galleasses along with Hawkwin's transports. Turning around, he looked south into the pass through the Alpas Mountains. It was a grand sight, with looming peaks that remained capped in snow even in the summertime. Duncan had never seen this before and he felt sorry to leave it.

Nearly two weeks had passed since the battle in the forest. Hawkwin had just arrived at Ravelin in force, and Duncan was preparing to return to Valandov with half of his battalion. The other half would remain here under Captain Blaine's authority until the Federate garrison built up to full strength.

"Don't be too quick to unpack your bags when you get back," warned Hawkwin.

"I left my pack in the grimal village," smirked Duncan.

"Funny," replied Hawkwin dryly.

"No, really."

"So you're telling me you haven't changed your clothes in two weeks? Jarren will be delighted."

Duncan cleared his throat. "Yes, well, the spring that supplies the fortress is good for washing..."

"Never mind. Just don't unpack."

"Yes, I know."

Hawkwin looked at him sideways.

"You're not the only one I report to," defended Duncan. "My reassignment to Torinn won't be official for at least three weeks. Someone must have played up our 'victory' here. You wouldn't have anything to do with that, would you?"

Hawkwin turned to him. "No, actually. And you shouldn't play *down* your 'victory'. The accolade is well-deserved. Torinn is far more difficult a post than Valandov. Governor Bernand is very exacting. The Grand-General needs a marshal there who can strategize in the political *and* military arenas, and with your success here, that makes you the best candidate."

Duncan groaned. He hated politics. "It wasn't a real victory," he muttered. "The enemy's still out there. They'll come back. They always do."

Hawkwin clapped him on the back. "Well, a few weeks from now that won't be your problem, will it?"

Duncan conceded this. "So who's problem will it be? Any ideas about who'll be the next marshal of Valandov Province? Maybe someone they'll let keep the post for more than a few months?"

Hawkwin ignored the quip. "Your soon-to-be-former first officer is a possible candidate, or so I hear. You think she's ready?"

Duncan considered this. Blaine had deftly taken command of half a battalion, and done so with success. "She might be. She's come a long way in the last six months."

"Sounds like someone else I know," mumbled Hawkwin.

Duncan glanced at him, but the usual twinkle was gone from the general's steely eyes. Instead, Duncan saw pride. He turned away, staring out at a mountain scape he was unlikely to see again after he left Ravelin. Torinn was more of a desk job than he had right now. To be sure, there would be a lot of military action, but Torinn was more central, more economically active, and more influential within the Federated States. Maybe it wouldn't be so bad, he mused. More desk work meant fewer missions, and fewer missions meant more flexibility for other things.

Jarren...

Duncan looked again at the grizzled warrior standing next to him, a man who had known the marshal since his adoption by Leodore Milius, the recently reelected premier of the Federate. Cyril Hawkwin stood there next to Duncan, his hulking frame leaning in a crenel, admiring the same breathtaking view, and scratching a full beard that had long ago turned grey.

Maybe Cyril's right, thought Duncan. *Maybe it's time for a change.*

Landing

A mild breeze blew off the Great Sea along the western coast of the Hansic Alliance. The sleek form of a Khadashite corsair seemed to glide across the surface of the water as it followed the current to its destination. Even with such a light breeze to fill its sails, the vessel moved faster than

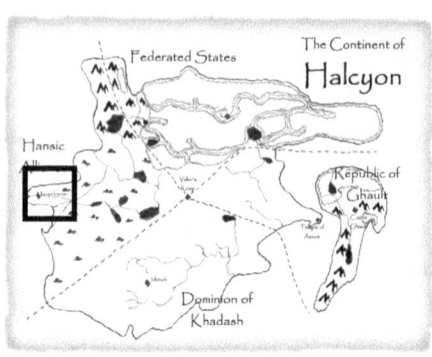

the quickest means of overland travel, but this still wasn't speedy enough for its anxious passengers. Premier Glendon Fortinbras and his delegation of negotiators, which included his daughter, Dannia, were on their way to Hansehaven to meet his Hansic counterpart, Chancellor Yarena Hanser. As Fortinbras stood at the prow and watched the twin cities

of Lubec and Rugen draw closer from the horizon, his meeting with Cain three weeks earlier weighed heavily on him. That the Champion of Chaos was on the move was beyond doubt. Now that the evacuation of Khadash was underway, the premier's mission to procure more food and raw materials was critical.

And now a delay!

As Rugen's pier came into view, Fortinbras shifted his bulk. Dressed in tan breeches, dark brown boots, and a red surcoat that did little to hide his generous frame, he hardly looked like a head of state. He noted the honor guard and the carriages awaiting them and nearly slammed his fists on the rail in frustration. Did the Hanse need a ceremony for *everything*? Was he not clear enough in his missive about the need for haste?

Soon, pier workers were tethering the corsair to the dock and a plank was lowered to allow the passengers to disembark. A voice carried over the entire waterfront.

"Present arms!"

As one, the honor guard drew its weapons and saluted the vessel.

"Company, at ease."

The soldiers sheathed their blades and remained standing rigidly. A herald moved to stand in front of the guards and announced a formal greeting. "To His Honor, Premier Glendon Fortinbras of the Dominion of Khadash: welcome to Rugen and to the Hansic Alliance."

The premier moved to the plank followed by his daughter and the rest of his delegation who had emerged from a lower deck.

A noble stepped forward dressed in a navy blue ceremonial outfit with a bright sash that ran from shoulder to hip. "Greetings, Premier Fortinbras," he said stiffly. "I am William Lessander, governor of the Great Sea District. Welcome to the Hansic Alliance. I hope your stay will be pleasant."

The plank groaned perceptibly as Fortinbras debarked. He stopped a few paces away from the governor and eyed the waiting carriages angrily. "I don't care who you are. I'm here to see your chancellor, but she's in Hansehaven, not Rugen." His booming voice carried across the entire waterfront.

Lessander's eyes bulged and his mouth gaped. "I was told that you were informed of the repairs currently underway to the pier at Hansehaven," he growled. "All naval traffic is being rerouted through Rugen and Lubec. These carriages are the quickest way to Hansehaven from here. I hope the remainder of your journey will be comfortable."

Standing a head taller than the governor, Glendon Fortinbras glowered at Lessander. "Fine. Have our belongings transferred to the carriages. I want to leave immediately."

Lessander replied to the premier with forced civility. "Very well. The journey to Hansehaven will take several hours. I'll send word of your arrival."

"You do that. Every second lost is a second wasted. I'll tolerate no more delays. The sooner I can speak with your chancellor, the sooner we can return home."

The Khadashite delegation was ready to leave in a quarter of an hour. As the honor guard formed around them to escort them to Hansehaven, the governor mounted his steed and returned to his keep, thankful to be rid of these guests.

*   *

Twelve hours passed. William Lessander looked down on the city of Rugen as the lights winked out one by one. His city and its twin across the river were going to sleep. Lessander's bedroom was very plain, with only some decorative weapons and medals adorning the stone walls. He had kept none of the paraphernalia amassed by the previous governor. A brazier sat in a corner under a ventilation shaft for Lessander's daily votives to the Spirits, though he was finding it increasingly difficult to Commune lately.

Dressed in his nightgown, Lessander was preparing to turn in when a page appeared at the entrance to his bedchamber and knocked. The governor responded with annoyance. "Yes, Douglas?"

"Message from Longpoint, your Honor. They require your immediate presence at the lighthouse."

"Longpoint? Can't it wait until morning?"

"No, your Honor, I'm afraid not."

*

"Ships, your Honor."

"That's what you called me out here for, to stare at a group of ships?" Lessander and the head watchman were observing the horizon from the deck on top of Longpoint's lone spire. It stood thirty meters from the ground and its large oil lamp was extinguished. The lighthouse was built on a small promontory just west of the mouth of the River Odra.

"The problem is, sir, that there weren't any ships scheduled to arrive tonight. And look where they're coming from — out west."

"Could it be the *Explorer*?" asked Lessander hopefully.

"If it is, they seem to have found some friends. There are a lot of them out there and it's impossible to tell which of them, if any, is ours. If they were coming during the day, I might be able to make out some markings, but right now it's too dark."

Lessander took the watchman's spyglass and raised it to his eye. He could barely see the faint outline of a fleet of ships stretched across the horizon in the full moon's light. After a moment, he said worriedly, "Send for the garrison commander."

Time passed and the fleet edged closer. Soon a figure appeared clad in his armor. His breastplate bore the emblem of a vulturn clutching a bow with a sword and pike crossed behind it. He was tall with watery-blue eyes and blond hair.

"Yale Hendricks, senior marshal of the Twin Cities Praetorian battalion, reporting as requested."

Lessander glanced questioningly at the Praetorian. "What are you doing here? I sent for the militia garrison commander."

The fighter treated this question disdainfully. "General Eigels escorted the Khadashite delegation to Hansehaven to attend the chancellor and Commander Frederick has taken ill. His senior lieutenant asked me to fill in."

"Very well." Lessander handed him the spyglass and he surveyed the advancing fleet. "How many ships do you estimate, Marshal Hendricks?"

The marshal surveyed the horizon for a moment. "About fifty, with more possibly following behind."

"Do you recognize any designs?" the governor asked the watchman.

"They're too distant for me to make out identifying features, but judging from the apparent sizes and shapes, they could be similar to ours."

Hendricks furrowed his brow and looked back out at the horizon. "How many people could be stowed away on board, if there were only supplies and no cargo?"

The watchman was puzzled. "Depending on how long the voyage was, I'd say between eighty and one hundred people, plus the crew." He suddenly understood what this estimate meant. He stared at his governor fearfully. "Your Honor, how can this be…?"

Lessander turned to his armored companion. "Marshal, I want you to awaken the militia and dispatch the soldiery. Rugen and Lubec are now under curfew. No one is permitted to leave his or her home for any reason."

Hendricks nodded. "That's sensible. I'll deploy the Praetorians to establish defensive positions. The militia will be kept free to evacuate people to the keeps if the need arises. Otherwise, they'll be used as backup. I want the Praetorians to be the first line of defense."

The governor nodded. "Okay, I'll leave it in your hands." Lessander entered the lighthouse, found some paper and a quill, and started writing. "I need some hot wax," he instructed the watchman. After a few minutes, with his letter finished, he dripped the wax onto the bottom of the page and pressed his ring with the governor's seal into it. He looked up gravely.

"All three of us must sign this. I'm sending it to Hansehaven immediately."

Hendricks accepted the note and quickly read it. He looked up at the governor grimly. "There hasn't been an attack on Rugen and Lubec in three hundred and fifty years."

Lessander stared worriedly at the western horizon. "I know, Marshal. I know."

*   *   *

The long, oak table in the dining hall was laden with food and clogged with people. Upon it were placed an assortment of cheeses, wines, and meats. Around it were seated Chancellor Yarena Hanser, Premier Glendon Fortinbras and both of their negotiating teams.

The chancellor and her husband, Lawrence, wore matching velvet robes, as was expected of Hansic heads of state. Upon the Khadashites' arrival, Fortinbras had demanded that they be taken straight to dinner, so the guests were still wearing their brown and tan travel attire.

The dining room was large and spacious and was lit by a glowing chandelier. It had a rustic feel to it, but so did the rest of the parliamentary island complex. Hansehaven was the oldest settlement in the Hanse. Its history could be traced back to the beginning of the Age of Disquiet, making it nearly five centuries old. At only two hundred years, the mainland city was still considered new.

The visiting Khadashites had arrived three hours earlier following a six-hour trek along the River Odra. Now, as the clock fast approached midnight, everyone seemed to have been sitting for an eternity listening to Fortinbras' forceful negotiations. The chancellor, having been caught off-guard earlier in the evening by the Khadashite premier's directness, was frantically rifling through reports and files with the help of her husband.

"This is appalling," rumbled Fortinbras. "I made it clear in my communiqué that I was coming to discuss terms for contracts to import coal, tar, copper and iron. You should have been prepared!"

The chancellor suppressed the urge to lash out at this man. "As I explained earlier, this was to be a social gathering. Neg—" She was interrupted by an aide who deposited another folder in her hand. She sighed before handing it to her husband. "Negotiations weren't scheduled to begin until tomorrow afternoon. The delegate from the Alpas district hasn't even arrived yet!"

"That isn't my problem."

"But it is," voiced Lawrence coolly. "If you want us to increase iron exports, they have to come from Alpas, so you're going to have to deal with that delegate."

"That's inefficient." Dannia Fortinbras had a dark complexion like her father, though her features were more angular. With her arms folded across her chest and wearing a smug expression, she had spent most of the evening sitting quietly. Her instructions from the Chieftain had been clear: observe and record, and leave the politics to her father.

Lawrence leaned forward, nonplussed by her attitude. "What's that supposed to mean?"

Dannia sighed. "This whole political system, this economic alliance. Every decision has to be made by consensus. It takes too long and creates unnecessary levels of bureaucracy."

"Our people have the freedom to elect governors who see to the needs of their own districts."

Dannia returned his look with a smug expression. "Our people elect a single central government with the knowledge that the premier makes decisions for the good entire country, decisions that may involve sacrifices from certain local communities. Your system favors local needs over the needs of the whole, and in doing so, favors mediocrity."

Lawrence was taken aback by this blatant statement. He eagerly leaped to his country's defense as Chancellor Hanser, Fortinbras and their two teams continued negotiations, ignoring the argument taking place next to them.

Presently, a cleric of Samlah entered the dining room. The platinum depiction of a closed fist, a symbol that Samlah holds the soul of every person in thrall, patted lightly against the skin around her neck as she approached a burning brazier in the corner of the room. She checked the flame's intensity before beginning the midnight ritual. She closed her eyes in silent prayer. Lawrence grabbed his wife's arm to get her attention, and they joined the other dignitaries in the devotion. The high cleric sprinkled incense over the brazier and muttered a short prayer for the goodwill of the Forum. When the odor from the rite dissipated, the cleric exited the room.

Several quiet minutes followed. Chancellor Hanser approached Fortinbras and laid a hand on his arm. He seemed about to recoil from it, but he held himself in check. "Premier Fortinbras, we've been at this for hours, and there's still much paperwork to do." He was about to interject, but she cut him off. "I know that you want to conclude these arrangements quickly, but we all need some rest. We've agreed on the basic terms. I'll have my people work through the night preparing draft contracts. They'll be ready for your review in the morning."

His expression softened. "I appreciate your effort to accommodate us. It's just that there are times when it seems as if we live in different worlds."

"Then we finally agree on something." Chancellor Hanser turned to accept a note from a page who came scuttling into the room. Worried that it was yet another misplaced economic statement, she broke the seal and scanned it.

"It may take some time for us to boost our production of some of these commodities," warned Lawrence. "Tar, coal, metals. Why do you need such drastic increases, anyway? You look like you're preparing for a war."

For the first time since he arrived, Fortinbras cracked a smile. "Maybe I am. Oh, there was one other thing. We want to import more grain."

"The Highland and Khadashite districts are exceeding their capacities just to meet the quotas you demanded last month. Can you afford this?"

"Let me worry about our treasury. Don't fret — you'll get your money."

"And with a twenty percent share of all contracts signed, your own account stands to gain quite a bit," added Dannia.

"That twenty percent belongs to the national treasury," defended Lawrence.

"Twenty percent less your own commission," she corrected.

Chancellor Hanser gasped. She grabbed her husband and thrust the note into his hand. Noting the shock on her face, he quickly read it before passing it on to one of Chancellor Hanser's junior delegates. He stood next to his wife, dumbfounded by what he had just seen.

"What's going on?" asked Fortinbras. 'What does it say?"

Lawrence maintained his composure, though his lips were pressed tightly together as he motioned for the note to be passed to the Khadashite premier. "This message just arrived by carrier bird from Rugen."

Fortinbras read it and his voice betrayed confusion. "I don't understand this. What does it mean? Who's attacking you?"

As one, Lawrence and Yarena Hanser marched briskly to the nearby balcony which faced west toward Rugen and Lubec. The chancellor's grim expression mirrored her husband's as the two gazed at the horizon. She turned to one of the aides. "Take this note from Rugen to General Galen at once. Have him send messages to every garrison on the Great Sea coast to put them at full combat readiness. Send reinforcements from Stettin and every available ship from Riga to Rugen and Lubec. Also, send copies of the note by carrier bird to the rural governors and instruct them that they may have to send for reservists."

The others had joined the leaders of the Hanse on the balcony to gaze at the dark horizon. Chancellor Hanser continued to issue orders. "General Eigels will take two regiments of the national militia and return in force to Rugen and Lubec. I want these orders written up and ready for my signature in one quarter of an hour."

At her chancellor's command, the aide darted past the meal table and along the corridor leading from the main dining room.

"We should also convene an emergency session of parliament," continued the chancellor. "We need to brief the members so they can inform their constituents of what's happening."

Lawrence turned to his wife. "We should send messages to every town and city in the Hanse and inform Valor's Keep. We may need immediate assistance."

Fortinbras interjected. "This all sounds very incredulous."

"I agree, but what choice have we?"

"It's probably a force of highland rebels or pirates. It seems to me that this governor of yours may be sounding a false alarm."

Chancellor Hanser shook her head. "You don't know Governor Lessander. He doesn't call false alarms — he's very careful. He trusts his own instincts and so do I. And you'll note that he has confirmation from the captain of the watch on Longpoint and the Praetorian garrison commander. We'll verify the signatures and the seal, but in the meantime we have to take this seriously."

Fortinbras sighed and looked out at the sleeping River Odra. Sporadic torch light reflected off its still waters. The invaders had approached the Hanse the same way he did. The Khadashite delegation — including his own daughter! — had missed being caught in it by a matter of hours. Keeping his feelings to himself, he responded, "It just seems so sudden."

The chancellor gave a long exhale. "That's what makes our assailants so dangerous. We never prepared for an invasion like this. Our coastal communities are only lightly defended, so even if it's a false alarm, we can't take chances."

Lawrence met Fortinbras' gaze. "Premier Fortinbras, I suggest that you and your daughter return home while you still can and shore up your defenses."

The memory of his last conversation with Cain nearly a month ago came back to the premier, and now, with this sudden attack, the immediacy of the Time of Meeting weighed heavily on him. He recalled his last question to Cain, a question that the Chieftain couldn't answer.

Tell me the truth, my friend. Will we survive?

Noting the premier's hesitation, the chancellor explained, "We're being invaded by an unknown force from beyond the Great Sea. If Governor Lessander's assessment is correct, a fleet of ships greater in size than our own navy is approaching our coast, and they could carry tens of thousands of troops. If the Hanse can't contain them, they may spread to your country."

"We're throwing everything we have at them," added Lawrence, "and we may have to request assistance from Valor's Keep. Now this city is likely to be the next target, so unless you want to find yourself in the middle of a bloody siege, I'd suggest that you and your people leave immediately. We'll arrange for transport to Raskilburg. You can take a ship home from there."

The chancellor of the Hanse shook her head. "What I don't understand is why us. Why attack the Hansic Alliance?"

"Maybe they're just starting here." Dannia's quiet words struck a disturbing chord.

The appearance of a dull orange glow on the horizon cut off any further discussion. "What's that haze?" asked Dannia.

Tears welled in the chancellor's eyes as she replied. "Rugen and Lubec are burning."

HERE ENDS HERALD,
PART ONE OF
HARBINGER'S END

THE STORY CONTINUES IN
HARBINGER'S END
THE TIME OF MEETING

PREVIEW OF

HARBINGER'S END:

THE TIME OF MEETING

A table and two chairs floated in the endless expanse, a place that was everywhere and nowhere. The playing area was ready for what was to come.

Soon two figures emerged from the surrounding nothingness. One, a woman of unsurpassed beauty; the other, a man with flawless features. They eyed one another warily as they sat in the chairs and waited. Until now, the game had swung back and forth between them with no clear victor. They were equal in intellect and ability, these two beings of power. Neither could overwhelm the other.

Now they would play a final round where there could be no stalemate. To lose meant utter defeat, to win meant eternal domination.

The players waited for the others to arrive. Then the Game would conclude.

THE MARSHAL

Three weeks after the attack on the Hansic Alliance, a different struggle was playing out in Torinn Province in the Federated States. Just beyond Torinn's city boundary, Marshal Duncan Milius was surveying his quarry from afar. He was accompanied by two lieutenants, Rand and Ilern. Both

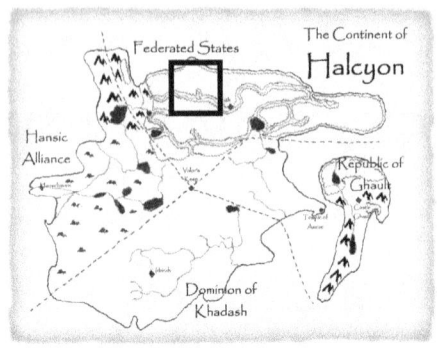

were long-serving platoon leaders under Duncan's predecessor who were close to completing their tours of duty.

Cramped on a ridge overlooking a shallow forest valley, the three of them used binoculars to watch a small band of grimals a short distance away. The grotesque creatures moved about their camp freely and silently, as if they were a

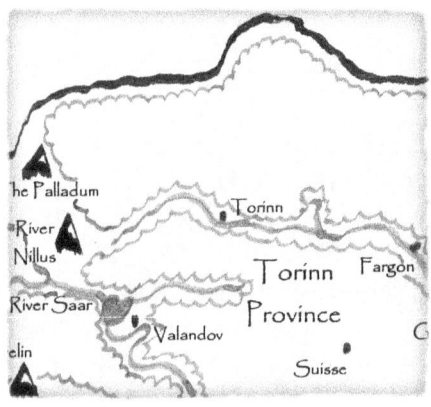

part of the woods. They were squat and lupine, had thick hides and no necks. Their incisors hung low over their jowls and their eyes were yellow slits. Because of their streaked fur, it was virtually impossible to spot them when they stood still. Occasionally, they hissed and made animal-like calls to one another.

"It's been several hours, sir," stated Rand in a hushed tone. "When do we move out?"

"In a moment." Duncan removed his leather helmet and ran his fingers through his hair. He had been hoping to avoid combat, but now there seemed to be no choice. This band was straying too close to human territory. He rubbed the scar on his left cheek pensively. Yes, action was required. His other hand touched a pouch that hung at his side. It held a grimal claw that was stained by blood from the lung of a dead Praetorian. He had kept it with him ever since the tragedy at Ravelin. How long had it been? *Almost seven months*, mused Duncan. So much had happened since then.

Duncan looked at Rand. "Search the underbrush to the north of their encampment, about four meters off the path. How many scouts do you see?"

"One… no, two. There's one in the tree."

Visually, Duncan confirmed Rand's assessment but the marshal's instinct told him something else. The first time this heightened awareness hit him at Ravelin it scared him, but he had since grown to depend on it. Duncan focused on the grimal encampment and saw the danger instantly. "There are four scouts: two in the trees, one crouching in the bushes, and one more lying on the ground just off to the side of the path."

"I don't see them."

"They're there, look closer."

Rand squinted hard. "I still don't — wait, there they are. How did you—"

Just then, a corporal scrambled quietly through the bushes and onto the ridge. "Our trackers have reported in, sir. They count a dozen grimals, including two scouts, one to the east and one to the south."

"Very good, Corporal," acknowledged Ilern. "Have Sergeants Willem and Baylor move their squads into attack positions."

The corporal scrambled off while Ilern turned to his commanding officer. "Sir, doesn't it strike you as odd that they would have a tighter northern defense when they know we have no settlements up that way?"

"I should say so," replied Duncan. "This is a new tactic they've employed recently. It's as if they're expecting an assault on the opposite front from us. Very strange, indeed."

"Looks like Governor Bernand is right. They *are* dumb creatures."

Duncan eyed his subordinate with reproof. Ilern was an effective soldier but he had proven himself incapable of working out strategies or tactics on a large scale. He would never amount to much more than a platoon commander.

"Look at the way they positioned their scouts," responded Duncan. "If I'd joined another platoon today, you would've walked into an ambush. Think, Lieutenant, and get to know your adversary. While you're doing that, inform Sergeant Willem that you'll give the order to attack once our signal is sent. Make sure you eliminate those scouts or they'll circle around and catch you from behind. I'll join you when the path is secure."

"Yes, sir."

A chagrined Ilern climbed down to the waiting Praetorians as Duncan handed Rand his short bow. "Lieutenant, you'll provide cover for the squad from here. I want those four north scouts taken out by the time our people reach the encampment. We can't have them hitting our exposed flank."

The two of them focused their attention on the first scout in the bushes. Careful to avoid touching the poisoned tip, Rand nocked an arrow in the bow. With a quiet twang, she let it fly. It darted unerringly toward the grimal and thunked into its hide. The creature slumped over and died.

Recognizing the signal, Ilern discreetly ordered that the east and south grimal scouts be quickly dispatched. Once that was done, Duncan slid down the side of the ridge as the squad moved on the camp. By now, Rand had refitted her bow with another arrow and fired it. It hit the tree near the second of the three remaining north scouts. The camp was alerted.

The forest came alive as eight camouflaged Praetorians leaped into the tiny clearing. Eight grimals were dispatched as they scrambled to their feet. The last two lashed out with their clawed limbs. They slashed wildly but, outnumbered, were quickly cut down by the attackers. Another thunk sounded from a third arrow as the north scouts noiselessly darted toward the fray brandishing their claws. Moving with inhuman speed through the trees, Duncan cut them off. As he parried a blow from the first grimal with his buckler, he whipped his dagger at the second, burying it in the creature's chest. The marshal drew his short sword and assumed a defensive posture. The first grimal followed through with another swipe, tearing into Duncan's armor. While the two struggled hand-to-hand, the marshal sensed rather than heard Rand release another shot from the ridge. Focusing on the arrow, he watched as it was seemingly guided into the shoulder of the final enemy scout. The poisoned tip went to work and the grimal toppled forward. Simultaneously, Duncan kneed his remaining adversary in the gut and brought his elbow crashing down onto the back of its skull, crunching its head on his raised knee.

From the time that the signal was given, the attack had lasted less than a minute.

As Duncan knelt to examine his foe, Lieutenant Ilern trotted in from the clearing, glancing in amazement from the grimal bodies to his commanding officer, who wasn't even breathing heavily. "I'm pleased to report that the enemy was dispatched with no casualties to us."

Duncan nodded. "Excellent work, we'll continue our reconnaissance. Send a runner to the other three squads — I want a twenty-kilometer sweep completed by 17.30 hours. Inform them to keep the grimal bands under surveillance until I advise them to do otherwise. Do not engage them except in self-defense! We're not going to have a repeat of the Ravelin fiasco."

"Yes, sir."

Duncan looked about and found a large tree stump. He approached it and removed a large rolled-up paper from his backpack. Using the stump as a table, he unrolled the map and indicated one of the squares on the grid. Lieutenant Rand joined them from her position on the nearby ridge.

"Tell Lieutenant Lowell to send two of her squads up the south side of this ridge. Now that we've cleared up her east flank, the grimms may have to regroup to a defensive position and try to take higher ground. The other half of her platoon will sweep around east and west of the ridge to try to catch them as they retreat.

"Lieutenant Rand, take your platoon and dig yourself in five hundred meters north of our current position. You're going to be a buffer in case more grimms decide to show up. Lieutenant Ilern, contact Lieutenant Knowles and coordinate a standard twenty-kilometer search-and-sweep pattern with him. Concentrate your efforts in this region northwest of Torinn. We don't want any grimms sneaking around the ridge and nipping at our exposed backsides. And another thing: the order is to hold these positions. Make sure Lowell and Knowles are clear on that. Do not pursue the grimms into the forest — God only knows what kinds of traps they've laid out for us. Remember that they're going to try to draw us out of position, so keep the squads together. They're most effective when they're able to divide us into small groups to pick us off. We can't let that happen."

"What about the regular patrols?"

"Leave that to the local militia. This is our fight. Return to your platoons. I'm heading over to Lowell's group to direct the engagement from there. Any questions?"

Rand and Ilern shook their heads.

"Good, off you go."

The lieutenants saluted and headed off to initiate Duncan's plan.

*

At sundown, Marshal Duncan Milius led twelve squads of weary Praetorians into the safety of Torinn's walls. They successfully completed their latest attempt to clear the region of grimal activity, and this was to be their first rest in more than two weeks. Like all settlements in the Federated States, Torinn was surrounded by a thick defensive barrier two stories high. In the smaller towns, the wall was a palisade that consisted of tree trunks that were bolted together, but cities like Torinn used a combination of wood and stone. The base of the wall was made of Alpas granite, but the bastions and towers that protruded from it were wooden, as was the walkway. The crenellated walls marked the city limits and formed a square all around it, and at each corner there was a square tower that stood three stories from the ground. The walls were dotted with archers' slits. The militia, being more numerous, was responsible for defending the settlements and their immediate vicinities and for patrolling the roads. The Praetorship, being better trained and equipped, monitored the forest itself and initiated any military action.

Fortified cities and towns housed the population of the Federated States. Each community was reasonably self-sufficient and produced much of its own food from farms that were located inside the walls. Being the second largest city, Torinn had a population of more than one hundred and fifty thousand people. Only Gath had more residents.

By the evening mealtime, Duncan had replaced his leather armor with a plain tunic and breeches. This night he was expected to dine with the governor of Torinn Province, Saulnier Bernand. He loathed these monthly dinner meetings. Every time they spoke, Duncan felt as if he was being scrutinized.

The Praetorian was admitted to the governor's keep to dine with senior members of the district legislature. Duncan presented his report while the others listened intently. When he was done, he waited for the criticism that was typical of all these dinner meetings.

"So what you're saying," clarified Bernand with a full mouth, "is that in less than four months you've managed to cleanse the vicinity of Torinn of a grimal presence which, until now, has been a match for our forces?"

"I wouldn't use the word 'cleanse', your Honor. The grimals know of our change in tactics and are likely avoiding this area. Tomorrow, Marshal Baldwin and I will start coordinating a sweep of the road from here to Fargon."

"I think you give these creatures too much credit. They're unintelligent and barbaric."

Duncan scoffed. "You underestimate our adversary."

Duncan noticed the city's mayor raise her eyebrows and exchange glances with a number of her municipal administrators. The governor didn't take kindly to rebuke or criticism.

The marshal continued. "They're well aware of our military strengths and weaknesses. I expect them to adapt to our change in strategy sooner than you think. Grimals are cunning and wily."

Bernand grumbled. "Perhaps you can tell that to Premier Milius when you see him."

"The premier requested my presence? That's odd. I report directly to General Hawkwin and to General Leyva at Valor's Keep." At the mention of Hawkwin's name, Duncan thought of Jarren, who was traveling as an aide to the general's inspection tour. They were due to arrive in Torinn in two days, and Duncan was eager to spend some leave time with her.

Unaware of the marshal's private thoughts, Bernand shrugged. "A missive arrived from Gath this morning asking for a direct report. It has to do with this nationwide rise in grimm activity, but I think I'll let 'Daddy' detail that."

Some of the senior members of the legislature grinned to themselves while others chuckled quietly. This was turning into a lively meal. Bernand's insult invited a glare from the marshal. It offended him when people brought up his familial connection because it implied that his status was due to influential politicking. Duncan had worked hard to dissociate himself from his foster-father's parliament. Bernand knew exactly what to say to get a reaction from him.

The governor noted Duncan's unease. "I understand that you're Teivan by birth."

It was a statement rather than a question, and it caught Duncan off-guard. Bernand had never wanted to discuss the marshal's childhood before. Why the sudden interest? The governor was in a feisty mood and his other guests, who seemed to enjoy the marshal's discomfort, were silently egging him on.

"What of it?" replied Duncan cautiously.

"It's nothing, really. I'm not suggesting that you're untrustworthy. Loyalty is one of the few positive virtues of the Praetorship." He leaned forward with his hands folded in front of him. "I'm curious: how is it that you became such an expert on the grimms? I assume it must be your upbringing."

The marshal took a bite of his food and chewed thoughtfully. He decided that he wanted to see where Bernand was heading with this line of questioning, so he answered. "From the time we're old enough to crawl, Teivans are taught to integrate with the natural world around us. That includes recognizing certain signs — indicators, if you will — of forest activity. Even young children are knowledgeable about the behavioral patterns of the life around them. Plants, animals, and insects all have predictable cycles and predictable reactions to change, and so do grimals."

"Of course this integration doesn't apply to cities and towns."

Duncan responded carefully. "Human settlement isn't natural."

"Oh?"

"Most humans don't exist in harmony with nature. They subdue it, reshape it to suit their needs. What they don't understand is that nature always has its own way. What we maintain is an illusion of control, nothing more."

The governor slammed his fist on the table. "Hypocrisy! When a bird builds a nest, is that not a measure of control? Nests don't exist naturally, nor do burrows or warrens!"

"Animals use only what they need to survive. Humans consume, and when they've drained an area of its resources, they move on to a new area and consume that."

"Don't Teivans consume? Their tribe-groups are constantly moving from place to place."

"We migrate according to the demands of climate and the forest around us. We don't clear-cut vast areas of land for our use. We leave the natural world intact!"

"We? What is this 'we'?"

Duncan was momentarily confused by the governor's sudden change of topic, and Bernand seized the opportunity. "You still associate with your former kin?"

"I'm a Federate citizen," the marshal spat angrily.

"And a Praetorian, as well. Your conflicting loyalties fascinate me." Bernand looked around at the councilors who were listening intently. "You see? They can be tamed after all."

Duncan tensed at the laughter that followed. He returned to his meal with a growing sense of humiliation.

The governor continued the confrontation. "I know these questions irritate you, but I've always wanted to know more about the humanity behind the legend of Duncan Milius. Tell me, are you a religious man?"

Duncan paused between bites. "My personal beliefs are just that."

"What a wonderfully neutral answer. It's all right to admit that you're religious — I do."

The Praetorian chuckled bitterly. "Then you're the only religious Federate I know. You must have Ghaultian blood."

The councilors blanched. Federates had long memories. They had endured deadly clashes and occasional wars with their neighbor ever since their ancestors were forced to flee the ancient city of Halcyon during the Age of Ruin. It was considered a great insult to imply that a Federate had a Ghaultian connection. Duels had been fought over such claims.

To everyone's surprise, Bernand merely ignored the quip. A part of Duncan was disappointed that he wouldn't have the opportunity to best him.

"Oh, I reject the idea of the Forum, just like you," stated Bernand loftily. "It's silly to imagine that an all-powerful deity would need to create twelve Spirits to govern the universe for Him. Then again, who are we to analyze God's ways?"

Duncan's patience wore out. "Is there a point to this?"

The governor scowled. "The point is, dear boy, that those who believe in nothing end up exalting themselves. The Praetorship is little more than an elitist club."

Pleased with himself, Bernand sat back. The marshal glared at him. The rest of the courtiers kept quiet until the governor broke the tense silence.

"So what do you believe in, boy?"

Duncan rose. This was a question he had never really considered and it wasn't something he was going to trouble himself with simply because this loathsome governor demanded it of him. He stared at the assembly of bureaucrats and felt himself flush. The marshal berated himself. He had addressed hundreds of soldiers without feeling anxious or nervous. He ordered people to their deaths without reserve. He didn't flinch when his career was on the line during Wallace's court-martial all those months ago. He never had doubts about leading a battalion of troops on the riskiest mission of his life to recapture Ravelin. So why did he feel self-conscious now? Duncan was squirming under Bernand's scrutiny and the governor enjoyed it. The marshal decided that it was time to finish it.

"I don't need your approval and I don't need to justify myself."

This ended the meal. The marshal spun around and headed for the door. Bernand called after him. "That may be, but you haven't answered the question: what do you believe in?"

The Praetorian halted, turned around, and met the governor's self-important glare. "I believe in humanity." With that, Duncan resumed the walk to his quarters.

*

At daybreak, Duncan relieved himself of duty and left his command in the capable hands of his senior captain. The summons from his foster-father and General Hawkwin was urgent.

Duncan boarded the corsair at the pier just outside the walls of Torinn. He wasn't the only passenger. He recognized Caren, a city councilor whose ward included most of Torinn's residential district. She was on her way to Relligen for business. There were also a number of merchants and commoners en route to various destinations. All of them were pretending not to stare at the marshal though he felt their inquiring glances all the same. It was unusual for a Praetorian to travel alone, much less with civilians on an expensive corsair. The marshal nodded curtly and tried to smile politely while muttering "hello" to people when he passed them. Privacy was a luxury that was hard to come by on a Federate galleass, but on a Khadashite corsair it was a standard feature. He found his quarters and retreated inside.

It was a small room that was just large enough for a cot, a low desk and a washbasin. Duncan lay down on the cot and closed his eyes. He absently rubbed the scar on his cheek and his thoughts strayed to his foster-father. His mind took him twenty-five years into the past. The newly elected premier was hunting in the woods surrounding Gath. Duncan was a young boy then, a Teivan child who had been left for dead following the murder of his parents. It seemed as if his life truly began when the premier stumbled over their bodies. A jagged scar on Duncan's left cheek, the result of a killer's thrust, was the only residual of the encounter. From that moment on, Leodore Milius, who to this day mourned the deaths of his own wife and unborn child, welcomed Duncan into his household and treated him as a son. Duncan adopted a Federate name and chose to remain in Gath rather than rejoin his clan in the forest — the memory of his parents' death was too painful to face. As he grew older, he learned Hansic and he tried to integrate into his new culture, but there was always a strong sense of his difference, and his accent never faded. The time he spent in the national assembly, not to mention his participation in two reelection campaigns, led Duncan to swear that he would never enter politics. Then again, had he avoided that world altogether, he would never have met Jarren.

He returned to the present and his mind reverted to soldier mode. The marshal tried to analyze his current situation but failed to arrive at a logical purpose for this trip. Why would a premier in need of military counsel send for a Praetorian marshal? The premier had always been careful to maintain a professional distance between himself and his foster-son. And what could be so dire that a man like Cyril Hawkwin needed Duncan's assistance? Surely, a grave matter faced them. Duncan's mind raced as the ship set sail.

INTRUSIONS

Cedric IV Deis, Padishah of the Republic of Ghault, wandered aimlessly as he was wont to do. He was short and rotund, and he carried himself with an air of arrogant disdain and bloated self-worth. As he strolled lightly through the corridors of his

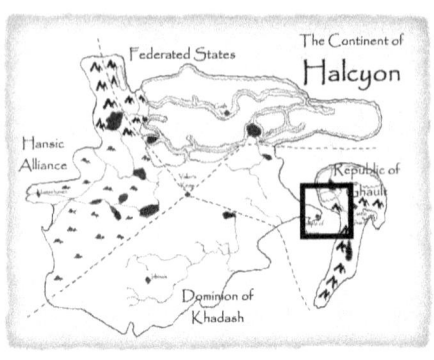

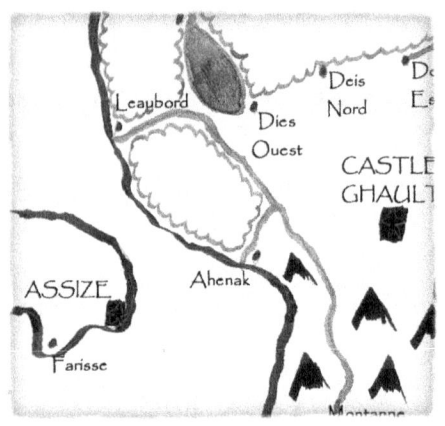

castle, people bowed in homage to His Grace, waiting for him to dismiss them so they could return to their work. He was followed by a train of handlers and servants who fussed over him and picked up after him. On most days, he held court with his advisors so that anyone who had a case could come and complain to him. Today, however, was different because it was a holiday.

The Padishah's purple robe rustled quietly as it trailed behind him. He was preceded by personal guards who made way for him in the wide hallways of the citadel, always ensuring that everyone except his handlers stayed the requisite ten paces away. He stopped for a moment at a large window and gazed outside. His entourage halted an instant later and backed off a bit. It was obvious that the Padishah was deep in thought. The sky was overcast, promising rain. In the city beyond the courtyard, his citizens were everywhere, running around to perform last-minute errands before the downpour.

Our people. See how they adore Us.

The citadel's baroness approached. Tasked with the responsibility of managing the household affairs of House Deis, she frequently sought audiences with His Grace. When she was stopped by the guards, she begged permission to speak to him and they let her through. He turned to face the brief commotion.

"Lady Delia, you disrupt Our musings." His voice was soft, his tone indifferent.

Maintaining the appropriate distance, she bowed her head and addressed him with reverence. "Forgive the intrusion, but someone wishes to see Your Grace in Your Grace's throne room."

The Padishah sighed quietly and appeared mildly annoyed. "Our court is postponed until the holiday has ended. Who is this person who disturbs Us?"

Lady Delia gulped and eyed the floor. "I am forbidden to speak his name."

The Padishah choked and stepped forward, forcing her to move back a pace. "You dare to speak thusly to Us? We have issued a command and We will be obeyed! Who is this person?"

Delia responded with a shaking voice. "He bade me to give him my countenance at the cost of my life. He said that for the sake of the Republic, he must speak with Your Grace alone. He invoked the Spirits."

The Padishah raised an eyebrow. After a moment's consideration, he responded, "For granting this countenance, your life may yet be forfeit to Us should We disapprove."

"It shall be as Your Grace wills."

"So be it. We dismiss you, Lady Delia."

The baroness bowed and left quickly. The Padishah headed off to his throne room, where he normally held court. He walked very lightly, and the soft pat of his slippers was inaudible amid the booted footfalls of his entourage. Since the throne room was not being used for the festivities, that part of the citadel was devoid of activity (the guests awaited the Padishah in the audience hall downstairs). The guards opened the massive doors and scanned the chamber. It was built to accommodate hundreds of petitioners, and as such, it was open and spacious. The only light came from a lamp stand next to the Padishah's divan. Apart from that, the place appeared empty. The guards checked the room thoroughly. Finding nothing, they returned to the entrance, awaiting orders.

The Padishah motioned to his guards to stand aside. He entered the chamber boldly, heading straight for the divan. He was furious — did he not specifically instruct his servants to lock up the room? If so, why was the light still on? He suddenly halted and turned around. Something wasn't right. He needed his handlers.

The Padishah's soft voice echoed through the chamber. "Close the door and wait for Us outside. Make sure that I'm not disturbed. I'll tell you when We're ready to leave."

Suddenly very frightened, the Padishah wheeled around. Who said that? The voice was his but he hadn't uttered a word. He turned back to run for the door just as it slammed shut. His guards and handlers were outside. He was trapped in his own throne room with the unseen intruder.

Then he noticed someone sitting on his divan. The glowing lamp revealed his features. The stranger wore a long crimson robe with a hood which was pulled back to reveal a wizened face and flowing white hair.

"I see the baroness found you. This is a nice divan. Big, spacious, lots of pillows. I like the way it's set on top of a stage so you can see over everyone's head when you're reclining."

The Padishah squinted and moved further into the chamber. "The Circle Chieftain!"

"Very good, Padishah Cedric IV Deis. I hope your guards didn't suspect anything. Mimicking the sound of a person's voice is easy, but the inflections are always tricky and my Ghaultic is a little rusty — I hope I got the syntax right."

The arrogant indifference returned as the Padishah realized that he was no longer in danger. "Why have you disturbed Us? Our presence is required at the festivities in the audience hall. Invocation of the Spirits is not an act to be taken lightly. To do so falsely—"

"Would involve immediate imprisonment for a minimum of thirty days, blah, blah, blah. I assure you, this is no joke."

Cain spoke while admiring the lamp. "I understand you've begun massive exports of foodstuffs and raw materials to Khadash. I'm glad. They really do need it."

"How came you by this knowledge? The Khadashite delegation insisted on the utmost secrecy."

Cain flashed a grin. "I know about many things, including the advances made in your arms industries, but that's not why I'm here."

The Chieftain reclined on the divan and motioned for the Padishah to approach. Cedric Deis' eyes flared — how dare he command the Padishah of the Republic of Ghault! Nevertheless, his curiosity won out and he complied. Normally he would never allow himself to stand so close to anyone but his handlers, but he didn't seem to have much of a choice.

When he was near enough, the Chieftain whispered, "There's news from the Hansic Alliance. They've been invaded by an army from beyond the Great Sea." There was a nasty grin on his face, as if he was waiting to laugh at the response.

The Padishah snorted derisively. "That is a matter for the Hanse to deal with. Perhaps if they expressed more than tacit devotion to the Spirits, the Forum would view them more favorably."

"There's more. The invaders are marching straight for Valor's Keep."

The Padishah stared haughtily at the Chieftain. "The problems experienced by the rest of the Commonwealth are no concern of Ours. The Spirits do not seek Our involvement. We would know if it was otherwise."

"There's one more thing: you should expect visitors soon."

The Padishah became wary. "What visitors?"

Cain stared down at him. "That is internal business for the Republic and certainly no concern of mine. I'm just passing on some information."

The Padishah looked away for a few moments to consider his options. He looked back and saw that Cain had vanished. After another minute, he called for his guards. He would consider this matter later. Right now, he had festivities to attend, though his thoughts remained troubled.

The story continues in...

Halcyon Chronicles:
Harbinger's End
The Time of Meeting

The story concludes in...

Halcyon Chronicles:
Harbinger's End
Endgame

Available Now!

www.halcyonchronicles.com

www.ingramcontent.com/pod-product-compliance
Lightning Source LLC
Chambersburg PA
CBHW060148130626
46556CB00006B/2543